THE WAY WE WERE

Prajwal Hegde is the author of *What's Good About Falling* (2018) and the *Times of India*'s tennis editor since July 2005. She began her journalism career with *Mid-Day* in Mumbai, before moving to *Deccan Herald* in Bengaluru. Prajwal has reported on all four Grand Slams – Australian Open, French Open, Wimbledon and US Open – for several years. She is on the International Tennis Federation's Media Commission and is also a member of the International Tennis Writers Association. The Association of Tennis Professionals awarded Prajwal the 2021 Ron Bookman Media Excellence Award, making her the first Indian and second Asian to receive the honour. She wrote the 'Steffi Graf' chapter in *Sportstars 40,* published by *The Hindu* in January 2020. She features in *Break Point,* the Leander Paes–Mahesh Bhupathi docuseries. Prajwal lives in Bengaluru with her husband, Dr Sanjay Hegde, a senior orthopaedic surgeon with Manipal Hospitals.

THE WAY WE WERE

PRAJWAL HEGDE

hachette INDIA

First published in 2023 by Hachette India
(Registered name: Hachette Book Publishing India Pvt. Ltd)
An Hachette UK company
www.hachetteindia.com

1

Section divider illustration from Freepik
Author picture by Om Prakash

ISBN 978-93-5731-191-5

Hachette Book Publishing India Pvt. Ltd
4th & 5th Floors, Corporate Centre
Plot No. 94, Sector 44, Gurugram – 122003, India

Typeset in Amiri 11/14.5
by Manmohan Kumar, Delhi

Printed and bound in India
by Manipal Technologies Limited

MIX
Paper from responsible sources
FSC www.fsc.org FSC™ C043100

For

Myra, Gulabi, Shambhavi...

If it's love, it's never lost...

Chapter 1

I knew the scent. A cocktail of cigarettes, lust and Davidoff.

Then I heard the name. Andrew Brown.

Perched on tables, staring at the rotating chairs with a 360-degree take, colleagues were in conversation, a hushed exchange of exclamations and bumfuzzled expressions. Only the name rose above the din.

Blue jeans, weather scarred. A hoodie. A metonym.

I thought I had swept it all into that bin of forgettable art.

'Myra,' I heard someone call, but I kept going.

The amalgam of LED bulbs and 11 a.m. light was blinding. The window shades should be free to do their job.

'Myra.'

I turned abruptly and crashed into a paper-laden office attendant. My iPad slipped from my grip, as did a file and my unzipped tote, the contents of which lay scattered around me like party confetti.

I don't usually walk around like a porter, balancing bits and pieces of property. I'm organized, everything has a place, is in its place. But this was *that* kind of a morning.

My head was heavy, my feet were slow. A muscle-relaxant-fused interlude. An electric current speared through my spine shattering the lull.

Hands reached out to help, pick up my belongings, gather the pages that had fanned out across the slate-grey flooring.

'Sorry,' I said to no one in particular.

'You okay?' Neeta asked, picking up my tube of Clinique. With her Sherlock Holmes air, she was holding up my lipstick, looking for the number to determine the exact shade of my pink.

I nodded. This was not the time for words. Neeta didn't need another peek into my mental state.

'Deep,' Neeta decided.

Intense. I threw a furtive glance around the cream-coloured interiors of our office space.

This was usually my favourite time of the day in a newspaper office. There's a crackling freshness to 11 a.m. It was early, but not too early.

It was when I embraced the day. A bawdy Bollywood number playing on my computer, AirPods snug in its case. Caffeine coursing through my veins. Head unwrapping an idea. Fingers hot stepping on a keyboard. An opening para that grabs the collar.

It was also when reporters trickled in, talking on their phones, a persuasive edge to their tone as they attempted to get their day rolling. The swagger was for later, when they had the story to flaunt. The features team had just about swiped in and were catching the breath they had lost in the race to record their entry. Photographers were talking pictures and assignments, or checking people's lipstick, like Neeta today. A few paginators were at their workstations, and the odd desk guy lingered, not quite knowing what to do. To commit to the day or not.

'Hey!' That came from across the office. I knew the voice. It was strong like the brew she was sipping.

'My alarm didn't ring,' I said without turning.

'That kind of a morning, eh?' Sudha, *Morning Herald*'s business editor, enquired.

Sudha was perfectly groomed, as always. Her salt-and-pepper bob matched the grey of her freshly starched cotton sari, which finished in a heavy red border.

'No coffee either.'

'That's brutal,' Sudha sympathized, taking a sip of her Starbucks. Once a lover of filter coffee, she had eloped with espresso mid-sip when deployed in New York for a year.

'Making a grand entrance?' the resident editor said cheerily, walking past us.

Sudha and I laughed politely.

For the record, I was seven minutes late.

I was headed in the direction of my cabin with my editor on my heels, rattling like an overloaded bus. Talking but not making sense.

I needed a few minutes to fix my head and grab a coffee. Not in that order. Today was too-few-hours Thursday, not can-afford-to-stray Tuesday. The weekend supplement is put to bed early on Friday.

How do you eat an elephant? One bite at a time.

I exhaled. It was forced.

I had written most of my story, which was on the resurgent culture of street theatre in Bengaluru. Student groups used this informal presentation to capsule powerful messages, raising awareness on burning issues. My piece was the lead until the chief reporter called me this morning, waking me up with news of a recent shenanigan. A bunch of collegians had been picked up by plain-clothes policemen during a recent performance. They had been charged with selling drugs.

I didn't need the company of a genial editor on a day like this. I was by my seat, facing my desktop. I refused to make eye contact with him, preferring to gaze at the xanthic panelling at the far end of the office.

I had ignored his knock, not that these subtleties ever worked in a newspaper office.

'My dear, I need to have a word with you,' he said, taking my iPad from my hand and placing it on the table.

Raj Kumar was a dapper 56-year-old, a thorough gentleman, which was the only reason his female workforce put up with his endearments.

'I'm not going to take much of your time. I know today is a busy day for you,' he said as he fiddled with a coffee mug that contained dry pens from maybe the last century.

'I wanted to tell you myself,' he said slowly, squaring his shoulders and straightening his back. 'Andrew Brown is joining us.'

There was only one Andrew Brown in journalism.

I tried to nod, but my neck was frozen. I tried to smile, but my lips wouldn't move. My eyes shifted between the computer screen and my boss before getting stuck on him. His chest had puffed, and his eyes sparkled with a weirdly happy look.

The scent was beginning to surround me. Again. Cigarettes, lust and Davidoff. Andrew Brown.

'Here? Is he?' Grammar had abandoned me.

Mr Kumar smiled. 'Obviously, you are eager to meet him, and why not? He's a good-looking chap,' he said with a wink. 'You probably know him. He did his schooling in Bangalore Scottish. You went there too, right?'

'Yes,' I said slowly. 'He, too, went to Bangalore Scottish.'

My school. This is my city, and *Morning Herald* is my newspaper. I'm not dead; I just haven't had coffee yet.

'There,' Mr Kumar said, smiling, rubbing his hands together, 'I knew you'd want to meet him.'

'I know Andrew. Who doesn't?' I said, summoning fake cheer, like the faux diamonds on my earlobe.

'He was here, completing formalities.'

I was on my feet, and Mr Kumar followed suit. My face had broken into a demented grin in a determined effort to commune with my editor.

'He's joining as political editor,' he said. Then added, 'That's for now; we have other plans for him.'

'Of course.' *How about plans for me?* That would be quadrillionth on the waitlist.

I waited for Mr Kumar to leave before dropping into my chair.

Hold on! When did this happen? My hand went to my desk calendar. January 2018. I only woke up 40 minutes late, not 40 years.

Until last week, Andrew was based out of New York, or so his column said. He was a successful journalist and co-author of the bestselling *India: She'll Unmask You*, a sketch of the political climate in the country that was churning out captains, not leaders.

I had followed Andrew's career as it skyrocketed. He had left Bengaluru eight years ago to do his master's in legal studies at Harvard. Outside of interning at a boutique practice in New York City, he didn't pursue the line he had chosen. What started as a dialogue on social media, when he was still studying, veered into a political blog. In an already simmering international climate, his aggressive stand was well received, not just in an informed global market, but more importantly, amongst the youth. Not long after, he was snapped up as a columnist by a prominent publication. There! I remember.

Rajesh Soor, the metro chief, entered my cabin without knocking or asking.

There was nothing Soor hadn't seen or heard around *Morning Herald,* including events that had never happened.

I looked up reluctantly. I wasn't in the mood for conversation. Not that my disinterest registered on him.

'I think,' he said, placing a steaming cup of filter coffee before me, 'he's taking over as executive editor.'

'Who?' I was irritated and let it show.

Rajesh had plodded into my cabin on the pretext of getting me an over-sweetened coffee he knew I wouldn't touch even with my pinky.

'Andrew Brown,' he said, adding, 'Didn't Mr Kumar just tell you that? He has joined us.'

'Oh yeah! He's going to head the political bureau or some such,' I said, my eyes going back to the computer screen.

'That's to begin with. He'll be taking over – captain of the ship – in a couple of months, if my sources are right.'

'Good for him.' The king of clichés was grating on my nerves.

'How can you say that? It's so unfair; everybody is so upset,' he said.

I was aware 'everybody' was probably just him, but he had stirred the pot, and I was curious. 'Why?'

'They should've taken someone in-house, like Sudha, or you maybe…' he said, pausing only to take in my reaction, 'or Saravanan.'

'Saravanan…' I shook my head. 'Sudha would've been great.'

'Or someone younger, like you.'

I smiled and decided to play along. 'Or you.'

'Or me!' He was beaming as he lifted his ungainly self.

It had been ages since I had played pass the parcel, but it was good to know that my skills hadn't softened.

I watched him leave my space laughing. On his way to another audience.

'Right,' I said. 'Coffee!'

But before that steaming stab of caffeine, I needed some air. A quick turn around the central business district (CBD), feeling the January sun on my skin.

While sipping my morning brew, I wanted to chew on everything I had heard.

Andrew Brown, I tried to say, settling into a randomly placed chair at a takeaway counter that offered the odd seat. It wasn't going down, not even with this scald-the-lips, burn-the-tongue concoction.

I'm in the business of news, and I had no idea. No fucking idea.

Chapter 2

I swiped in early the following morning. I was to rewrite some data-based copy on migrant labour. It was the best fit in terms of size and content to replace my argument on the case of students turning the street into a stage.

I was vexed at having to put my story on hold. I had done the reference and spoken to a dozen people. I had written most of the feature. But how do you fight an issue, especially when arrests had been made?

'Myraah...'

The call crashed into my thoughts. It brought down the sheesham-panelled walls that flanked me. I didn't need to look. Naked without the boundaries of construction or distance.

I recognized the voice. The way my name finished on his lips, a triumphant 'ah' rather than an 'a'. A knock had preceded the call. I knew that too – one firm rap. He was conscious of his surroundings, wary of disturbing people. There was never more than one attempt unless it was an emergency.

I continued to work on my keyboard, which, like me, had known better days. I needed time to fix my expression.

When I looked up, I saw that God had framed the entrance to my cabin. All 6'4" of him. A black tee that said nothing and blue jeans that had weathered a storm. I wondered if the blue hoodie, stray filaments of which sat stubbornly on the right shoulder, was draped across the backrest of his chair. The sharply cut sleeves revealed sculpted, slightly hirsute arms. His lips had broken into a lopsided grin.

No, not cool, I wanted to say, except that I knew that wasn't what he was trying to convey.

Andrew Brown wasn't big on appearances. He would never use 'handsome' or 'hot' or any such lame adjective to describe himself or anyone else. If he liked something, he served it plain; embellishing wasn't his style. Any time I complimented his looks, he'd change the subject even before I could catch the colour that stained his cheeks. His manners were faultless, but I can't remember ever hearing a thank you. That's how he had been, at least.

'Myraah,' he repeated as he walked into my cabin, crowding it. That loose-limbed, commandeering gait was engraved in my memory.

He had used my name twice in two minutes, which was already too many times for a month maybe.

The copy I was editing was forgotten; the hole in the page was lost on a screen that was now in sleep mode.

Myra Rai on deadline. *That old stubborn she?* I had no time for her.

The generous light of the midday sun flooded our editorial spaces, countering the aircon that had doubtlessly been turned to some permafrost temperature.

Andrew put his hand out, and I stood up to meet him halfway. It was a firm grip, just the way I had known it. Slowly, we broke from the hold – me first, I think. I may have fronted a blank look, but I was breathless. I needed water. I was going quietly crazy.

Some not-so-delighted office folks had filled me in on the details of the Andrew Brown hiring. The chairman had apparently flown to New York with his flunky, *Morning Herald*'s marketing head, to convince Andrew. He supposedly had more than one offer from India. Andrew went with the most lucrative pitch, which was also from the only newspaper deal he had before him. There was one from a magazine; the rest were net properties. According to the rumour mill at No. 7 MG Road, he had agreed to move only for a year. He was testing the waters to see if he could make the switch to a medium that had long been outpaced in the race to grab eyeballs.

I understood why *Morning Herald* wanted him, but I had my reservations about these postulations.

An institution built on tough-as-nails journalistic principles, which was born during the country's Independence movement, was looking to sharpen its game. A last-ditch effort to attract young readers before committing to digital space.

Andrew was a political pundit. He'd bring much-needed gravitas to the pages of any newspaper in the country. But as far as I knew, he hadn't spent much time in fickle, under-pressure newsrooms, the pillars on which an organization's reliability rested. It was where split-second decisions on stance, what to highlight and where to place the decibel were taken in the dying hours of each day.

I had woken up with a start this morning. Was this new colleague actually *my* Andrew Brown? No longer mine, I reminded myself. Same name, different gents? An imposter, a charlatan?

The man I knew had left home a long time ago. He had thrived, made a name, but not once in those eight years had he looked back. Andrew was a sought-after brand in media today. Why would he choose to return now when he could be anywhere he wanted to be? It didn't add up. Just like that decision to leave law and pursue journalism.

'So, it's really you,' I said, my bored smile in place. I'm better at expressions than doing my make-up. My hands shake – 28 going on 98.

'Unfortunately, it is,' he said, nodding before turning away. Sometimes, when he gestures, he doesn't look at the person he's in conversation with. Reporters do that, too, using the few seconds to take in nuances, but his is an old habit.

Unfortunately, he had said. I was not going to correct him.

His appearance was eloquent. He was taking it all in his stride – the envy-stained synthetic shirts and every pair of kajal-lined eyes that filled the bays of our newsroom.

There were more squeals than story ideas coming from the female section, and suddenly, lipstick-kissed tissues were lying all over the restroom.

'Back in Bengaluru. Welcome home,' I said cheerily.

He was watchful. Every twitch of my lineless face had been noted and filed away.

I was taking my time. Andrew knew me as an easy-going soul, and that was all he was going to see.

'Thank you,' he said, settling into the lone chair that faced me.

His arms were folded across his chest. His eyes scanned the walls of my cabin. To his right were three frames of blooms, *Tabebuia rosea* in yellow and pink and the gulmohar. My favourites, my pictures. He knew it. On his left was an abstract painting by a friend. I could see that he was straining his eyes, trying to read the name of the artist. I let him. He may not have trained as a journalist, but he had learnt quickly. We sniff stories before we hear about them.

'I didn't think I'd be back so soon either. It was always my plan to come back home eventually.' He spoke suddenly, his eyes roaming the length of my desk. They lingered on the back of a heart-shaped frame that faced me. Only decorum stopped him from turning it around.

I nodded. His vacillating plans were of no interest to me. *Not any longer,* I told myself.

'I like the look,' he said, pointing at my hair, moving his fingers like a pair of scissors.

I had chopped my tresses a few months ago after wearing my hair long for most of my life. My mother had loved my hair. Hers had been straight and silky; I got my father's curls, or at least what he once had of it. I'd never had a hair opinion for as long as Mummy was around; she took care of it. In the last year or so, I had the itch to experiment. I coloured it, streaked it in shades of wine, but while it looked great, it had ruined my hair. My soft ringlets suddenly felt like straw.

'Oh!' I flicked aside his compliment. 'It's the result of an experiment gone wrong.'

'Short hair suits you. Not everyone can pull it off.' His dark eyes sweetened like chocolate. I tasted the compliment. I wanted to do a shampoo ad then and there, but I shrugged instead. It was awkward, in step with the erratic beat of my heart. I hated how my body was betraying me in his presence.

Wait! Did he think I had done this for him? Visited a salon a week ago to give myself a new look.

'I had it styled a few months ago,' I said. *Why was I offering an explanation?*

Andrew's grin was galling. His eyes danced as they studied me. Dangling filigree earrings, bare neck, just a watch on my wrist.

'I committed to returning a few months ago, too.'

'Lucky *Morning Herald*!' Damn the teasing.

I consciously didn't take a deep breath but did the mental equivalent of the same. I pressed the reset button in my head, not to start again but to take a step back, to relax. I needed to be in charge. My mind was moving in a hundred different directions. *Was he married? Did he have a family?* I crushed the questions before they found a voice to break into the open.

He smiled. 'No place like home.'

I wondered where he was staying. He had sold his family's crumbling mansion in the CBD before he left for the United States. A high-end apartment complex had come up in its place. I knew he had been offered a flat by the builder as part of the deal, but I wasn't sure how that had panned. If he had taken ownership of the 3,000-square-foot facility on offer or if he had banked the equity.

'I would agree, even though I don't really know any other place other than home,' I said.

'You should try your wings. Test yourself.' He wasn't mocking; the tone was encouraging. Still, it wasn't his place to advise me.

'Some of us fly in our own spaces, but fly we do.'

'You certainly are,' he said. 'I was reading some of your stuff before coming here. You've captured the people's market, shifted the dialogue back from trends to people. Your crime series is outstanding.'

My smile was slow to show. How long had he been reading my pieces? Was he surprised when he saw my byline for the first time? I hadn't decided on print journalism when he was in Bengaluru, but that was the direction I was headed in. I had a job well before his blogs struck a chord in influential corridors. Maybe I was his role model.

I was delirious, drifting like a sun-kissed wave. *Myra!*

'Is crime your beat?'

'No,' I replied, startled by the question.

I reached for my water bottle and took a swig. A drop dribbled down my chin. I'm clumsy. Put your last rupee on me dropping something every day, and you won't be poorer. Several times each day actually. As I returned my bottle to its place, I noticed Andrew reaching forward. I pushed back in my seat, panicking, and wiped the stray droplet with the back of my hand. *What was he thinking?*

He'd done it every time I drank from a bottle when we were together. Sometimes, he used a tissue, but most often, it was just his hand.

'I'm in features,' I said, before correcting myself, 'heading features. That's just a column I write.'

'Your USP.'

I smiled. 'You'd recognize quite a few of the stories,' I said, refusing to let this charming little interlude waylay me.

'Some are big cases from our younger days. I'm trying to track the journey of this city – once a quiet cantonment town, to the bustling metropolis it is today – through its crime scenes. Does that make sense?'

Andrew nodded. 'It's not the most innovative idea, revisiting popular crime stories, but I like how you've linked it to the city, cultural backdrop, economic growth. It is a secondary character almost.'

I was smiling. Hopefully, in my head only.

'How did it start?'

It wasn't fortuitous play.

Days after my mother's death, I started scouring crime stories, sections in newspapers, segments in the news, and as much of the meta space as I could get to, looking for answers for what I believed was a motivated homicide.

My parents were locked in a heated argument the night before my mother was mowed down. I heard the words 'loan' and 'not cleared'. I had put it down to my dad's fitful dalliances with funds at the time. He could never get that right.

Though the accident in which I lost my mother was declared a drunken-driving case a few months later, I wasn't convinced. The file was closed, but my doubts were open wounds.

Drunk at 8.30 a.m.? He would've been lying under a couch, dead to the world, not behind a steering wheel.

A couple of years ago, I even took it up with a cop I had befriended on the job. There were no loopholes in the case, no openings to claim doubt.

'It was clean and clear,' the policeman had said.

Those were the bare facts.

'I was looking to give the pages an edge,' I said. I ignored his question.

Andrew nodded. His eyes were on me.

I exhaled. An anodyne sound escaped my lips.

'It can't be a random death…' Andrew said. He stopped and smiled, letting the shift in mood complete his sentence. No death is random. 'It has to be a sensational case – one people will bite into.'

'Yes,' I said, 'there's something ugly about this profession.'

I was so focused on not stumbling that I hadn't noticed his gaze had dropped to my collarbone.

My left hand rushed to the rescue of my suitably uncovered clavicle, dislodging the keyboard in the process.

Was that a smile on Andrew's perfectly sculpted face?

It might've been a whole different view he was looking down at had we been on our feet. This civilized posture of being seated on a chair had its merits.

I needed to keep talking, that was my only out.

'It was a stressful time,' I said. 'Digging out details was the toughest part. How did you discover the body? What did you see? Who did you call? What did the message say? The details that are needed. I took a month off after writing those seven pieces. I was exhausted. That bank had busted me. Only when I returned to work did we launch the column.'

'Are you okay?' His right hand reached across the table but stopped midway.

'Some of these guys are psychopaths; they have no remorse. It's kind of crazy. While there are others who look regular, like you and me, even after 10–15 years in jail. They planned these elaborate murders, which they may have actually got away with if not for a twat here or a turn there.'

When I looked up, I noticed that he was staring at me intently. His eyes were of such a deep hue, they would've passed as my coffee. They stirred strange sensations in me.

'Politics is the hard stuff supposedly, and features are fluff,' I said, holding his gaze for the first time since he walked into my cabin. 'Quadrupled whisky to gin and tonic.'

I caught a flicker, a light I hadn't noticed before. My eyes dropped. It might have just been a shaft from the window behind me.

Andrew's face crinkled with laughter. 'You have changed. The fierce Myraah.'

Slayed! He was reading me faster than a graphic novel.

'We only show the world what we want them to see.'

'We,' he repeated after me, tasting the word. There was an intangible sadness to Andrew Brown 2.0, or was that a sagacious air? Something lost, something gained.

Looking at him seated across from me, the visual treat aside, I was glad *Morning Herald* had invested in real talent rather than technology in their last defence of the physical property. Whether or not Andrew Brown was capable of leading that fight is a different debate, but I liked the choice my organization had made.

'More serious, too,' he said.

We had hardly met, but he had made all the right deductions while I had more unasked questions in my head than words for this piece I was rewriting. I laughed out loud. I had to rebuke myself. Come on!

It doesn't always have to be a hundred, Myra!

'Want to come and have a look at my space?' he asked suddenly. 'Show me around the office maybe?'

The gall of the man! I was on deadline. I had a story to finish. He walks into the place and thinks he can own my time? What did he think? Only he wrote for the newspaper while the rest of us flipped burgers while we waited to fill the G-strings between advertisements?

'I would've loved to show you around, Andrew, but I am on deadline.' I lost the laugh; my smile was salty. This was easier. I should try trading insults in the next round.

He nodded quickly. 'I'm sorry,' he said, straightening up to his full height.

'Don't be,' I said, sweetly. 'It'll catch up with you, too, Mr Political Editor.'

He laughed again. That slow, rhythmic laugh.

Chapter 3

Andrew Brown was my first crush. He was the boys' school captain at Bangalore Scottish. A topper in academics, he ran a mean 100 metres and played on the right wing for the hockey team. I was blushing within minutes of being introduced to him in a light-flushed quadrangle. I was 12 and new to the debate club where he was already a senior at 14.

He had started inhabiting my dreams a couple of years before that introduction. It was the name that intrigued me initially, the Anglo-Indian in him grabbing my attention. My classmates were Anita or Sita or Akila, and the boys' school, which was across the road from us, had its share of Stanleys, Sureshes and Shoaibs. There was a distinctive ring to Andrew Brown.

I told no one about my crush. Not even Meena, my closest friend at the time. There wasn't much to say, outside of the warm welcome he had given me to the debate club. He had done the same for almost all the other 64 people in the guild; besides, half the girls in school had the hots for Andrew. All of which I chose to ignore, playing that greeting in my head every night as if it were a sonnet penned just for me.

I had no plans of acting on my feelings. I was content with spotting the waistband of his underwear that popped out every time he bent during debate club meetings. On the odd occasion he passed me on the street, I followed him at a distance. He, of course, barely noticed me outside school. I was fine with that;

he wasn't seeing anyone. Had Andrew Brown bought so much as a leaf, never mind a red rose, it would've been the lead story of our campus weekly.

My crush, however, came undone a few years later, on the night of the school's annual ball. Andrew opened the floor with the girls' school captain, Manisha Seth. She was in an Anita Dongre dress. If I had the means, that was what I'd have worn. It was electric blue with self-colour detailing.

After the first song, he walked in the direction of where the bulk of the girls were seated.

Meena was not with her regular fashion clique; she had chosen to sit with me. I was elated. She was in a cream Chanel dress that skimmed her knees. She could've worn any outfit and made it look grand, but that deliciously fresh shade, almost the colour of her skin, was a standout choice. She paired her skyscrapers, which had a dainty red strap, with a clutch of the same shade. She whispered the brand name of the footwear in my ear, Manolo Blahnik (it sounded like a European variant of Hakka noodles).

Meena was in a particularly chatty mood that evening. I tried to keep up with her words, make sense of what she was saying, even as my eyes got busy. Andrew looked exactly like he had in my dreams. Never mind the corduroy blazer, which hadn't seen a lint roller since it was first put together, or the ill-fitting black trousers. His steps were light and quick; there was a rhythm to his stride, as if he were already dancing.

When he was almost in line with the row in which I was seated, I felt my stomach churn. It turned into a tight knot, a cricket ball. I began sweating. I wasn't prepared for this. Andrew Brown, the hottest boy in town, was going to ask me, this skinny, awkward girl, for a dance. He was actually going to ask me. I was going to break into grateful hysterical sobs.

My dress was new; my mother had bought it for me. It was loose in all the wrong places, but I loved it. I had borrowed my mother's sandals, and her lip gloss was the only make-up I had used.

She said I looked lovely, and that was good enough for me when I left home earlier in the evening. But with Andrew standing before me, I wished I was better dressed. Wearing something sharp. I should have listened to my mother and bought a nice pair of stilettos. I had saved money for it but got lazy in the end.

Who would have thought that Andrew Brown would ask me for a dance? I didn't think he even knew my name. I stopped breathing when he paused by my chair, standing in front of me. I wasn't sure if I was already dead, so I instructed myself to inhale, exhale. Go through that stuff that living, breathing creatures generally do. Just to be sure. I inhaled him. Dettol soap, perhaps.

Andrew bent down to my level and smiled. I promise, the rising sun was the colour of melting chocolate. I tugged at my dress, preparing to get up.

'Excuse me,' he said softly. A ton of bricks might've felt lighter.

He had moved past me to Meena, who was still in her hundred-word-per-minute mode.

I tried hard to forget what followed... But how do you wash away a rubber stamp on your heart?

Andrew stretched out his hand; his palm was open. In a flash, Meena was walking beside him. 'Bye,' she turned to tell me, delighted by her conquest.

I can't recollect much of that evening except that Andrew danced with Meena all night. He had eyes only for her, even if hers were wandering.

The next morning, the student's edition of *Morning Herald* carried a picture of Meena and Andrew, captured between the railings of the school gate. It was all the photographers could get of the closed-door affair, a marked event on the city's social calendar.

I was also in the photograph, somewhere in the blackened background. Like a balloon deflated with a pin.

Chapter 1

I had taken refuge at my workstation an hour ago, but it felt like 10 minutes.

I scrolled through the breaking news stories on social media.

An actor was getting married. She was wearing an ornate diadem because her name rhymed with 'tiara'.

A batter had scored runs and a bowler had taken wickets.

Somebody was making pickles and elsewhere people were raising funds for world peace.

Social media took care of my anxiety on days I didn't run.

From the far corner of the table, a photograph of my mother was smiling at me. My lips twitched.

My landline blared, cutting into my calm like a motorist on steroids.

Who could that be? This wasn't an internal call. I cast a glance around me. The editorial was moving at a glacial pace. The office was empty when I arrived a little before 10 a.m., but there had been a considerable spill of people since.

'Hello,' I said. I was breathing heavily.

'Are you okay?' It was Ravi. He sounded worried. I reached for my mobile instinctively. I had three missed calls. All from my boyfriend. My phone was on silent and inside my tote.

'Where have you been?'

I'm not a fan of that question. Only my mother was allowed to pin me down like that, but even she didn't get an answer. It was an unfair tackle. Ravi's tone, as always, was sweet concern.

'My phone was on silent.'

'Where are you?'

'You are calling my landline.'

Ravi laughed, and I joined him.

'Welcome back!' Ravi had been travelling on work the last couple of weeks.

'I'm around your office. Are you up for a coffee?'

I had been ready for coffee ever since I parked my bum on my seat an hour ago, but I was too lazy to get up and make it happen. Reasons to get that first shot of espresso in you before the day surges ahead. Crimes can be committed.

'Good,' I said, standing up immediately.

Ravi wasn't big on the chain outlets scattered around Morning Herald Towers. He had joined me once at my favourite coffee shop, Perky Grace. It was located at the helm of Church Street, some 800 metres from my office. It was semi-outdoor, the tables were nicely spaced, and stone benches and star jasmine vines gave it a garden party vibe. The brewers are sturdy, and the servers are gentle. The bakery will make it to my crime series one day.

Let's just say Ravi liked the coffee and not the cup. Too public, he called their space. He preferred his five-star privacy. Every time, thereafter, he drove me to the coffee shop of a luxury hotel some five minutes from my office.

As I walked out of my cabin, I heard my name being called. I winced.

It was white-tee day today; no blue or hoodie of any other hue, I gathered.

'I was coming around to your cabin,' Andrew said, walking up to me. I wished he would sit down and not walk.

I nodded. This was bad timing. Not the coffee but his wanting to come around to my cabin.

'Work?' I asked, grinding my feet to the ground. What else could it be: *Myra? Your dating plans?*

Andrew laughed.

'Where are you going?' Andrew asked.

Boundaries. I blinked to buy time.

I was going to get a coffee but not really just get a coffee. Andrew was not my boss. He may have been in a super senior position, but we were not in college.

'I'm going to get a coffee.'

'You've only just got to work.'

He was questioning me. And because I hadn't logged in, he was assuming I had just arrived at my workstation.

My gaze shifted from the 6'4" tower of dubiety before me to the brightly lit floor around us. We had the interest of the business bay, which we now faced. There were seven men and two women. Fingers on keypads and eyes on the white tee. Sudha was in her cabin, hammering away.

'So?' I asked, turning on my heels.

I did a flip-flop as soon as I sat down. I suddenly wanted to do a takeaway.

'Why?' Ravi asked. He looked so forlorn that I changed my mind again and said we could do a quick coffee. 'Very quick,' I added, just as he started to smile.

'I know you're a busy lady,' he said, keeping the smile, meaning nothing more than what was articulated.

That run-in with Andrew had unsettled me.

'Andrew Brown has joined the paper,' I said. I don't know why, but it felt like dropping the joker from an already disconnected hand in a game of rummy.

I had mentioned Andrew to Ravi when we started dating. I had lauded the man's brilliance, even introduced him to Andrew's blog. I had also said we were close friends who dated briefly before going back to being friends. The mood was light and the fractional disclosure somewhat flippant. Ravi didn't pose Andrew Brown questions that day or any other time.

'You are reunited with your friend!'

Friend? I laughed. It was a hollow sound.

Ravi was the most uncomplicated person I knew. It might have something to do with him being an on-the-surface kind of creature. Not in a frivolous way, only that it is his core. He didn't feel too deeply. He didn't bleed, at least where people and relationships were concerned. My antithesis.

Hari Rao, Karnataka's longest-serving chief minister, who walked away from politics after three successive terms, is Ravi's 'grandfather'. Hari Rao lost his son, daughter-in-law and two grandkids in an air crash towards the end of his third term in office. Ravi was rumoured to be Rao's wife Kamini's nephew. He was adopted a couple of years before the horrific accident. The family referred to him as the grandson, presumably because of the age difference between him and Rao's progeny.

That Kamini was an only child further fuelled the parentage debate. There was some talk that Ravi was a distant younger relative's son. He had Kamini's eyes and nose (I downloaded a picture of the former CM's late wife and held it against Ravi's profile picture). They had the same square build, were of middling height and were remarkably broad-boned.

Ravi had told me that he was Hari Rao's grandson shortly after we became friends; that was enough of a personal introduction. He had gone to medical school only because his grandfather wanted him to. The Raos owned a chain of multi-speciality hospitals around the state, which also catered to the economically challenged sections of society.

I put down Ravi's on-the-surface personality to his early life. Just as well, actually, that he wasn't the touchy-feely sort. To be adopted, and so publicly at that, with his grandparents ostensibly being the only parents he knew. Then to have those second set of parents lose their only child. I didn't broach the subject of his biological parents after the first time I had involuntarily asked who they were. Not quite a do-you-prefer-cheese-or-whipped cream-frosting question.

It was the third or fourth time I had met him. He repeated that he was Hari Rao's grandson and sat there smiling like some sort of a phantom.

Yeah, but what do your parents do? The question had almost slipped out of my mouth. I'm slow sometimes.

Hari Rao had all but thrown in the towel after the death of his son. Barely living. As heavy as that loss was, I've often wondered how Ravi didn't ask, *What about me?* Was Ravi inconsequential? Didn't he want more? Quite the opposite, he's superbly adjusted. There are pictures of him breaking down after he lit Kamini's funeral pyre (googled that, too; it makes my world go around).

'Yeah,' I said, taking a sip of my coffee. 'I'm reunited with my friend, except that he's more boss than friend.' The caffeine trickled down my pharynx. The heat of the beverage warmed my spirit, calmed my nerves.

'How is that?'

I explained Andrew's hiring to Ravi, adding that he could take over as the executive editor of the newspaper soon. I had repeated all of this so often in the last few weeks, I was simply reciting it now. As if it were a poem that didn't rhyme.

'You guys were classmates, right?' Ravi asked.

'Schoolmates.'

Ravi came into my life the day Andrew exited it.

It wasn't easy allowing him in. Not just because of what I had shared with Andrew, but for about a year, I had harboured hopes that Andrew would call or message. How could he not? I swallowed the question with another sip of the brew.

Looking at Ravi leaning back on a library chair, I thought this friendship wouldn't have been possible with anyone other than Ravi.

We are antonyms; if we were typefaces, we'd be Bold and Light. I could get lost in a book; he hadn't read anything long form beyond a college textbook. Movies were not his expression, and I relied on them to get me on my feet on a bad day, feeling them in my step. He had no interest in politics; I was in the business of news. He never had a job. Not the 9-to-5 variety or even the 11-to-9 kind – his MBBS degree was never really put to use. But I always yearned for financial independence. I knew I needed a job the moment we laid my mother to rest.

It was his personality, however, that allowed me to take the chance.

About a year or so after we started dating, Ravi told me that it wasn't easy for him to trust because he wasn't sure what women – or in an arranged set-up, the families – were after: his inheritance or him. I didn't ask, but I figured he had been let down in a few relationships. That day, as he dropped me home in his car, he reached across and kissed me on the cheek. He gave me a ring the following year.

I never wore the ring, and he didn't ask me why. Not once. It is ornate, and I'm sure there are people who think it gorgeous, but it wasn't my style or size.

'How come you were around my office today?' I asked lamely. I wanted to get off the topic of Andrew.

'I wasn't really around. I wanted to meet you today. I got ready early, and that's when I started calling you.'

Ravi met me for coffee once a week. We usually met in the first half of the week, when I was breathing a little easier. And it was always at the start of my working day.

Our time together was pleasant. Ravi wasn't much of a talker, but he had a measured opinion about most things. He was equally adept at losing himself in thought, and we would drift into our own worlds. A parallel space.

It was one of those times when we were drifting, some six months ago, at this luxury hotel, sitting in this exact same spot, that he had proposed.

He drummed his fingers on the table and asked, 'How about we get married?' It was asked in much the same tone he used to ask me if I wanted another coffee.

I hadn't thought about marriage, even though he had been hinting for a while.

'Of course,' I said, not knowing what the hell I was saying, except that I knew that I didn't want to break this lovely man's heart. 'But we should talk about it another time. You know, give it a real thought.'

'Of course,' he said. His smile didn't dim.

'You should come home,' I told him.

'I would love that,' he said, his eyes brightening.

He gave me the ring anyway. A second ring I couldn't wear. Hopelessly loose.

Looking at his mauve shirt, full-sleeved and of superior weave, and his perfectly fit form, I realized that Ravi didn't complete me. He balanced me. She of the boyfriend jeans and thigh-length shackets. He was the perfect antidote to the whirlpool of emotions churning inside me. The grieving daughter, the slighted girlfriend. The woman who wanted to be.

All that he is. All that I'm not. An equation that balanced. How I longed to be a mathematical sum.

Chapter 5

The wind-blown look was working for Chhaya Mehta. Her kurta and dhoti pants billowed with a passing drift, which had dislodged her dupatta. Her hair was an unquiet wave.

My eyes shifted to my wrist; she was late again.

Chhaya laughed, unfazed by my subtle attempts to guilt trip her.

I hadn't seen my friend in a while. I was out of town for a week, chasing a story. When I returned, she was busy, sucked in by family and work. Each time we decided to meet, Chhaya would ring at the last hour to call it off. She was dealing with one kind of emergency or another. We hadn't communicated much in the last three weeks, outside of the odd text.

Over the years, Chhaya and I had fashioned a little tradition. Every Wednesday, we met for breakfast at Perky Grace. We'd been doing this for five years. We met otherwise, too, if life permitted, but that midweek outing was our time.

The scheduled hour was 9 a.m., but invariably, I reached a few minutes earlier and she came in humming her favourite tune of the time at least 20 minutes late.

We would order one plate of English breakfast and an egg puff. There was no need to go through the menu; it was always the same pick. We'd peck at the food while downing a few rounds of hot beverages, pretending we were lactose-intolerant after the first. The generous tip we left behind was for the brewmaster, who knew just how to wake a girl up. A strong cappuccino.

I usually drove down from the gym, where I showered and changed into office wear. Home was just two kilometres away, but it wasn't an option. Weekday traffic. I arrived balancing two big bags, laptop in one and Eves Essentials in the other. I'm not comfortable leaving valuables in the car, unless I've dunked them in the boot when no one was watching. Stealing from cars is like slicing bread, it's all in the technique. Not surprising then that weights are an all-day feature for me.

Chhaya would park at her office, located two buildings from Morning Herald Towers, and walk over with no more than a clutch, which she promptly placed next to my voluminous tote. 'You and me,' she'd say with a laugh. The sum of our differences.

Chhaya only carried a big handbag on night outs. All she needed in the day were a few relevant cards, a lipstick and some change to tip the parking attendant, besides her phone and car keys. But on a social outing, she carried her whole house. A shawl, a vanity kit, a book to read (no idea why she packed that in because she was always the last to arrive), an extra pair of ballet flats in case her stilettos (that cost as much as my second-hand car) gave way.

Chhaya headed her family's business empire, Mehta's Limited (ML), which she sometimes called 'unlimited'. It included cinema halls in upmarket malls in Delhi, Mumbai, Kolkata, Pune and Bengaluru and a chain of 30-odd eateries that dotted highways in the southern half of India. Mehta Express had corrupted taste buds with their wallet-friendly north Indian pickings that attracted all sections of society. ML also owned petrol bunks and 24x7 medical stores in four metros.

Chhaya and I go back 14 years, when the Mehtas shifted to Bengaluru. Our paths crossed in high school, but it took a while for our friendship to warm up. Back then, I had a friend, and she had several pals. I would've liked to be popular, but I was the basic model student. Chhaya and I moved in the same circles but in different directions.

I remember Chhaya's first day at Bangalore Scottish; she made a striking entry. She was the only new entrant to Class IX that year, and I couldn't take my eyes off her. Most of the students were engaged in an eager exchange of opening-day pleasantries when the teacher's voice rose above the rest, calling for silence. She made the introduction soon after, telling the room of 30 teenagers that Chhaya Mehta would join our section.

'Wow!' a random voice from the back rows exclaimed. It might've been mine.

She was tall, having grown most of her 5'10" by then. My height made me awkward, hers gave her a *Teen Vogue* air. Her wavy brown hair was tied in a loose braid. I preferred the green of her eyes to the shade of her tunic, which was different from the rest of the class because she had gone with a lighter weave.

She had only just stepped into our midst when she was expressly roped into the fashion clique, a group of girls who had everything money could buy, including boyfriends. They called themselves the 'StyleStahs'. I wondered if the second half of the half-baked acronym was 'sisters' or 'stars'. They were four in number until that June morning.

I was at the periphery of this bunch of expensively-turned-out teens by default. Meena Iyer, who was the epicentre, was my closest friend in school.

Ours was an unlikely association. I didn't have the fashion sense or hail from that kind of money that gives one admittance into these leagues. But Meena was a generous soul. She looked out for me. If I didn't tag along to their outings every time she invited me, it was only by choice. I had no great longing to be a charity case, even back then. I took care of Meena's homework. She attempted it most days but couldn't complete it. Juggling outings, outfits and boys was time-consuming.

When the StyleStahs fragmented two years later, following the Class X board exams, each going separate ways, Chhaya and I drifted towards each other organically.

Unlike Meena, however, Chhaya rarely telephoned me once she was home. She came home often though, dined with us, slurping glasses and glasses of my mother's 'sumbarrr', which she later bastardized for her eateries, calling it exactly that.

My first visit to the Mehtas was years later, after I joined *Morning Herald*. Chhaya had invited me to lunch with her family. I used to think Chhaya lived in an apartment complex, not as tired looking as ours, but a flat all the same. However, she lived in a bungalow with a circular driveway. At the centre of the lawn was a marble fountain. Liveried guards manned the gates.

Chhaya greeted me at the door, standing a little behind her uniformed housekeeper, Mrs Molly.

As she led me to the formal dining hall, she apologized for her father, who was away on work. A giant door opened into the grandest room I had ever seen, fit for a state banquet. My whole house could flow into it comfortably. My eyes were so busy taking in the walls and the high ceiling that I failed to notice the two people seated at the other end of the mighty teakwood table. A lady in Juicy Couture tracks and an awkward-looking boy. Chhaya introduced me to her mother. I smiled involuntarily. My eyes were still on the boy.

'And this is Chetan,' she said, 'my brother.' She smiled as she spoke; I heard it in her voice. Chetan made snorting sounds. His eyes were like Chhaya's, his skin was pale, and his neck didn't hold.

I had thought that, like me, Chhaya was an only child. I would joke about it when we were in school, and she never once corrected me, going along, even teasing me.

'Chetan has cerebral palsy,' she said softly as we settled into our chairs, 'but we're making sure the palsy doesn't have him.'

I turned to my friend and smiled. She responded with a laugh.

It was then that I saw for the first time, beyond the mesmerizing colour of her eyes, a quiet sparkle that reflected in everything she did.

Long ago, the Mehtas had made a family decision not to talk about Chetan. They never hid Chetan, but they didn't advertise their life either. They wanted to protect their daughter.

I stole glances as mother fed son, making soft, cooing noises, comforting him. She was telling him about me, 'didi's best friend'. He tried to get up from the chair and move towards his sister. His mother didn't stop him. Instead, she followed him, and his sister rose from her chair and reached out to him. She ran her hands through his hair and pecked him on the cheek.

Later that evening, as I chatted to a photograph of my mother, I told her that, like me, Chhaya had everything.

Chhaya and I were similar people with distinctive tastes. She drank tea, and I was a coffee lover; she had a sweet tooth, while I devoured savouries; our political ideologies were not opposite but different; reading habits, Hardy and Austen. She liked milk chocolates, and I enjoyed them dark and bitter; she flaunted easy lines, and I liked my clothes fitted, but we were united by a toughness we instantly recognized in the other.

As she settled into a garden chair opposite mine at Perky Grace on this windswept Bengaluru evening, I was quick to verbalize the elementary questions of 'how' and 'why'. I forced her to speak first. I was buying time.

We had broken with our Wednesday breakfast tradition, reuniting as we were after three weeks. Any time of day or night would do.

Chetan had contracted a virus; his body temperature had risen to 104 degrees. They thought they had lost him. He cried all day and night, his limbs wracked in pain. He would scream and turn violent even. Chhaya and her mother took turns nursing him, and her father never left the room.

They could afford all the help in the world, but the Mehtas took care of their own.

Chhaya was exhaling. Her eyes widening in terror, her fuchsia-stained lips twisting, her voice strained in part until it gave way to laughter.

I rode the roller coaster with her.

As I drained the last of my once extra-hot, now ice-cold cappuccino, my eyes were still on her.

'Enough about me,' she said suddenly. 'What's going on with you, babe?'

The drama in my life didn't compare to what she had gone through these last weeks. I was caught between a sob and the excitement that was growing within me. I didn't know what to say.

Chhaya stretched out her long legs and wrapped her arms across her chest.

'What's that?' she asked.

I had a choice, of smiling and putting it all off for later, or I could just tell her. I chose the latter. It would be a good distraction for her, and it would make me lighter. Win-Win.

'Andrew Brown has joined *Morning Herald*.'

My revelation was met with radio silence, which is Chhaya's standard reaction to an unexpected shift in conversation.

She needed time to digest. A whole tea cake could be sliced in the interim.

'Who?' she asked lamely, holding my gaze before her eyes shifted to a spot beyond me, as if she was trying to place someone in the distance.

I nodded.

'What?' she asked as she pulled herself together, sitting upright. '*The* Andrew Brown? Our schoolmate?'

'The very same.'

'Are you happy? Wait, you have to be happy... No... Savage!' Then finally, 'But where has he been all these years?'

My friendship with Chhaya had gaps, from when we first said hello to each other to when we started chatting. Then, again, after school. Chhaya pursued a business management degree, which at first took her away from Bengaluru, after which she sought a transfer and came home, while I studied humanities at a local campus. We didn't drift apart; we just didn't keep in touch after stray attempts in the early months. She got busy with her course and family while I was otherwise engaged.

Some three years later, a chance meeting on MG Road got us back on track. I was rushing to the office with a takeaway coffee in my hand when I heard someone call, 'Myra.' Chhaya had stopped her car in the middle of Bengaluru's busiest road and was hollering. I turned abruptly, and the coffee was all over me. 'Wait right there. I'm coming in a minute,' she said. Just like that, we were back in each other's lives.

Her eyes widened briefly, replaced by a wicked smile.

'He's a super-successful journalist,' I said.

'And so are you.' She was laughing, but it had a hysterical ring to it. 'Have you met him?'

I nodded.

'The ghost who walks!'

'I'd have stopped at ghost.'

I gave her the lowdown on the Andrew Brown hire, the money and the madness.

I listed the pros and cons of *Morning Herald*'s most high-profile addition to the editorial team in recent times, but I kept going back to how the whole exercise had flown over my head. I'd had no idea, none at all.

'Is he married?' Chhaya asked, her eyes twinkling.

I shrugged. Like men wear mangalsutras!

'Is he dating?'

'How would I know?'

'What's he joining as?'

'He's not the peon.'

'Myra!'

'For now, as the political editor, but the plan is to make him executive editor or whatever. If he st–'

'Have you guys spoken?'

I nodded slowly.

'What the fuck! When... How did this happen? Why didn't you call me?'

I shrugged again.

'The dress,' she said, looking at me like she was seeing me for the first time. She was pointing at my navy-blue outfit that had ridden up my legs.

I didn't adjust my skirt; there was only that much of it.

She was smiling now. 'I don't remember seeing it before,' she said, leaning forward.

She hadn't. It was new.

Chapter 6

Four years may be a long time, but not distant enough to forget your first crush. It was a Saturday night in March 2007, and I was at one of the most happening nightspots in the city, The Colour Black.

There were two groups of students, one a bunch of 20-odd boys and three girls who had gathered for a reunion. The other was us, an all-girl group of 15 from St. Mary's, celebrating a birthday.

It was past 11 p.m. The place was fast emptying, but DJ Ivan Roller wasn't ready to quit. One of my friends started tapping her feet to a catchy nineties tune. Within minutes, we were all shaking our booties, moving as much to the beat as to the liquid diet we were on.

It was then, as I was shaking and two-stepping, that I first noticed Andrew. The brown eyes that carried a hint of winter chill were on me, too. My heart skipped a beat, and my feet weren't quite as light any more. It was two years since I had passed out of Bangalore Scottish. Despite both of us living in Bengaluru, within a two-kilometre radius of each other, I hadn't clapped eyes on him since the night of the annual ball, a little over four summers ago. I had heard of his exploits. He was blazing a trail at the National Law School and was equally active on the dating scene.

He was the first among the boys to walk up to us. Andrew tapped me on my shoulder and mouthed a hello before introducing himself.

'Of course, I know who you are, Andrew.' Only the weak take refuge in coyness.

He towered over my 5'9" frame, and I was instantly lost in him as we fell into step. My grip firmed against his light touch, just to make sure it was all real.

My mind went back to that starless night four years ago.

'Hello, Captain,' I said, happy to get back to scratch if that's how he wanted to play it. 'I'm Myra. You might remember me from Bangalore Scottish.'

Back in the time when you are scaling grades, it doesn't get bigger than school captain. That changes expeditiously in college, but in some cases, auras don't tail off.

'Myra Rai,' he said, smiling, before twirling me around.

Although I was salivating all over the wooden tiles in spirit, I was holding my own in appearance.

We burnt the spaces between the tables, moving like we were glued at the hip. Our eyes locked from time to time. I felt him, and he felt me. He was a superb dancer, and in his arms, I discovered I could keep pace. Our friends had lined the wall, clapping and whistling as we kept the crowd – plumped by the staff – entertained.

'When do we meet again?' Andrew asked as we called it a night. My heart was racing, and my head was spinning. Too much alcohol. Too much Andrew.

'I'm sure we'll meet soon.' I played it cool. The question had taken me by surprise, and it was all I could do not to bounce up and down and shout, 'Yes. YES.'

'Nice try,' he said. 'I'm not so easy to get rid of.'

I knew Meena and Andrew were not in touch. He had approached her and tried to make a go of things, but Meena wasn't interested. 'Not worth the trouble,' she had said.

'It'll be tough, Andrew,' I parried.

'Give me your phone number.'

I made my way to the waiting cab. Then I snuck my head through the window and shouted, 'It ends with one.'

Andrew stood there looking delighted. Make that delicious.

Not very long ago, on a night like this, I was a mess. My heart had been shot to pieces. But as my mother had promised, the wheel had turned. She hummed a soothing track from a time when reel life was black and white, *'Malagu, malagu charulathe ningu neralide.'* Sleep, sleep Charulatha, there's some shade for you, too.

Chapter 7

That was how we got started – at the end of one day and the beginning of another. On a makeshift dance floor.

Andrew was in his final year at the National Law School, the country's premier institution for legal studies. I was in a similar stage of my bachelor studies; I had taken up journalism.

Only, I had no plans to work in media, or for that matter, anywhere else. I was remarkably without ambition at the time.

I had won an essay writing competition in school, writing on locals adept in the art of selling ripe, almost rotten comestibles. Why fresh and tender was made to age. I had linked this slant to the city's 'adjust maadi' culture. Nowhere else in the country would this kind of nonsense be tolerated. The Bangalorean, instead of charging the cashier to pay them for clearing their diligently accumulated waste, would not only look the other way but even cough up cash for it.

A bag of rancid potatoes going at…

The future of marketing. It wasn't until you were home that you realized you had been played.

That piece was followed up with a letter to the editor on a missing stray. The few paras I hammered out and the picture got a special mention in *Morning Herald*.

It led my mother to believe I was Pulitzer-winning material.

Mummy nudged me towards the media when I was deciding which column to tick for my degree application.

Mummy, much as I love her, was not the reason why I chose journalism. I liked that all the cool people in college had ticked this option.

I was a regular girl. Not straight-silky-hair regular but ringlets-down-to-the-hip regular. I wasn't a topper in anything, but if I put my mind to it, I could be quite a force in academics.

I was going through a rebellious phase when Andrew danced his way into my life. I was fixated on everything I didn't have. Meena's family had moved to the United States, where her father, a head honcho in the IT industry, was to be based for a few years. My dad couldn't hold a job. Meena had the best clothes, her gadgets were top of the line, she could afford to go anywhere she wanted, eat any meal, splurge on spirits. Buy anything, including affection.

My annual shopping budget could buy her blush brush perhaps.

Andrew was the one person in my world who had less than me. He didn't even have a dad or a pre-used car with a disobliging back door. His mother, rumour had it, died in childbirth.

Andrew embraced my life, my parents, my home, the food Mummy laid out on the dining table every time he visited (when it was just the three of us, we ate in the kitchen). Our crockery was middle-class melamine, but it was attractive; our linen was old, but the stubborn stains were adequately covered.

Andrew and I never spoke about what we had or didn't have, but by allowing me into his home, a barely standing bungalow of more than a hundred years, paint peeling, cracked floors and broken windows – an advertisement for derelict disrepair – I saw everything life had afforded me.

Andrew came over whenever he wanted to, even when I wasn't around.

I was good with that. When he accompanied me, we made sure that he kept his hands off me. We were touchy-feely people:

his right palm spread on the small of my back, his thumb hooked into the waistband of my jeans. He'd throw an arm over my shoulder for no reason. I didn't want to alarm my parents with how comfortable I was with his touch. On me, in me.

On a dank afternoon, Andrew recounted how, despite topping not just Bangalore Scottish but all Bengaluru schools in the ICSE (X) and ISC exams (XII), he chose to study law instead of going with popular choices like medicine or engineering.

'I think my mother would've been happy with my decision,' he had said, leaning against the wall in my bedroom.

I clutched my half-empty mug and sported an even expression.

Why would it please his mother?

Did she study law? Or did she want to study law?

I swallowed the questions. What he'd said didn't go down easily. I was born curious. I told myself Andrew meant to say grandmother, not mother.

There was an unspoken agreement between Andrew and me. He never asked where my dad worked, and I didn't probe about his father.

It was common knowledge that Andrew and his grandmother, whom he called 'Nana', owned Bengaluru's number one address, on Rest House Road, a bare-necessities structure that was waiting to be blown away. The Browns could sell and bank the cash at some point perhaps, but as things stood, they were stretched.

I was taking little sips of my black coffee, frustrated that we couldn't talk freely about something that was essentially who we were.

Ask me what my father does for a living, I urged him silently. *Let's bring the dam down.*

Andrew's eyes were fixed on the wall behind me.

'What about your father?' The question slipped out of my mouth.

'Bubbs,' he said, his voice dead. He was shaking his head.

He called me 'Baby' most of the time. 'Bubbs', that cuddly nickname, was, ironically, a sign that shutters were being brought down. The conversation wasn't over, but it would be if you couldn't redeem yourself. That was the last I heard of the Browns.

I stayed over at Andrew's place a number of times, helping him with something or the other, like applications for his master's. Nana was always around, refilling water bottles and making us coffee, which we had with the packets of biscuits my father slipped into my bag.

There was a haunting emptiness to the house. The walls were bare, and there was minimum furniture. Sometimes, when his grandmother, Noelene, opened the door, it felt like I was walking into nothingness, fanned by a draught coming through a window that couldn't be shut. A whisper of an embrace. It felt less empty when Andrew answered the doorbell, which was only once in a while.

I remember the day he got into Harvard. He had come to St. Mary's to tell me about it at lunch break. He didn't call; he borrowed a friend's bike and rode halfway across town to let me know. Andrew was interning with a law firm at that time.

He had some notes in his wallet, which he used to bribe the watchman. I was walking down the college driveway, and he picked me up, hoisting me. When he put me down, he kissed the top of my head and whispered, 'We made it.'

Every pair of eyes on the campus was on me. I still feel it.

'Have you told Nana?' I asked of the only family I knew he had.

'I will,' he said, running his finger down my cheek. 'I have the rest of the day.'

He had the day but not much more time with Noelene.

Chapter 8

It was one of those rare nights when I had gone to bed early. My parents were attending a wedding, and I had drifted off to sleep reading.

Andrew was watching a tennis match, the French Open, in which I had little interest. The trill of the phone woke me up.

'Nana, Noelene... collapsed.' Andrew was at the other end. He was shouting.

I wondered if I was awake. I was, and I was shaking.

I washed my face before locking the flat and heading out. It was only when I exited the lift in the basement that I realized I was in pyjamas and chappals. I was carrying money, but I wasn't in a fit state to call a cab. I decided to run the two kilometres to Andrew's place.

The air was wet. To distract myself from the weather, the catcalls and the bikes that kindly stopped to ask if I wanted to hop on, I thought I might actually like running. One foot in front of the other, listening to the wind hiss, feeling the droplets, tasting them. Wet feet, muddy bottoms. Weather-beaten.

This wouldn't rank among the smartest things I had done. I knew that even as I started running, but Andrew needed me.

The ambulance reached just as I arrived. I climbed into it with Andrew. He hugged me so tight, I thought he had squeezed the living breath out of me.

'Are you carrying some water?' I asked out of habit.

'She won't need water,' he said, crying silently.

Chapter 9

I couldn't get to the 19th Floor quickly enough. My shoes were stalling me – too steep for the pebbled pavement.

I'm normally sensible in these matters. On days that required getting around, which is most workdays, I wore sneakers. Only on occasion did I indulge myself. Looks over comfort.

I hadn't factored in the one-kilometre hike from office to the resto-bar today. Too close to taxi and too far to totter. Blame it on Meena Iyer.

I was meeting my oldest friend – we'd been together since kindergarten – for the first time in nearly a decade. Her family had shifted back to Bengaluru a couple of months ago. Meena had invited Chhaya and me for drinks.

I was excited to see Meena, but equally, a sense of dread had been building inside me after I'd heard from her last week. My heart felt impossibly heavy.

Words were swirling around my head.

The pin that burst the bubble.

A brouhaha I didn't want to acknowledge.

I pushed that draught of grotty air into my recesses and impelled a smile.

There was much to look forward to this evening – the reunion of friends.

That's when the heel of my shoe found the edge of a crevice on the pavement. I was tilting, dragged down by the bulk of my tote, when a firm grip on my elbow steadied me.

As I straightened to my full height, my eyes met rapidly darkening almond-brown pools. The lost notes of halcyon.

The late-evening westerly was playing mind games with me.

'Are you hurt?' Andrew asked, his palm warm around my elbow. I felt his strength.

I inhaled his perfume. I needed air to dilute the effect.

Andrew's eyes caressed the length of my legs. 'Are you hurt?' he asked again.

I hadn't seen him in office today. I had thrown more than a few furtive glances in the direction of his cabin. I didn't want to run into him in the middle of the editorial again.

I wanted to say something, anything… but those words that came cold through the telephone line some eight years ago rang in my ears. Like a cross-connection.

I was torn, shredded into a hundred pieces.

Andrew was now looking at me like I were a book, the pages of which he couldn't turn.

Other women...

Over you...

There was more.

The words settled on my tongue, refusing to leave it like a stubborn stain. I was sweating.

Andrew was saying something. I think he was asking me if I was heading out on work.

The question rang like a timer.

I stepped aside, forcing him to drop his hand, which was cupping my elbow. I swallowed the bitter aftertaste and made my way past him.

I felt his eyes on my back.

I gave myself a once-over in the full-length decorative mirror at the entrance of the resto-bar that had recently featured in Asia's top-10 nightspots.

I was in my go-to black dress, an angular hem that finished well above my knees. I was looking sharp. Andrew's eyes had told me that. I checked my watch. I was on time.

Chhaya had informed us that she would be late. Maybe she'd be in time for the bill!

'Oh my god! Oh my god! You look stunning!' Meena was standing with her palms pressed against her cheeks.

I paused mid-stride and looked around me before covering the few steps between us and enveloping Meena in a hug.

My ankle felt fine, but there was an anxious strain inside me that was threatening to break.

We stayed that way for a whole minute; it was comforting. Meena set me aside and wiped off a stray teardrop.

'Look at you!' she said.

Compliments made me cross-eyed.

'You, too, gorgeous.' I attempted a comeback.

Meena was wearing a linen dress. She looked like she had walked off the pages of one of those glossies she deified.

'I love your shoes. You've changed fully, Myra. You're a whole new woman.'

A whole new woman?

'Tell, tell, tell. When did all this happen?' Sometimes, she had an accent; at other times she sounded just like she had in school.

Meena's decibel level was rising. That's when I noticed the glasses on the table; there were three. Even assuming one was water served in the wrong glass, that was bottoms-upped, too. She was already on her third drink.

There was a bowl of untouched peanuts in the middle of the scattered crockery and cutlery. I reached for it as I seated myself. I was starving. 'Let's order some food,' I said, trying to shift the topic from me and my clothes.

No sooner had we placed our order for food and drinks than she wanted to know when the makeover had happened. 'From ugly duckling to swan. What triggered it?'

Ugly? Was the emphasis on 'ugly' or was it my imagination? Or the slant of her smile.

'It must be your success as a professional. You're working, and you have some money. That always helps. It ups your confidence,' she said, smiling.

'Or I just grew up.'

'And got rid of your clown wardrobe.' She was laughing, flashing pearly-white teeth.

Where was Chhaya when I needed her?

This was a first for the three of us. We hadn't dined together before. When Meena was in Bengaluru for her summer or winter breaks, the two of us would have sleepovers, chatting into the wee hours.

She caught up with Chhaya and the rest of her fashion clique over lunch or dinner.

'This is the first time we are meeting of whatever was left of the group as adults, Meens.'

I don't know why I said it; maybe because I was thinking of it this morning.

'Remember the stuff you wore in school. It was like you had emerged from a dive into a paintbox. We always wondered if you got your clothes from a stall in Shivajinagar.' More laughter.

It was as if Meena couldn't stop herself. The more she drank, the louder she laughed and the deeper she cut.

I love colours, I have to admit. Sometimes, all of them equally and at the same time. But garish? Even though we all have mirrors in our homes, some of us need help, especially at an age when you tend to gloss over the image before you.

I often bump into people from my past in Bengaluru – classmates, school and college, teachers, friends of my parents. Almost every time, I'm told how much I have changed. 'How lovely you look now…' Compliments. Unfinished sentences.

Meena's index finger was tapping her right cheek. I could tell she was thinking, weighing. 'So, naturally, you have a boyfriend now,' she deduced, as if she were tracking the *Homo sapiens* evolution.

'Is that what you wanted to tell me? Your big secret.' She was laughing again.

I started to tell her about Dr Ravi Rao, the man I was dating. He had been the unflinching light on my darkest day.

'Hmmm… Doctor means money bags,' she calculated.

I smiled. He was not just moneyed; he came from seriously influential stock. I had wanted to tell Meena that, but seeing how the evening was unfolding, I changed my mind.

'How long have you both been dating?'

'A few years now.'

'You should push for marriage. You're not getting younger, and it's not like a ton of men are waiting for you.'

Incidentally, Ravi, too, was pushing for marriage. And it was *moi* who was dragging her feet.

It was desi night at 19th Floor, and the foot-stomping Kannada song '*Alladsu Alladsu*' was playing.

'*Jeevna tonic bootli, kudiyo munche alladsu*.' Life is a bottle of tonic; shake it before drinking.

Everyone around us was on their feet. It was a loud and busy space.

I wouldn't have picked a bar for this meeting. It was Meena's choice. Suddenly, I was grateful for everything I had objected to – the volume and the strobes. The buzz about meeting my oldest friend had dissipated.

'How are you doing, Meens?' I asked forcefully, picking up a honey-coated cauliflower floret, urging her to eat. She hadn't so much as touched any of the plates we had ordered.

As perfectly as her make-up was done, I noticed a puffiness below her eyes. 'How is married life?'

For the next half hour, Meena told me about her divorce. She was married to a software engineer in Chicago, who was so obsessed with her that he became suspicious of her every move. The way she wore her hair, the timing of her supermarket visits... he even monitored her phone calls. He was so far gone that he disguised himself to spy on her. She fled to her parents' place six months ago and filed for divorce. The marriage hadn't lasted a year.

'Hellooooo,' Chhaya cooed.

She swooped down to pull us together in a tight embrace.

Meena was quickly on her feet, returning the hug with air kisses. I didn't move; I was drained.

Chhaya had chosen drab for the day. She had been on the field, having scheduled visits to a couple of troubled highway outlets. One had been burgled and the other had complaints of food poisoning. She was not just a hands-on captain, but where quality was concerned, she gave it personal attention. She had driven 400 kilometres, and she had neither the time nor the energy to change into something more suitable for an evening out.

'Are you getting ready for marriage, too?' Meena asked after she filled Chhaya in on her divorce.

'I wish I was,' she said, grabbing at a plate and waving to a waiter all at once. 'Why, who else is?' she asked as soon as she settled into her seat.

'Our lady here got herself a makeover and money-bag boyfriend followed.'

Chhaya turned to look at me but was distracted by my phone, which was lighting up. The network was unreliable in this part of the building. After a spell of quiet, WhatsApp messages were pouring in.

Meena's eyes were on my phone, and before I could react, she picked it up. 'You have a message from an Andreeww,' she said, handing me my phone. Her eyes were glazed.

After Andrew was added to the various *MH* groups, one night, when I wasn't at my best, I opened an independent contact page and saved his number.

Good interview, Myra. Andrew was congratulating me on my piece on a female lawyer who had taken on the bar in fighting for a rape victim. I had chased Harini Parekh relentlessly. She hadn't spoken to any media outlet until she decided to speak to me.

'Andrew Brown?' she asked.

'Yup, the very same,' I said.

Chhaya added, 'He joined *Morning Herald* recently. You remember the fellow from school, right?'

'You didn't tell me.' Meena was pouting now.

'You were in the throes of shifting, babe, and I thought I'd tell you once you were here.'

Why was I making an excuse? It wasn't like we spoke every day. We had been reduced to exchanging messages two to three times a year, birthdays mostly.

'He's doing his politics stuff?' Meena asked.

'Politics stuff?' Chhaya's laugh was a bark.

Watching her shift in her seat, it occurred to me that Meena was a creature of intent.

When we were growing up, I'd thought she was moody. What she wanted to know, she took pains to get a clear understanding of, but the rest, she was hazy about. She needed three to four promptings to answer a question like, *Where are we meeting?* It would start with, 'Someplace close by,' to, 'Oh, let me check if my driver is available,' then, 'Gosh, it's so sunny,' or, 'I could've walked.' Then finally, she'd tell you where she would meet you. God help you if you were in a hurry or it was not where you wanted to go.

'Yeah, he's the political editor,' I said.

'What's the reaction been like?' Chhaya asked. 'I've been meaning to ask.'

'You knew?' Meena questioned Chhaya. 'You guys meet often?' she pressed, waving her index finger at us like we were a pair of errant six-year-olds.

Chhaya smiled.

'Actually, you could say he's doing his politics,' I piped in. 'His joining *MH* has shifted the balance somewhat, putting certain oldies on the ropes.'

Meena nodded. 'I've been hearing he's doing really well at work. I thought, initially, his shift from law to media was tame. Clearly, there's money to be made in reporting, too.'

'Journalism is his calling,' Chhaya said. 'I've read some of his work. He's good.'

No one was contesting Andrew Brown, political analyst, but editor was a whole different game. A field without goalposts.

'Editor? He's just reporting, no?' Meena asked.

'He has an entire political team, some 40–45 reporters all over the country, reporting to him. That's for now, but there is talk of him taking over as executive editor.'

'Andrew Brown.' She said his name and shrugged. They were a couple for an evening, a lifetime ago.

I noticed the growing flush on Meena's cheeks. Not even the dim lighting could hide it.

I coughed; it was engineered.

I shut my eyes and recalled those words that had come down a telephone line seven summers ago.

Meena had told me that Andrew had hit on her, among others, after he had moved to the United States.

'Sorry, Myra, he has moved on,' she had told me.

'Hopefully, I will not run into him here,' Meena was now saying between gulps.

'Why?' Chhaya asked.

While I had relayed almost everything Meena had told me about Andrew, I hadn't told Chhaya about Andrew flirting with Meena. That was hard to admit, even to myself.

'You know.' She shrugged. 'What's there to say to him?'

Chhaya's lips twisted. She had caught on.

For most of the evening, Meena flaunted an ascendency that was typical of the woman I thought I knew. She was always in charge. In the last few minutes, however, I sensed a discomfort, an awkwardness.

'He's not really a nice guy,' she said.

A nine-year-old's summation of her bench mate.

'You were lucky to be rid of him at that point. See how nicely settled in your job you are.'

Hornswoggled by a carnival barker. 'Am I?' I asked.

'Of course, you are,' she said. 'You are doing damn well. Look at you!' She was almost shrieking.

'Andrew is a user. Every time we met, he made me pick up the tab,' she continued.

Meena had told me they had met for a couple of coffees. It came in random messages. *I bumped into Andrew today. We had a quick coffee.* She would refuse to dwell on it even if I brought it up the next time she called. I wasn't sure if she was trying to protect me or if she was just being her selectively abstruse self.

'Come on! It's not much if he made you pay for a couple of coffees. He had just moved to the US, and he may not have been high on cash at the time,' Chhaya said.

'What coffee?' Meena asked, her eyes sparking a fury I hadn't seen in her before. 'There were lunches and dinners almost every day for months and months.'

'What?' What was Meena talking about?

'Yeah... You know how much he likes his drink; he didn't hesitate to order that, too. And I was paying for everything.'

I was confused. Was the woman so drunk that she didn't know what she was saying?

'Are you drunk?'

'Not at all. You don't believe me? That I paid his bills? I even bought him an iPhone for his birthday. The same one with which he blocked me on WhatsApp...'

My head was reeling. I wanted to scream, *What were you doing? Having all those lunches and dinners with my boyfriend?* He wasn't yet ex-boyfriend at the time, not in my head at least. I couldn't spit the words out. They were sitting on my tongue, and my mouth was open.

'What are you talking about, Meena?' Chhaya asked.

Meena must have noticed the shift in mood. She was shaking her head. 'Yeah,' she said, smiling suddenly. 'Let's change the topic. Let's not talk about that creep.'

'But,' I said, still in a daze, 'what were you doing having all those lunches and dinners with him when he was the one who was hitting on you and you were ignoring him?'

'You know how it works, hon.'

'No, I don't. Tell me.'

'We were mates; it's not like we were strangers. We had to meet. He was in a big city, and I tried to help him out. You know me; I'm the friendly, helpful sort.'

With every word Meena uttered, a layer of her mask was peeling off. It's incredible what you see when you view people without spectacles powered by affection.

'Why would you give him an expensive phone on his birthday? Why would he block you?' The words came out of my mouth really slowly.

It was late now, and the bar was slowly emptying. Meena's hand was on her knee; she looked like she was getting ready to get up.

'How does all this matter now? You and Andrew are history.'

'Were you and Andrew in a relationship in the US?' I asked.

Meena blinked. 'We were friends, we always were. Even when the two of you were dating.'

I was freaking out; my hands were shaking. 'So you had a fight? A falling out?'

'Listen, I'll be very happy if we stop talking about Andrew. He's nothing to me, and hopefully, nothing to you. It was an ugly chapter in my life, and if you must know, he chased me, relentlessly. I was fobbing him off because I knew how deeply you felt for him.'

'But you bought him an iPhone…' Chhaya said. I think she was screaming, too.

'He asked me to buy it for him.'

'Low maintenance! Buy me a Jag!'

Nothing of what Meena was saying was making any sense to me.

Andrew had chased her, hit on her.

They met for countless lunches and dinners.

She gifted him an expensive phone; he blocked her on WhatsApp.

'Why?' I asked the question.

Meena lowered her head and looked directly at me. 'My relationship with Andrew is mine; yours is separate. If you have any questions, you ask him,' she said.

Chapter 10

I was wriggling my backside into running tights when my phone lit up. One of my social media handles was on fire.

I was obsessing over a kurta a Bollywood actress was papped in after a family function. It was vanilla edged with sprinkles. I couldn't ascertain the label even after reaching out to her agent. That's how hard I tried.

I wanted to know the price. Instagram had worked it out for me perhaps. An arm and a leg.

I'm not a kurta person, but there were days when I romanced it like no one before me. I didn't run around trees, singing songs. I sashayed between desks, taking my time, and sometimes, on an evening out, I held it up with a glass of fine gin. I don't wear traditional attire to hide behind it, go out and about in it.

I tapped my phone, and Andrew Brown's angular face was smiling at me.

Well, good morning, even though it was a little too late for that. But what in god's holy name was Andrew Brown doing on Pooja Patil's – PPpicks – page?

He was standing tall, broad shoulders narrowing down to unbuckled jeans. Bare-chested. The coveted V-shaped torso. A ginormous roll of polka-dotted fabric was on its feet beside him like a vassal aligning allegiance.

The modal cotton in deep navy was draped daintily on Andrew. It dropped off his almost bare shoulders in a cascading fall that was arranged in a stylish heap.

The annotation extolled the merits of the textile, calling it 'smooth as sin' and 'easy on skin'.

Silly, I thought.

Andrew Brown, political editor going on executive editor, was making a case for the polka print.

I tossed my phone aside and squeezed into my tights. I liked how I was looking. The mirror gave me an objective picture. A deep-purple tee and matching hand band. I wanted to go live instantly.

I picked up my phone and scrolled through the verbose text. Pooja called this 'one-off shoot' a victory for her 'persuasive skills'.

I clicked on Pooja's handle; she had 57,143 followers, and I was one of them. The most recent maybe. Andrew at ABrownsss1 had 101. It was an unbalanced equation only because Mr Political Editor used Instagram to scroll for work.

He of the many parts. Pooja Patil's bare-chested muse.

Pooja had three sets of photo dumps of the shoot – same fabric, different angles. Only one was without a shirt. No, wait, there was a shirt; it was unbuttoned, the sleeves rolled up. Whatever.

Who was Pooja Patil? I had a vague idea. She was a fashion blogger who also lived in Bengaluru. I had hit her page last week while searching for that kurta I was going crazy over. I noticed that Sudha was following her and decided to do the same.

I slipped my phone into a side pocket and pulled on my shoes.

I wandered into the dining room of our home and looked around hopefully. I needed conversation, a tête-à-tête to get away from stuff. Home, however, was an empty space at 10 a.m. on a weekday.

My dad had left for 'work'. I looked around our living space; everything was in its place. The bookshelf, the crockery cupboard and a vase of fast-drying flowers. There were six pictures of me in this room, all from my childhood, my mother's favourite shots. There were a couple of my parents.

I turned on the radio. A saucy advertisement for apartments was playing. I switched it off.

On the fridge was a pink slip of paper, my father's note, telling me where my breakfast was. It was always in the same place, to the left of the stove. Eggs made one way or the other and bread. Butter was in the fridge. Papa didn't have to tell me, but he did, every day. It was how we started communicating after my mother passed away. He makes breakfast, and I put something together for dinner. Rice and… We take it as it comes.

I did the grocery shopping most weeks; occasionally, we did it together. My dad was notoriously thrifty while buying ration; Mummy and I were the other extreme. The economic continuum was adequately covered in the Rai household. Father and daughter made detailed lists, just like Mummy did, but in twice the time. We were constantly drifting off at the mention of a fruit or vegetable that she liked. We argued over recipes we didn't know a fig about but agreed on my mother's excessive use of turmeric. Her panacea.

My mother's favourite breakfast tray consisted of an egg-white mushroom omelette (she hated yolk), grilled tomato, a lightly buttered slice of white bread and black coffee. When she wasn't feeling her best, Papa brought it to her bed. When he was in a particularly amorous mood, he'd throw in a blueberry muffin, which he'd pretend to have made himself.

We never spoke about what we did for lunch. Mummy took the greatest pains over that meal, even if we were only eating it from a lunch box in various corners of the city. She had it all planned in the night – how many palm-sized rotis for the each of us. Rice, multi-grain ragi or jowar, embellished with herbs and grated vegetables. When we ate them six hours later, they were still soft.

I subsisted on coffee, a bag of crisps, maybe, and if I was really hungry, a chicken sandwich. I had no idea what my father did; I never asked. Maybe he helped himself to the leftovers in the fridge or he was skipping lunch. His belly had almost disappeared. He was by no means lean, but he was slighter now compared to the generous frame of his younger days.

Until that day in August, eight years ago, my mother used to pack lunch for both of us and leave it on the dining table before she headed out to work, no later than 8.32 a.m.

The bus stand was a 10-minute stroll from our house, and she caught the 8.50 a.m. bus to her office, which was two stops away. My mother was a banker and the centre of our world. She was the provider, the problem solver, the go-to person. For as long as I can remember, she was the main breadwinner, oftentimes the only one. My dad couldn't hold a job; each time he appeared to settle down in one, he'd have a brainwave for a novel business venture that, of course, didn't go anywhere. Only, he'd quit his work, and more savings would go down the drain. But theirs was a happy marriage. He was proud of his wife, who had worked her way up the ladder in the patriarchal set-up of a nationalized bank to the position of associate finance manager (South). His wallet was empty, but his heart was bursting with love.

My father walked his wife to the bus stop most mornings, carrying her lunch bag. Occasionally, maybe because he had woken up late, or had wasted too much time in the loo with the newspaper, my mother carried on at her scheduled hour. She'd give me a quick hug and remind me for the tenth time that my lunch was on the table while my father stood by, watching the rush and roll of the woman he loved.

That morning, the sky was threatening and there was an uncomfortable chill in the air. She had worn her favourite silk sari, maroon with a mustard border. She was smelling of roses. When I complimented her, she repeated what she always told me, 'I had a similar combination in college.' With a smile that seemed to climb all over her face like a naughty child on the monkey bars, she ran her hand over the pleats of her sari.

That is the last image I have of my mother.

Every time she went alone, she called my father as soon as she reached the bus stand. She dialled her husband that day, too, and as always, he answered on the first ring. Only, strange noises came from the other end. He disconnected and dialled again and again but couldn't get through. He cursed the connection and did what he generally does when the lines are bad. He dialled her office number and left a one-word message, '*Baleh*,' ('baby' in Tulu) on her answering machine. It was a reminder to call him as soon as she got to her seat. Not that she needed a reminder.

I was in my bedroom, in front of the mirror, wondering what to do with my unruly hair, wishing I had taken up Mummy's offer to side-braid it, when our doorbell sang its 'Mamma Mia' tune. It was a little after 9 a.m. My father had just asked me for the third time if my mother had called. 'It must be her at the door,' I said. 'She must've forgotten something.' Barely had my father pulled open the metal contraption than I heard him scream, 'Whhhheeerrrreeee? Durgggaaaaaa...' The sound emanated from his deepest depths, ascending, then descending, like a dying storm.

A drunk driver had mowed down two women, injuring three others at the bus stop. My mother was one of the two women. She was rushed to SBM Hospital, where she was declared 'brought dead'.

Neither of my parents came from large families. My father had two spinster sisters, whom I had met just once, and my mother lost her only sibling a little before her 18th birthday; he had drowned. They only had each other. And me.

My father wouldn't leave my lifeless mother's side. I left Andrew with him to pursue the paperwork that needed to be completed. We had to take her home.

One of the doctors in the administrative line helped expedite the laborious process – Dr Ravi Rao. This is how I knew him then. I was able to get my mother home by the evening because of him. He dropped me home later that afternoon and stayed for the last rites.

Mummy, for whom punctuality had been the deity she worshipped every waking moment, was cremated on time, shortly after she was brought home for the last time.

Andrew was one of the men who carried my mother's flower-bedecked body to the waiting hearse. The vehicle for her last journey was decorated with her favourite flowers – Mangalore mallige. In my memories, it was this jasmine I confused with that last living memory of her when she asked me not to forget my packed lunch. In my head, her departure began with that goodbye.

Andrew was in the front, along with my father, holding the tightly woven mat of plantain palms on which she lay.

I didn't need to look at my watch. I knew it was 5 p.m. We had the last slot at the crematorium. Andrew's flight to Boston, Massachusetts, was in five hours. I was supposed to have been with him, to help him complete his packing and close the house. My parents were supposed to pick us up and drive him to our place, where we'd have an early dinner before we dropped him at the airport.

I walked up to Andrew and told him he should be on his way.

'I'll push my ticket back,' he said.

'No,' I heard myself say. 'Just go.' I didn't turn to look at him.

Please go while I have the strength to tell you to go.

The key to getting me started on the days I was iffy about going for a run was stretching – a set of six exercises. The moment I felt my quads and calf muscles, an alarm went off in my body. I was ready.

That post of a certain bare-chested mammal had set me back this morning. Like there wasn't enough on my mind already.

Pooja Patil looked young. Very young.

My phone was in my pocket, and I was not pulling it out again. Not for a while.

Just before I left, I stepped on my balcony and made a 15-second video of the bougainvillea that swept across the terrace. It was picturesque.

Meena Iyer. Pooja Patil. Days turn to weeks, to months, to years. And answers slip between the cracks.

I had started running after my mother's death. It is my time with her. I hear her in the rustle of low-hanging branches or the whistle of the wind. I see her in the stray leaf that drifts and settles on the ground before skipping along with me.

I run on weekends, but when my head is buzzing, I hit the road four to five days on the trot. Any time, afternoons even. It's as if I'm looking to catch an answer that's floating somewhere in the troposphere, hoping my toes will carry me to it.

I couldn't feel the world around me like I usually do this morning. The sound of whirring vehicles, the shuffle of pedestrians, the kid on the bike, the lush pink carpet of tabebuias or the sharp rays of the sun, all of which I usually carried with me. My two-kilometre loop around Cubbon Park, which led me past the State Library and out of the grounds, was the favourite part of my routine. Sometimes, I ran that loop four or five times.

I stopped for the flora and fauna, on occasions, to watch how and where the light fell at different times of the day, like it were making a point, closing an argument. Offering closure?

Today, it felt like I was seated before a monitor displaying two pictures – Andrew Brown and Meena Iyer. No matter how much I ran, I couldn't get away from them.

Meeting Meena the previous week had parched my spirit. At first, I couldn't think or feel. I was numb. Then it all came rushing to me, a gargantuan wave.

After Mummy's death, every now and then, a bloodied picture darted in and out of my mind space like an erratic wireless signal. It stirred violent thoughts. I wanted to crash my head against a wall, crack it in two. The frequency had reduced over the years, but in the last few days, there was a new trigger. Twice during my run today. Already. The first time, I flinched. The second time, I hit the pavement and grazed my right knee and left palm, ripping my favourite tights.

My friendship with Meena was a chequered space, a chess board. We had our moments as friends. The odd chat at the school cafeteria, a few sleepovers, her material generosity and her openness in wanting to include me in outings with the StyleStahs. The rest, the times she ignored me, fell in the dark squares.

My only exposure to friendship as a schoolgirl was that of being a project. Meena was trying to make me better. She was teaching me style, moulding me, making me presentable.

'You should wear more shorts,' she would decree, pointing at the length I needed to achieve. More like a waist belt. The two pairs of shorts I owned were right for havildars she told me. 'They're called shorts for a reason.'

Meena was constantly correcting my posture, and then, as we grew older, my pronunciation. When there wasn't anything to correct, 'Lower your volume,' she'd caution me. My decibel level was barely above a whisper.

I was an oddball growing up, even in my tiny family. My mother was the social one who had a lot of friends, college pals from her Mangaluru days she stayed in touch with. She had quite a circle at office, too, most of them women, who came home for tea and snacks after work sometimes. My father had a couple of pals, with whom he went out for a drink sometimes, but he always knew what to say to whom.

I didn't have my mother's charm or my father's comfort level around folks. When we were invited as a family for a meal, I stuck to my mother; it was only after a lot of cajoling that I would leave her side. Once I mixed with the other kids, exhausting most of Meena's tips, I would play the circus clown, not knowing how else to communicate with them.

My mother embraced me whole and soul. She didn't try and change me, make me like the daughters of her friends, one of whom was in the movies. She let me be.

Andrew espoused me in the same fashion – the dinks and dents. He didn't talk down my scattered communication skills, my vacant expression or my hesitant social manner. 'Your strength,' he had told me when he was just 21. I had no idea what he was talking about then, but I have an inkling now.

My mother had been wary of Meena. Meena had come home a few times over the years, for juice or biscuits or just a sit-down. She always brought tons of snacks with her but partook of nothing from my mother's kitchen. Chhaya came calling a couple of years later, swinging her hands. She devoured everything that was placed before her. Mummy loved feeding guests.

I didn't want to weigh the revelations of that evening, see if the pieces of our friendship fit, consider the what and why of my romance, search for answers in the rubble. It was all too much.

So, Meena and Andrew had an affair? My knees wobbled.

Meena hadn't admitted to the affair. She had only alluded to it. She was drunk, she was my oldest friend. Was I being fair?

They had a relationship. An affection, an attachment. No one gifts stuff like that for a lark, not even Meena Iyer.

We were friends, we always were. Even when the two of you were dating.

Meena had called their relationship a 'friendship', an uber-modern expression for an affair (not my proudest eureka moment). My breath caught in my throat, and my feet struggled to move. Did this appalling sequence (whatever it was) play out after Andrew had left Bengaluru, or were they in touch when he was here?

What had he told her?

Did they discuss me?

I didn't want to go back to that moment when Andrew told me he loved me. He was in me, and his eyes held mine. He hadn't repeated those three words again. Not to me.

My legs broke into an unkind pace precipitously, my arms kept with the tempo, and my mind raced back and forth. I was ignoring what I didn't want to deal with: Andrew's part in the mess. It felt like a rhinoceros was sitting on my heart.

Meena's actions had defeated me. But as close a friend as she was, Andrew was the soul connection. His part in the act had destroyed me.

Images of Andrew – what he had come to mean to me in those two years – flashed before my eyes. My hand was on my chest, and I felt the emptiness I had carried within me for eight long years. The emotion, its intensity and depth, was similar to what I felt for my mother. I'd have given my life for Amma, stood between her and that drunk driver if I could've saved her...

That's why I had hoped Andrew would push back his ticket, even though it was I who had told him to go. That's why I thought he'd understand when I didn't pick up his calls. And that's exactly why I had to block him out of my mind and get on with the business of living when he didn't respond to my calls or messages.

Andrew had tried to get in touch with me as soon as he got a telephone connection, which was the day he landed in the United States. He called and messaged incessantly for about 10 days. After a couple of weeks, a month maybe, he mailed, asking why I was reading his messages and not replying.

I wasn't thinking of Andrew, or anyone actually, at that point. My head was a dark cloud. After a couple of months, when I tried to get in touch with Andrew, by calling on the same number, I got no response.

Why hadn't he replied to my messages? I had sent him two lengthy ones, putting myself out there.

I had tapped Meena in the hope of getting through to Andrew. She knew we had been seeing each other and how into him I was. At first, she casually let slip that they had bumped into each other, then she dissuaded me from messaging or calling, saying if he wanted to get in touch, he'd have done it.

At that time, the loss of my mother had dulled the sting of Andrew not bothering to reply to my messages. It was forgotten even... almost. Despite all that I missed and yearned for in that relationship, the cruel finality of my mother's death was what I was dealing with. Losing a parent, in the way I had, in a matter of moments, was like a half-done amputation. It was a shock at first. The pain was for later, for life.

Had I let her braid my hair that morning, she may have been running with me now...

After a year or so, when I started work, my father and I learnt to live again. I got myself into a routine. I had new responsibilities. I wondered about Andrew, but it wasn't so much the betrayal as I knew it then, but rather about how he was doing. I dwelt on our time together, the places we'd been to, the paths we had walked.

Now, eight years on, I was almost engaged to Ravi. He was the man I was going to marry, whenever we decided to get married. But there was this dull ache, a door half-closed. A wound that refused to heal. Andrew and Meena. And now, bare-chested Andrew and a roll of cloth. Love in the time of polka dots.

Chapter 11

There was this sagging sensation in the pit of my stomach.

What had I forgotten? My coin pouch kept coming to mind. I reached for it as soon as I got into the office, even though I had no use for it this day or most days. I don't know why I've employed this little pocket I've never quite committed to. I stretched for it again later in the afternoon and felt it full and bulging, held together by a metal clasp.

That's when I heard the knock. A firm rap. Just audible. My neck snapped back in recognition.

I had shut my cabin door. I only do that when I'm 'breaking stones', as Sudha and I call the writing process. It's hard labour. The closed door was my DND sign, not that these hints work in a newspaper office where everything is about here and now. The deadline was yesterday.

It was Wednesday, and I had a full day. I had come in early to finish my story and start work on the pages. That means going to war for advertisement positions, which, most of the time, is extreme, one way or the other. No one taught these marketing chaps 'balance', not their neighbourhood schools and definitely not those institutions from where they secured those big-ticket degrees. Editorial–ad department face-offs are as old as the caste system and as new as brand battles. They don't die. It's all about the moolah for them. Don't get me wrong. We like money, we know how to enjoy it, we can run tutorials on that, but our world spins on an axis of mind over material. We tolerate them; they wish we didn't exist.

After that verbal tug-of-war played out across three floors, which could go on for hours, I had to sit with the paginators and plan the layout.

Andrew and the chief reporter, Dinesh Reddy, were at the door. I had no choice but to wave them in.

My coin pouch again.

Sometimes, an oversight or omission has the amygdala on overdrive. Inconsequential items I own keep popping up in my head until the mystery unravels. It was a tray cloth two weeks ago when I had left home with both sets of house keys.

'Have you filed the piece?' Andrew came straight to the point. He had picked up newsroom etiquette quickly.

'Hello, Andrew, Dinesh,' I said, buying time.

'Hello, Myraah.' Andrew returned my smile. It wasn't of the same cheesy genre that had popped on Pooja Patil's page.

No one looked at me like Andrew Brown was doing now, like I was the only one even in an overcrowded, super-interesting radius. His eyes were light on my skin, like night cream.

I blinked and busted the duet. What was this about?

Andrew's eyes were scanning my desk now. They fixed briefly on my open notebook, maybe because he wasn't in a position to see what was on my computer screen.

This lip-smacking construction of a man was looking for something, and it wasn't me.

'Are you writing it?' he asked, pointing at my desktop.

'I'm writing it,' I said.

He was in a round-neck FC Barcelona tee. It was a forever enthusiasm.

My coin purse flitted across my mind space. Something had flown over my head.

'You've forgotten,' Andrew decided.

There was an edge of desperation to Andrew this morning. It reflected in his manner. His hands were in the pockets of his jeans.

Andrew turned to Dinesh, who was inching forward in my direction. He was almost in line with my computer.

I liked Dinesh. For some reason, even though we've been working in *Morning Herald* for the same length of time, we haven't gone beyond polite greetings and story briefs. He was a poor writer, a great reporter and the sharpest dresser on our floor. And he was chivalrous. Maybe that's why I liked him. I have my faults.

'Okay! She's finishing it,' Dinesh announced. The animation in his voice was marked.

Dinesh motioned to Andrew that they should leave me to it.

'Finishing what?' My piece was for my pages, which had nothing to do with Dinesh, much less with Andrew even in this to-be-editor mode.

The coin pouch. Again. That's when the light bulb flickered to life.

An 86-year-old woman's body was discovered in her home in a posh Bengaluru suburb last week. The death had been dismissed as a home-alone report in all the newspapers, which claimed the lady had no kith or kin.

A couple of days after the municipal authorities had performed the last rites, a neighbour called Dinesh to apprise him of the deceased Venkamma Achar's story.

The octogenarian lived alone in a rundown home that stood at the centre of a massive 100x180 square-foot property. Her sister had passed away a year ago.

Her brother, a hoodlum in his youth, was fighting for the property, which was estimated in excess of ₹20 crore. The house had been willed to the spinster sisters by their parents with a clause that if it survived the duo, it would go to their only other sibling. The brother, who had squandered his own considerable inheritance, was eyeballing his sisters' property. His family had prevented the sale of the house even when his ageing sisters had approached him with an agreement that would benefit all of them equally.

Venkamma had never worked; she had no friends or cash reserves. Her sister had been a teacher, and for as long as she'd been around, they'd got by on her pension. After her demise, Venkamma subsisted on her neighbours' generosity. She hadn't disclosed her dire situation to anyone. The condition of the house, the state of total disrepair it was in, hadn't gone unnoticed, especially after the older, more social sibling passed away. People, however, attributed it to her age rather than her finances or the lack of it. Things had gotten so bad that even the water supply and electricity had been cut. She had been dead for a week when her body was discovered.

Dinesh had told me that it would be a good story for 'Crime 3.0' at a later date. He had even given me the telephone number of his contact. This was two days ago.

Andrew, who was privy to the conversation, had cut into the exchange. He had said, 'In interesting or unresolved cases, after sufficient time, say a week or 10 days, has elapsed, the story should be laid out with as many details as possible.'

Stories that our reporters miss could be fleshed out and retold. Not reported but articulated comprehensively.

He was clear that it wasn't for the column, just yet at least, nor could it be dismissed in brief. He was looking at a 600-word story, a nice connect between daily reporting and 'Crime 3.0' that would appear on the feature pages.

At no point was I told to write the story. I hadn't forgotten; I relegated the obsequious coin pouch from my mind.

I had agreed with Andrew's argument; it was a line of reportage that wasn't followed to the full. Not just *Morning Herald,* but most media platforms were guilty of that. Readers are interested in people stories more than infrastructure or boardroom politics. They want to know what happened; often, it is curiosity, sometimes concern. In the case of Venkamma, was there no one she could turn to for help in this city of some eight million people?

No other daily had the full story, it was our exclusive – Dinesh or his team's exclusive. I thought they were ascertaining facts before filing the story, that's why it was taking time.

'You are writing the Venkamma Achar piece, right?' Dinesh asked a little uncertainly.

'No.' Dinesh's shoulders fell like a penny stock.

'Why not?' Andrew asked. The tone was frosty.

I shrugged. 'I'm not the crime reporter.'

Andrew's eyes were playing darts on me. Not in admiration. I wanted to giggle. I liked where this was going.

'Yeah, but Dinesh gave you the contacts last week and asked you to follow it up for your column.'

'Column? The column isn't scheduled for this week. Next month's piece is ready,' I said, meeting Andrew's gaze.

Dinesh was nodding. He had done the math; he understood what was happening.

Andrew's discomfort was uproarious.

'What's the confusion? You were supposed to write the piece.'

Andrew and I could always talk. We spent hours in verbal combat – an idea, a political stand, a cappuccino – only to agree to disagree. We emptied ourselves. I'm a good listener. He's not bad most times, but he tends to cut in every now and then, questioning, asking for clarification and throwing you off your thought process. Those chats mostly ended with a dry 'yeah'. An

Andrew special. His occasional bullshit. Today, he just couldn't find the right words.

I had boxed him into a corner without meaning to, and he was beginning to see it. Andrew was still a newbie in newsroom delivery. Normally, I would've explained this to a new recruit, perhaps during that exchange two days ago when he joined Dinesh and me, but I had stuff on my mind. And *Morning Herald* had never hired someone who was just cutting their teeth in this business right at the very top.

'I wasn't aware of having to write the piece for the daily. It was supposed to be for my column–'

'Yeah,' Andrew cut in.

Meet the bullshit listener of the new millennium; he won't let you finish a sentence. I was going to say, 'Down the line, as you pointed out.' This business of butting in might work brilliantly on another turf, when he's interviewing hard-nosed politicians, going at them from all directions, but with a colleague, it's off-putting. He knows (or at least he thinks he knows) what you're about to say and is bursting forth with a counter because he has long gone past what you have to say.

'I told you it would be a better follow-up piece.'

'Yeah, you said that.'

Even God in a beige tee better mind his manners if he wants more from me.

'Then what's the problem?'

'You should be asking the crime department that because they are the ones who write follow-ups.'

I had turned and was facing my computer.

Dinesh had exited the cabin. Like a good reporter, he understood there was no point hanging around haranguing when there was a story to be written.

'Myraah,' Andrew said. His fingers were gripping my table; they were white from the exertion. 'Dinesh had given you the details.'

'Yes,' I said sweetly, even smiling for effect. I could see his chest.

'I know initially he had asked you to write it for the crime column,' he said.

I wanted to butt in here to say, 'Because that was all Dinesh was allowed to do – make suggestions.' What appeared in the feature pages was outside that nice man's jurisdiction, but I let it slide.

Meanwhile, Andrew continued without pausing for breath. 'So, when I said it could go as a follow-up, I meant for you to write it. I was looking at you, speaking to you.'

'I'm not contesting what you said, what you might've meant or not meant.' And I was looking at you, too.

'I was addressing you,' he said in classic Andrew Brown style.

'So? I have no idea what's going on in that head of yours,' I said, spreading out my hands for effect.

'You knew what I meant.'

'Are you accusing me of shirking work?' My voice was dripping sugar.

'This is such bullshit,' Andrew growled. 'I can't understand why you couldn't have told me earlier that you aren't writing the piece. That you can't write the piece.'

Can't or won't? I cocked an eyebrow, letting the unasked question stoke his depleting reserves.

'As far as I know…'

'What you know is not important; it's what you had to do.'

I smiled, not for effect.

If there was an emoji for interrupting, it should look like Andrew Brown. I'm raising a public interest petition.

'The only reason I'm not writing the follow-up or whatever it is that you want to call this piece is because I wasn't asked to write it.'

'I asked you to write it, ba… Myraah.' His hand was on his chest, and his eyes were burning bright.

'Nobody asked me to write it, Brown. You only said it should be written.'

'If you had a question, you should've asked me.'

We were friends, we always were. Even when the two of you were dating.

Andrew closed in on my space and rested his hands on my desk. 'This is the problem with you,' he said. 'Your communication skills are zero.'

I looked up from my computer screen and let the laugh out of me. It started as a bark and finished on a hysterical note.

'Touché!' I exclaimed. 'Only that it's what I do for a living.'

'I mean it, you can't answer a telephone call or get back to a text. You don't want to tell people where they stand in your life. You don't want to communicate.'

'Excuse me!'

'Why can't you just pick up the phone and call? Or message? Why can't you ask a question, clear your doubts? If there was any confusion, and you thought…'

I was wearing my bored expression now. I had worn it well, I could tell by the look in his eyes. Andrew Brown doesn't do shows, but he was so lost and splashing about that it was ridiculously funny. A grown man in polka dots. 'I didn't think I had to do the piece. In my mind, there was no doubt at all.'

'I don't understand,' he said, shaking his head. 'How can you do this all the time?'

This wasn't about Venkamma Achar. May her soul rest in peace.

A man caught in dense weeds. A part of me felt for him. But the other me was angry. Livid at the lies and hidden truths. Livid that he had the audacity to demand explanations when he never gave one.

'Next time,' he said, 'don't assume or think… Don't give me the "I thought this" or "I thought that" excuse.'

'I didn't think,' I said. 'That's you, Andrew Brown. Entirely you.'

'I'm not the one who hasn't written the story I was assigned because "I thought".'

'No,' I said, 'I wouldn't ever confuse who you are.'

Andrew flinched. His palms were off my desk.

I hope I was smiling. I couldn't feel my face.

Chapter 12

I caught my reflection in an ornate mirror. Light from crystal chandeliers danced on it, giving my half-naked right leg the look of a painting.

'I have great sticks,' I said as I uncrossed my legs.

Chhaya roared her approval.

She had jumped at my suggestion for drinks and dinner, making it her treat. I protested, but she overrode it with typical Chhaya logic. Buy the bank if you can afford it. This ultra-luxe space in a seven-star hotel, the most happening nightspot in the city, Only Nights, was the upshot.

I looked around. The place was packed; I could tell by the din every time the music dropped off. The tables were tucked away in such a manner that it was hard to say if the space was full or not. This is where Bengaluru got away when she didn't want to get papped. This is where real money hung out.

Chhaya and I had met twice after our reunion with Meena a little over a fortnight ago. Both times for our Wednesday breakfast. I didn't bring up either member of the lovers' circle and neither did she.

A drink or two down – gin and tonic with a wedge of lime being my poison of the evening and my CEO pal on the rocks, which was beginning to show in the wondrous disarray of her neckline – Chhaya leaned back in her seat.

'She all but told me they were together. It should've clicked, babe. I should've known.'

I had told Chhaya everything about Andrew and me when we reconnected after completing our studies. I even told her that Meena had been in touch with him in the US. I had said it all but for the bit about him hitting on her.

'What exactly did she tell you?'

'That he hit on her.'

'And?'

I couldn't quite remember what followed, but those four words – HE HIT ON ME – had been ringing in my ears like a faulty alarm clock since our meeting with Meena.

'I don't think I said anything. I just laughed maybe.'

Chhaya's expression was kind.

'I told myself it was one day. I thought he was mad at me for not responding to his messages, picking up his calls.' I slumped in my seat.

Initially, I'd thought Andrew would buzz me back, reach out, but as the weeks rolled and the seasons changed, I didn't wait to lose hope; that would've been too painful.

I shut the door on Andrew Brown.

'When did she tell you about him hitting on her?'

'I can't say when exactly,' I said, letting the sentence hang on the uncertainty of my memory.

It wasn't that I had spoken to Meena, or anyone for that matter, a ton at that time.

I had two, maximum four, conversations with her then.

'Did she call when Sambrani passed away?'

That herbal essence was Chhaya's moniker for Mummy, *Sambhar Rani* shortened.

'Not on the day, but around that time. She didn't persist, but after a few weeks, a month or two maybe, she called again. That's when we spoke a few times.'

'This is what I think,' Chhaya said, pushing her hair back. 'When you connected and she told you about Andrew, they were in a relationship. Already. That's why he didn't answer your calls.'

Was he with her when I called? When I messaged?

'I don't think theirs was a long-drawn affair,' I heard Chhaya say.

I tilted the glass involuntarily, spilling some of the water on my lap. I felt it drip between my thighs and into the sofa.

'Babe, my broken pieces, you pick them up

Don't leave me hanging...'

Maroon 5's 'Sugar' was breaking those walls that were not brick and mortar.

I shut my eyes and went back to a time when Andrew and I were 'us'. There was nothing transient about us. We were never a couple for a reason or a season; we were going the distance. Bottled and sealed, no expiry date.

Andrew was clear about going abroad to study. He would return or I would join him, and we'd be together again.

When he was accepted by Harvard, his going away became a reality. We met later that evening to celebrate. My heart may have crashed to the floor of my stomach, but I was proud of him.

'So, you're going!' I was smiling, and it wasn't a sad smile.

'I don't have to, baby,' he said, cradling my face in his palms. 'I can get a decent job here.'

I wondered what he called her. Baby? Bubbs? Or Myraah when he was in her?

Chhaya snapped her fingers, and I opened my eyes.

'Don't go there,' Chhaya said, as if she had read my mind. 'We don't know the truth, babe. We only have her version, what she chose to reveal.'

'Why did she say he hit on her first up? Why didn't she just tell me the truth?'

'Because she didn't want you to know the truth. "He hit on me" was her half-arsed attempt to be a friend while carrying on with your boyfriend.'

I took a deep breath.

'He didn't tell you either, Bae,' she said after a while.

'I know, but we were not in touch at that point, Bae.' Chhaya sometimes called me 'Bae' and I enjoyed turning it on her. Completely original.

'Like for what? Two months? Which was the most traumatic period of your life.'

'He did try to get in touch.'

'But when you called and messaged, he didn't respond.'

They hadn't thought about me, not my best friend, not the love of my life. That was hard to swallow.

'That's what happens when two people get together. They're not thinking of the mess they're leaving in their wake.'

My fingers were drumming on the armrest, soft, the dissonant notes of a dull ache.

Chhaya had long raised questions about my childhood friendship, just as my mother had.

Why was it that what Meena did for you always more than what you did for her? Just because there was a price tag attached?

Chhaya laid the cards on the table. A little carelessly.

There was Meena Iyer and there was the image, a gilded frame – sophisticated, generous, loyal, kind. The two – who she was and who she liked the world to see her as – were inconsistent. But so thorough was that drill that she actually believed the picture was her.

Meena liked to think of herself as a gentle soul who reached out to those in need. She'd get out of her chauffeur-driven car and help a blind man cross the street. She pointed out potholes to kids. But that was what she did in the public eye. What about her private, private self? Who was she when the doors closed and she was alone?

'Maybe he was guilt-ridden, even shamefaced. Or he thought that connecting with you at that point would ruin your friendship with Meena. It's possible that he thought Meena hadn't told you about them and… he didn't want to tell on her or didn't want to rock that boat…'

I knew all of what Chhaya was telling me was a possibility.

'He faltered, he let you down, but it was an honest mistake,' she said. 'I'm not sure if I can say that of our one-time friend.'

What Chhaya left unsaid was playing on my mind. *Why was Andrew back in Bengaluru?*

There was a tentativeness about Andrew 2.0, an air of ambiguity. It had replaced the calm, the certitude of his youth. I'm not sure, though, if Andrew was ever really young; he was born old. This air of disquiet just couldn't be the result of an affair or even a series of transgressions. It's like he was not sure about something. He was anxious, searching, looking, reaching… There was also anger. It resonated in his tone, his fidgety body language. Atypical.

Did he know Meena was also in Bengaluru? Was that the reason?

'You were lost to him, but had he reached out to you then, he would've had to come clean, or at least that's what he'd expect of himself, and that would've ruined the friendship you have with Meena. Maybe in his own weird, convoluted way, he put you above him.'

'Maybe it was his ego. He didn't want to come crawling back; he didn't want to apologize,' I said, picking up the last of the stuffed mushrooms.

For a while after my mother passed away, I couldn't relate or associate with anything or anyone she had approved of; it may not have been every single thing or person, but there were some things (like a comb the two of us shared, like TV shows that sometimes kept me away from her, like Andrew, whom she approved of) I needed space from, to let the biggest loss of my life weigh me down. And then accept it.

'This is what I think,' Chhaya said, not for the first time that evening. She was considering a french fry, which she held between her ring and index fingers. 'Andrew didn't get back to you only because he didn't have a face to come back to you with. What could he tell you? Sorry, babe, while you were mourning your mother, I was fucking your best friend? From what I can tell of this man, he wanted to tell you, he understood the importance of being honest, but he didn't have the guts, at first.'

I shrugged. I was empty, I was excited. I'm a walking, talking contradiction.

Chhaya had moved forward in her seat. 'It's an awkward situation, but he's trying; he's reaching out to you.'

'I feel about as welcome as a fart in a spacesuit.'

Chhaya laughed.

I pulled out my phone and went to Instagram and opened Pooja Patil's page. A planet of looks and likes. Andrew's picture, the bare-chested one, had 40,431 likes.

I passed the phone to Chhaya, saying, 'Little Miss Polka Dots.'

'Get out!' I think she was screaming. She was out of her chair. 'You can't be serious?'

Chhaya was in polka dots, too; hers was a knee-length dress in red and white.

'My undergarments too!'

We just couldn't stop. We had turned this sophisticated set-up, where you might hear the folks in the next booth but didn't necessarily see them, into a market square, cracking tawdry jokes.

'And this when he looks like a million ball-locks!' She let it drag.

'Mr and Mrs Polka Dots,' I said.

After every stupid line that escaped our lips, we took another sip from our quickly disappearing stock.

'Who is this person anyway?' she asked.

I explained the business of fashion blogging to my friend, describing how these bloggers influenced the agile dynamics of the industry.

'What does she hope to achieve with this pic?' Chhaya asked, waving my phone, before adding, 'As good as he looks.'

I was feeling light – the polka-dot effect. 'This blog is about the various types of cotton fabrics in the market. She's extolling modal here, saying it's eco-friendly.'

'I'd say she's more enthusiastic about the model.'

'Savage!'

'But why would he fall for something like that?'

'Polka dots,' I said, and we were laughing again.

'I'm proud of you. You're handling this well,' Chhaya said.

She was sitting up now, determined to give her alcohol-infused words a backbone. 'I know Meena's actions were apocalyptic in that she transgressed a trust. I also get that since you have Ravi now… Still, Myra Rai!' Chhaya said, picking up her empty glass.

I swallowed something back. It wasn't the drink; there was none of that left.

'By the way, I like this new shade of lipstick.'

It was Dior's 999. Chhaya had bought it for herself but found it too heady. She had forced it on me, insisting I ditch my pink and brown tubes, which I had refused to do until now.

'Like you've tasted blood,' she said.

Chapter 13

I was just settling into my seat when Andrew's cabin called out to me. It was a luminous space. Unmellow yellow at a little over 11 a.m.

My legs have a mind of their own. They were bounding along towards that incandescent stretch even before I had placed my tote on my desk. It was now lying on the floor agape.

That was the angle of my jaw seconds later when my eyes clapped on a wholly distasteful sight. Below the belt in more ways than one, especially at this hour. And that was my mien when I arrived at Andrew Brown's cabin door. I took a few seconds to bring my lips together.

I didn't knock. The light beckoned.

My evening out with Chhaya had reminded me of unfinished business. Andrew and I had been lovers once, but we were colleagues now. I was determined that the old association wouldn't resurface like some architectural palimpsest in my professional life now. He had crossed lines.

'This is a whole different pin code,' I said as I walked in.

Andrew had barely raised his head. A benign smile was playing across his face. His eyes shifted across the room.

There was someone else in his cabin. I smelt her before I saw her. I couldn't turn my neck; it was suddenly stiff.

Andrew was on his feet; his hands were in the pockets of his cargoes. The black hoodie hadn't met an iron box in this life.

'This is Pooja,' Andrew said to me. He was smiling. He had more kinds of smiles than warm breads in a bakery. 'And this is Myraah, our–'

Pooja didn't let Andrew complete his introduction. 'Of course, I know who she is. She follows me on Instagram!'

I wanted to say that was only because Sudha followed her, but fortunately, I wasn't allowed to speak.

'She was following me even before you modelled for me,' Pooja told Andrew as she crossed and uncrossed her long legs. Her skirt finished where her thighs began. 'I followed you, too,' she said in that sing-song way of the carefree. Or was it the careless?

'Lovely shoot!' What else could I say?

'You won't believe it! I chased him for a month. Called him every day, knocked on his door every day.' She was swaying now. 'He was kind of rude, too!' She was simpering.

I wanted to ask her what this shoot had achieved, but that would be hard on the kid. Unfortunately, I couldn't manufacture a gentle question at this point. I had different thoughts in my head. I wanted to make a video of this scene and send it to Chhaya.

'All my friends were asking me, "Why Andrew?"' Pooja said.

I was determined not to look at Andrew. At least she wasn't calling him Andy! I sent up a prayer of gratitude.

'Obviously, he's eye candy and all, and there's no need to be shy about that.' She had turned to Andrew now. 'You're obviously more than eye candy, you know that!'

I wanted to laugh so badly, I was scared I'd pee in my pants. I bit my lip instead. The four incisors from my upper jaw had sunk into my bottom lip.

'He needs that approval,' I said kindly.

I heard a rumble; it came from my right.

'So, when you take two beautiful things, an unlikely combination of things, and put them together, the effect is magic! I cannot tell you the number of calls I got.'

I heard the door open behind me. I heard Sudha before I wheeled around. It was the rustle of the business chief's crisply starched sari.

'Auntie,' Pooja said and picked up her bag that wasn't any bigger than her skirt. 'I was getting ready to come to you when Myra walked in. She follows me, too, you know.'

'Cool beans!' That was for me.

Sudha waved Pooja out of Andrew's cabin and followed her, winking at me before she turned.

I waited for a whole minute after the door closed, and then I laughed.

Andrew's eyes were on my face, his hands were in his pockets.

'Entertaining,' I said, sitting on the sofa before which he was now positioned. 'You're more than eye candy, you know that, right?'

Andrew shrugged.

I was back on my feet. 'I could kill for confidence like that! Oh to be 21!'

'How do you know she's 21?' Andrew was quick on the buzzer.

'That was a guess.' I shrugged.

'You were close; she's 22.' Andrew smirked.

A lot of information. 'Anyway,' I said.

Andrew nodded.

'You didn't ask me to write the Venkamma Achar follow-up. We are clear on that.' I stated my case.

'I did ask you to write–'

I did an Andrew Brown and interrupted him. 'Yeah, but not the follow-up.'

'I asked you to write a piece on Venkamma Achar's death,' he said.

'I'm not a crime reporter.'

'I asked you to write a piece on Venkamma Achar's death,' he repeated. 'I decide where it goes.'

He turned and walked back to his seat behind his desk.

Wow! The arrogance. I took my time walking around the only chair that faced him and seated myself carelessly.

'Let me explain to you how these physical spaces in journalism work,' I said, pulling out a newspaper that was on his table. It knocked down a couple of books. Neither of us moved to retrieve them.

Andrew's smile mocked me.

'This is the masthead.' I pointed at the upper deck holding up the newsprint. 'There are various sections in here, including city, nation, business, culture and sports. Later in the week, we have weekend spreads, pull-outs; eight pages, but we've even gone up to 16.'

'Thanks,' Andrew said. His eyes were cold. Dead winter.

'Now, a business story cannot figure in the city page even if the corporate is headquartered in Bengaluru, just like, how do I say this simply, you cannot hang lingerie in the men's section of a store.'

'Not even if I owned it?'

'You could, of course! If you don't want to sell it,' I said, adding, 'which is exactly what I'm coming to – poor business practices.'

Andrew didn't like what he was hearing and was on his feet. It was his way of telling me it was time to leave.

I leaned into the chair and put an order to my posture. 'It would be unbecoming of the editor-in-waiting to indulge in amateur praxes.'

I looked around his space one more time before getting back on my feet. 'The devil is in the details, Brown.'

Chapter 11

I'm not a morning person. It's not when I'm alive and kicking. I'm not a night owl either. I'm a tweener. A spirit of the daylight hours.

I sometimes wish the day would stretch, like an English summer day, when the sun forgets to set. A series of extended coffee breaks when I could lock into what needed to be done. Today ran out on me like one of those social media stories I forgot to hold.

Each time my thoughts drifted in the direction of the why or what of the affair, someone knocked on my cabin door or I was called into a meeting or there was a public relations person hawking shoelaces.

I wondered if Pooja would've been a factor if Meena's betrayal hadn't socked me in the gut. I shook my head. Pooja didn't count because of Ravi. *Pooja is the present,* I want to say, *Andrew is in the past,* but I would only be lying to myself. Wounds should be allowed to heal.

I pulled on my running shoes a little after I unlocked the door to my apartment. I was spruced up in running gear that lined my contours. I started slowly, but as the conversation of a couple of yesterdays ago with Chhaya turned in my head, my feet picked up pace. I was pushing without feeling it. My teeth were grinding, and my nostrils flared. It wasn't for the physical effort.

Did Andrew hit on Meena? Was that where it all started?

Was he the game? The estuary of the affection.

It was a beautiful spring evening, as are most days at this time of year in this city I love to distraction. The wind was soft, a little wet, and it was constantly rearranging my curls. I had pushed them back with my mother's handkerchief (she actually carried that stuff around, beautifully embroidered maybe, but...), which I had converted into a headband.

Why had he done what he had done?

Did the 'what' actually matter? A rope I could use to hang myself with.

Why? A million times why.

I had run for more than an hour and stopped only once to take off my running jacket and wrap it around my waist. I stopped again, this time at a roadside stall, one of the many that dot Bengaluru's undone pavements and bought a bottle of water. I did a bottoms-up with the 330 ml container and looked around me. There was nothing familiar. It wasn't the same tin box I stopped for water at whenever I ran. I had no idea where I was. I remembered then that I hadn't taken my usual route. I probably turned left once I exited the apartment. I normally turn right and run along the CBD before getting into Cubbon Park and cutting across it. I had probably run some 10 kilometres, which meant I was in a suburb.

In a sense, learning of their affair was liberating. Strangely so.

I had wondered: *What happened to him? To us?* We hadn't broken up; we hadn't drifted apart. Yet I hadn't heard from him. I swung back and forth between concern and curiosity until I spotted his next byline. I was tempted to mail him...

I had written a great number of emails, which, until they disappeared, lay in the draft basket of my mailbox.

Dearest Andrew, Dear Andrew, Andrew...

How do you address one who was once a part of you?

I'm one of those creatures who walk around with a shawl or cardigan all day, all year. That's the reason I own a running jacket, living in Bengaluru. I have an aircon blasting inside me. I always feel cold, but Andrew only had to throw an arm around me, and I was instantly warmed. It was the same in spirit.

Then he was gone.

Now I know what happened in that time – those eight years were accounted for. Not all eight, but I didn't need a count for the seasons that followed. Suddenly, the ache gave way to anger that erupted in my head in unfettered waves. Expletives were flying across my mind like rockets against a dark sky when I heard my name.

'Myraaaahhhh – aaahh.' It carried in the evening breeze like a cry. It came from somewhere behind me. Was it Andrew or was it the wind? It was blowing a gale. I heard it more than felt it. I couldn't stop though I was tiring. My heart was heavy, but my feet kept going. My nails had bitten into the palms of my hands. I felt my eyes burning. I wanted to stop, to lean. I wanted to be held, but it was only the cold embrace of twilight that I was surrounded by.

'Myraah! Is that you?'

It was him. I slowed down and then nodded into the darkness. I didn't want to see him.

As I turned, I felt a stiff wind rustling through the branches above me. I sniffed rain and caught a whiff of his fragrance before my eyes found him.

'You look a mess,' Andrew said. I remembered I hadn't taken off my kajal. Or my lipstick even. Dior 999. He was in front of me now and wearing an undecided expression. Like he wanted to smile but wasn't sure if he should.

I pulled on my jacket. To look less of a mess maybe.

Andrew was the safe haven of my youth, and I was precipitously transported to that time. I wanted to close the space between us and throw my sweaty self at him, have him hold me forever. These are thoughts that should have no place in my head, now that I am almost engaged. Sometimes, though, the past catches up, no matter how hard you run.

'Th... thaannks,' I managed.

I wanted to ask him what he was doing there, but I had no idea where I was. I looked around for a sign, a hint, but it was dark and there were no street lights.

Andrew was driving back from a political meeting when he caught my gait. I was in the opposite direction of the traffic. I had broken from my run. He drove past thinking I was on my evening stroll (as if I'd ever do something as weak-hearted as an evening walk). After he'd driven for a kilometre or so, it struck him that I didn't live in the direction I was headed in. He took one U-turn and then another and was behind me again.

'I followed you from a distance, not wanting to intrude. It's late, there were some men around, I wondered where the hell you were going,' he said, pointing in the direction of his car.

We started walking towards his car. Sweat was streaming down my face, or was it tears? I noticed a half-constructed wall, and suddenly, I wanted to sit down. I walked ahead of him and perched on it.

I would've loved a coffee, but it was too late for that. Something more potent perhaps.

'That was quite a pace. When did you start running?' Andrew asked, joining me on the parapet.

'While you were away,' I said. I was smiling. I was feeling light-headed. Blame it on the endorphins.

He nodded.

Andrew was always a relaxed presence around me, even in public. He wasn't stiff, putting a distance, pretending to be indifferent. That was him, Andrew Brown. Remarkably without affectation.

I told him about running, it being my refuge, and also my time with my mother. I nudged him, tickling his ribs, and told him he was intruding. He bowed in mock apology.

Everything was forgotten. I was living in the moment. The credo of a pop psychologist who never lived.

I had made peace with the world. Had Meena passed me now, I would've jumped up and enveloped her in a hug.

'How much do you run? Miles?'

'Depends,' I said, looking at my watch to check the distance. 'A little over 12 kilometres.' I stressed the measure as a reminder that he was in India and not the United States.

'About eight miles,' he said, refusing to budge. We played these little games. A word here, a point there. Mental Monopoly.

'You don't listen to music when you run?'

'No. Not most times at least. It's a prop people use to take them a little further. One more song. A bubbly beat. A distraction to fatigue or boredom. I just want to be with my thoughts… and my mother.'

I didn't have a target, and the music of my life would suffice. He nodded.

'Besides, I don't run such great distances.'

'I'm not sure this is a good idea. I don't think it's safe,' he said, suddenly, looking at his watch. It was close to 9 p.m.

'Five more minutes,' I said, tugging at his sleeve. Had I drummed up that ready-to-eat empire idea, it would've been plated in five minutes. That's my pace.

Andrew turned and looked behind the wall, using his phone as a torch.

'Why are you here, Andrew?'

He turned instantly. His gaze met mine.

'Not right here, but here in Bengaluru, in *Morning Herald*?'

Put like that, the sum had a whole different look.

'Why did you decide to come back?'

'Family.'

Blood is thicker perhaps than those connections that run their course. Reasons and seasons.

'There was the house,' Andrew said, 'I could've done all that online.'

I nodded. It had nothing to do with me.

A sharp evening drift swept past us, clearing the space between us.

'How many times I called and messaged. You could've told me you wanted to be alone. I would've understood,' Andrew said finally.

'Really, Andrew? Did I need to tell you that?'

His eyes were clouded. 'I thought it was rejection,' he said. He was looking down at his palms. 'You, too?'

Why would he feel rejected? And why me, too? Because Meena dumped him not once but twice?

'You didn't want to have anything to do with me,' he said.

I wanted to remind him that I had just lost my mother in a way nothing in the world would've ever prepared me for, but he put his hand up for right of way.

'With Noelene gone too...' he said, shaking his head, 'I was alone, all alone in this world, without a next of kin. I had no one.'

Yet he had returned to Bengaluru, India, chosen to work in *Morning Herald*, because of family that did not exist.

Andrew turned away, looking into the darkness.

I felt the hollow within him.

Andrew didn't bring up my asking him to go. He hadn't forgotten; it was deliberate.

'Myraah.' He breathed my name. 'Believe me, please.'

Andrew and Meena and now Andrew and Pooja. The wind was playing havoc with my nerves. I wanted to run; I wanted control of my senses at least.

Andrew exhaled.

I was on my feet, and Andrew followed. I motioned towards where his car was parked, and he followed me.

He held the door open and waited for me to get in before following suit. I noticed a bottle of water in a side pocket. I took a swig and spat it out.

I sank into the seat and threw a glance around me before determinedly engaging my mind with the interiors. Andrew's car wasn't one of those flashy vehicles, even though his salary would allow for that. It was a mid-range sedan, but it was prized, I could tell, just by the way he put the car in gear and let it glide before he stepped on the accelerator. I wondered how much it cost and then looked around me again. There was a pen drive, an unopened box of Marlboro Gold and a lighter on the ridge that divided the front seats.

We were quiet for a while, and then I exhaled.

'Why didn't you reply to my messages?' My tone was casual.

'What messages?' he asked. He was smiling.

'My messages to you, Andrew. I sent you two of them.'

'You never messaged, you never communicated; you just let me fly away like a kite and then cut the thread.'

'I had messaged you, Andrew. How could I not?' *We're only separated by the physical miles. I love you, and I know you love me.*

Andrew pulled up at a dimly lit side road and turned off the ignition. I didn't have to tell him that was how I had signed off my first message.

'Messages... two...' He had turned and was staring out of the window. The night was dark, and I was beginning to see the light.

Please reply, if only to say you're doing okay. That was how my 203-word second message had ended. My body still recoiled at the memory of the day I wrote it; the pain had permeated down to my bones.

'I never saw those messages, Myraah.' He grabbed my arms and was shaking me. 'They never reached me.'

I could still see the blue ticks.

'Are you sure you sent them to...' His fingers tightened around my arms. I didn't flinch. 'You did send them to me?'

Andrew and I both chose not to mention Meena, for different reasons. I wanted him to tell me about that relationship, only because those are the norms for trade.

I was sure, though, that Andrew hadn't seen my messages. Meena had deleted them. I was sure of that.

Chapter 15

Rajesh Soor was ubiquitous any time some tittle-tattle was in the air. *Morning Herald*'s resident gossip placed a cup of direly sweetened filter coffee before me and made himself comfortable in the spare chair. My cabin suddenly felt like the Majestic Bus Station. The odour and the order.

Soor flashed what he thought was a debonair smile, a cue for when he had something malicious to share. My eyes were on his oily curls; the perfumed grease would darken the stain on the backrest.

He slurped the syrupy concoction. I sighed.

Soor had no sense of personal space, physical or otherwise. He was happy to encroach, making it all about him. What he had detected, what he wanted to say. All words, no ear.

Had he seen me with Andrew last night? Was that what the smile was about? I inhaled, held my breath, exhaled. I returned the smile.

Andrew and I were colleagues. We were seated apart, not leaning into each other. The wind had blown between us. I had felt it more than once. In the guidebook of business etiquette, was that improper? Even when not in office?

'I tell you,' he said, slapping my desk, making me jump and grabbing my attention all at once.

I cast a quick glance around me, wondering who else had heard that clap of thunder.

The general desk was only just filling up; people were drifting in, dropping bags and turning on machines, enjoying the reprieve air conditioning gave them. The afternoon sun was harsh in April. That's when I noticed he had shut the door on his way into my cabin. He was squiggling in his seat, trying to move forward. He had spilled some of the coffee on himself.

'If Brown doesn't get the interview, he'll be blacklisted,' he said, pausing, waiting for me to applaud his pun.

I exhaled, relieved that he hadn't spotted us, but that was not the reaction Soor was looking for. He continued to wait as I replayed Andrew and me last evening, Andrew walking back to the car, a few steps behind me, jogging the last few yards to get ahead of me and open the car door, waiting for me to sit down, securing the door before walking around to the other side.

I thought I had smiled, but a laugh escaped my lips to the delight of the man seated before me.

My phone pinged. It was Sudha. *What does the Boor want?* This was our nickname for Soor, whose other areas of specialization included walking into people in near-empty spaces. He'd hurtle towards you with a doubt or question, and god forbid there was no furniture separating him from you.

'Can you imagine the plight of the poor woman in bed with him?' Sudha once raised the point as if it were a toast. Her eyes twinkled and her cheeks coloured. We laughed ourselves hoarse, pondering positions, reinventing some.

'There's no chance of him getting that interview. How is it possible? Tell me.'

I forced myself to focus on Soor. He was asking me a question, and I didn't know what he was talking about. 'Who?' I asked lamely.

Soor was frothing. He had heard from his sources, who, please be warned, were as flaky as his smile was synthetic, that

Andrew was desperately trying to interview Karnataka's former chief minister, Hari Rao.

Why would Andrew chase Hari Rao? He, of all people, should know the man had stopped giving one-on-one interviews since the death of his son more than a decade ago. He had only recently started addressing press conferences.

'He probably wants Hari Rao to address the media as a whole maybe.'

I wanted to take those words back, almost as soon as they were out of my mouth. It was possible Andrew thought he could get through to Hari Rao. Be the chosen one. Why wouldn't someone of his standing not think he could bag that exclusive, the first interview since canned beer!

I leaned back in my seat as I came up with a counter in my head. Andrew was probably thinking of a select interaction, with a handful of journos perhaps, as a nudge for Hari Rao to be open with the media again.

The boor snorted. 'What is the point in paying him all this money and bringing him here if he can't deliver? He doesn't even know the politics.'

My phone was pinging again. It was Chhaya. I had told her last night about my running into Andrew.

Just asking, did anything happen?

I excused myself to respond to Chhaya. It was a one-word, two-letter reply.

No sooner had I placed my phone on the table than it lit up again with a string of messages. The last one was from Sudha.

Kick him out! Let's get that coffee. I have to tell you some Andrew Brown gossip.

My face must've sparked a serious note because Soor now wanted to know who was messaging me. 'Is everything okay?' he asked, but what he meant was, what have you heard? When I didn't offer him information one way or the other, summoning up a smile instead, he pressed forward with his claims.

'He calls himself a political analyst when he doesn't even understand the climate. It must be too hot for him,' he said, laughing at his own joke. 'He doesn't even know he can't get the interview. When you can't get it, why commit to it in the contract? There's only so far an American degree can take you in this country.'

American degree. Harvard. Hmm...

Getting interviews had little or nothing to do with being a political analyst. Apples and oranges. But I suddenly found myself at odds with the situation, Andrew Brown in trouble? Sudha's message had pushed me on the defensive. *Morning Herald*'s metro chief had caught onto something, a strain maybe. Still, Andrew's contract revolving around an interview sounded wildly discordant.

But why was my heart beating faster and harder than usual? It felt like alarm bells, a definite percussion. This had nothing to do with me; this was happening to my ex-boyfriend, who was now my colleague.

'Maybe Andrew is just trying,' I said tamely.

Soor shrugged, bouncing on his fleshy bottom. 'That he should've thought about before taking the job,' he said. 'It's normal that editors will ask him to deliver when he's collecting a big pay cheque. He's not delivering. Do you know how much he's earning?'

I wanted to remind the man that Andrew was an editor already.

'You don't know?'

I don't care. 'Come on! They've hardly given him the job because he could cajole Hari Rao to give *Morning Herald* an interview.' *Why was I getting into this?*

'That's what he told them. That's how the deal was signt.' Soor couldn't pronounce signed. I'm not sure he could spell it either.

Soor reached for the steel tumbler he had placed in front of me before pulling himself up. 'Since you're not having it, I will,' he said. 'We must not waste.'

That was the only part of the conversation I agreed with him.

I waited for Soor to exit my cabin and only then got on my feet. Sudha had messaged me to join her downstairs. I caught a glimpse of her as she left the floor, draped in a crisp green sari. Sudha rarely wore colours. I made a note to tell her that she should rest her black, white and beige saris. I was so wrapped in Sudha's sari that I almost stepped on the pleats of my own. The women in *Morning Herald* had decided to drape the 100-day sari challenge (in a year) our way – all 101 women in the organization were in the six yards today. Given our work schedules, the places our jobs took us to each day, it was pretty impossible to wear one every third or fourth day, but even this decidedly watered-down version took effort. It was an annual affair, and in the last couple of years, we had done quite well.

I was wearing the only sari I had ever bought. It was the exact replica, at least as far as I could tell, of my mother's favourite maroon-and-mustard sari, which went with her. I had no intention of buying a sari, but one day, on my way back from an assignment, I passed a sari shop where a mannequin was draped in this sari. That was about a year or so after she passed away. It was only recently, however, that I got a blouse made for it.

I was holding my pleats together and patting them down, and then suddenly, I knew I wasn't alone in my space any more. I got a whiff of him.

'I'm sorry! I forgot to knock,' he said, moving his hands vaguely in my direction. I knew it was me in the sari that had numbed his tongue, but my face gave nothing away. Andrew stepped back and waited until I signalled for him to come in.

He walked towards me. I was still in my cabin, and I took a step back instinctively. The heel of my footwear found the border of my sari.

'Careful,' Andrew said, reaching out, his right hand on my left wrist in an effort to steady me. Double shot espresso. My pulse quickened – must've been hitting a 100 or a 1,000. I quickly held the table for support, and Andrew shoved his hand in the pocket of his denims.

This is why I don't wear saris more often; there is just too much to it. The pleats, the *pallu*, what you tuck into the skirt and where you pin it to the blouse, what you hold up and what you don't... give me a pair of jeans any day. But a sari is style on two legs, and when you're done, it reflects in someone else's eyes. I didn't need a mirror in my cabin today.

'Saris really suit you, Myraah,' Andrew said as he retreated.

'I was going down to grab a coffee,' I said, ignoring the compliment. 'With Sudha,' I added.

He had seen me in a sari once before when I was in college for Ethnic Day or some such celebration. He had used my father's car to chauffeur me back and forth.

Andrew apologized and made way for me to exit the cabin.

'Where have you been?' Sudha asked. She had already picked up her second coffee from the vending machine. The empty, lipstick-stained mug by her side was her first.

I opted for an Americano and followed her to the corner of the executive lounge, open only to the senior staff.

I liked how far I had come in weaning myself off milk in my coffee.

All I ask for is a strong, steaming cappuccino. Make that Grande. You'd think that's easy to find in bean town, but you'd sooner hit a traffic-free road than a café serving cappuccino the way I like it. Too much milk or froth, and listen to this, luke-bloody-warm. South Indians like their cappuccinos extra hot and strong.

I can't make myself a cappuccino at home. I tried a couple of low-range machines, which I then had to junk before I went with black coffee. So here's how I work with coffee now. If I can't get a cappuccino the way I like it (please don't tell me cappuccino is a warm coffee and if I want a piping hot mug to get a latte blah, blah, blah, because I don't care. I want a cappuccino the way I like it, period), I'll go with an Americano. And this one in our lounge tasted good. Bitter, not burnt.

'What I wanted to tell you,' Sudha said, pausing before lowering her already faint voice. She looked around the lounge, making sure we didn't have unwanted company. 'I think Andrew is planning to quit,' she said.

'Whaaaa...' I pushed the steaming mug into my mouth to keep myself from talking. It burnt my tongue and so shut me up. Andrew had barely been here for six months. So what Soor was babbling about was right. He was in trouble.

'Careful!' Sudha cautioned, reaching for my cup.

My expression was salty. I could tell by her reaction.

'Have you burnt yourself?'

I shook my head.

Sudha laughed. 'Such a klutz!'

I joined in the laughter.

'Please don't step on your sari now.'

'I've ticked that box already.'

Sudha had heard from 'a reliable source' that Andrew wasn't happy in *Morning Herald*. Whoever it is she was hearing stuff from was generally in the know; I could vouch for that. Andrew was apparently not enjoying managing pages and the administrative responsibilities that came with being an editor. His first few months in *Morning Herald* hadn't afforded him the time to pursue what he wanted.

'What exactly was it… ah, "suffocated" is the word he had used,' Sudha said.

'I told you, about the time he joined us. He had absolutely no experience in print. He's a political pundit, but I'm not sure his résumé is cut to take over the newsroom.'

'I remembered that,' Sudha said. 'That's why I wanted to tell you the moment I heard.'

Sudha could well be right because, in the last couple of weeks, I noticed that the editor was on tenterhooks, tailing Andrew, trying to ensure he was comfortable.

'But you'd think he was smarter than that, that he'd have done his homework, known what the job entails, decide if that's what he wanted for himself. Who'd move halfway across the world, even if he was coming home, without being sure if it would work for him?'

I shrugged.

'Also, it's not just about Andrew,' Sudha said. '*Morning Herald* paid shitloads of money to get him. They need to justify the hiring to employees. Not verbally, but the economics, especially at a time when our industry is struggling. He's got to be worth the deal, right?'

I nodded. 'Already, people like Soor are walking around asking what he's done.'

'There's a rumour doing the rounds that he's under pressure to prove himself. I'm sure that's what Soor was telling you,' Sudha said. 'I don't think that's true. I think the people around him want him to stay. I think he doesn't want to.'

I nodded. 'And if I know Brown at all, he won't do anything he doesn't want to.' *What a stupid comment, Myra. You might as well have confessed that you are lovers.* WERE lovers. I cohabit in another tense.

'Brown, eh?'

Sudha was on too much coffee. 'An old joke!' I sneered. At least that was the intention. Apologies if it sounded like a squeak. I had rolled myself under the bus. India has talent.

'I keep wondering if there's any other reason he'd have made this move for.'

I shrugged.

'He's single?' she asked.

Was this an enquiry for Pooja?

'Yes, as far as I know,' I volunteered. 'But maybe there's a girlfriend or partner I don't know of.'

'I haven't noticed a ring. How is he still single though?'

I smiled. 'Maybe he's not single. We just don't know who his partner is.'

'It's easier to move the way he has, just up and leave, shifting jobs and homes if you're single,' she said, nodding. 'Still, I can't wrap my head around why he did this.'

I shrugged. Why had Andrew moved back to Bengaluru? Why *Morning Herald*?

'I introduced Pooja to him thinking he was single.'

I nodded.

'She's my best friend's daughter, and she's coming off a nasty break-up,' Sudha said. 'Her parents live in the same apartment building as Andrew.'

I was listening.

'She came gushing to me a little after he had moved here. She wanted him to model for her.'

'Maybe he's coming off a bad break-up too. Who knows?' Why was I talking? Why couldn't I shut up?

'Maybe.'

'They make a handsome pair,' I said. Sometimes I knew what to say and how to say it.

'They may look good together, but I don't think there's a pair there or there's any chance of that.'

I exhaled. Living in the moment. Heard of that?

'He's an old 30, she's a very young 21 or 22. Too much Gen Z.'

'Too bad!' When did this go from a slightly uncomfortable conversation to an enjoyable one?

'Were you guys friends?'

I told her we knew each other. How quickly the weather changes in Bengaluru!

'He's a super smart man, Myra.'

If she was hawking him like home-grown produce in a market square, he had impressed her, which wasn't easy to achieve either. Sudha wasn't given to superlatives, in life and in her stories. She was the very definition of a reporter.

She obviously thought I didn't have a boyfriend. Ravi Rao's and mine was a noiseless affair. We didn't stroll the streets hand in hand or otherwise, and as a couple, we didn't have a social media presence. It's the way both of us wanted it, but it was more me. I didn't want people to know, particularly because I was in the media. Once we were official, engaged, maybe it would be okay to make it public, but before that, it was best to fly under the radar.

I smiled. I needed a rocket out of this personal space we were in.

'What'll he quit and do? I'm not sure if people are waiting to take him back from where he came?'

'He'll write columns, books, cover elections,' Sudha said. 'This level of expertise is always in demand. There are too few of them in the ecosystem.'

I nodded. 'They'll have to afford him.'

'He could freelance. There are organizations that don't cost cut on intellect.'

I was beginning to wonder if Sudha's source was Andrew Brown himself.

'You probably know him longest,' she said.

I nodded. She was waiting for me to add to it, but I forced my backside off the settee to get more hot coffee to burn my mouth.

'If Andrew stays, he'll make it worthwhile for *Morning Herald,* but I don't think he wants to stay,' she said after I took a sip of the boiling hot black liquid.

Then he won't, my lips were too scalded to say.

Chapter 16

I sat heavily at the breakfast table Ravi had picked for us. There was a lot on my mind; most of it was Andrew-related.

Were Sudha's sources right? Was he going to quit? It had nothing to do with me, which was an issue by itself.

Andrew either wanted to up and go because this wasn't what he bargained for or was being pushed into a corner as Soor had asserted. I was leaning towards the former only because of where it came from, but who's to say? It was like looking into a kaleidoscope, disjointed bits of a story floating around, parts of which I recognized.

That Andrew had no idea I had messaged him had crept up on me like a snake. Poison.

What kind of a relationship were Meena and Andrew in?

How deep was their love if his phone was with her? If she knew the passwords to his phone?

My airways felt constricted. I needed air.

Andrew had given up on us only a few months after he left Bengaluru.

Ravi reached across the table and squeezed my hand. I returned the squeeze, exhaling. Divinity was in the pacific.

My mind wouldn't stop going back. Each time I managed to drag it forward, it found a way back. I could feel the surge of emotion; it was showing in my eyes. I could tell.

What brought Andrew back to Bengaluru? Or rather, who?

I wanted to stop these questions because they did not matter. I was almost engaged. I had finally found some peace after my mother's death and Andrew's hasty exit from my life.

Closure is not for all things and everyone. Sometimes, you just move on.

My head was spinning, and Ravi was smiling as he always does when we meet. It made me want to smile, too, but all that I could manage this morning was a half-hearted response.

We weren't at our usual 11 a.m. coffee-break table. We were early, but our spot was taken by two men in slick business suits. House rules ignored. I grumbled to Ravi, who contributed to the charade with no more than an eye-roll.

We don't do breakfasts; we meet for lunch or dinner whenever possible. But that mid-morning coffee break is our time.

When Ravi called last evening, asking if we could meet for coffee, I suggested breakfast, and he readily agreed. My body didn't need nourishment until midday most of the time. I drink gallons of water, have fruit – an apple or guava – and a mug of black coffee with a splash of milk, and I'm good most mornings. I save the egg my father fries for me for dinner. Lately, however, I've been experiencing hunger pangs early in the day. That's why I suggested breakfast. It might have something to do with my running, which I was becoming increasingly regular with.

We hadn't decided on a place, maybe because we didn't need to. Ravi offered to pick me up at 10 a.m., giving me fair room to drop my bags in office.

'I want to eat their blueberry waffles,' Ravi had said as soon as I settled down in his car. He hadn't even greeted me.

'Someone is hungry.' I was speaking for myself, too, and this was after I had already gobbled a two-egg omelette.

'They must be the only people on the planet who make it without any added sugar or sweetener. The moment you said, "Why not breakfast", I knew what I was going to order.' Ravi was beaming.

The food arrived at the table almost as soon as we settled down, and quite a spread it was. The plump walnut and raisin waffles with maple syrup and a fluffy egg-white omelette, condiments and a large breadbasket.

Ravi was digging into his food the moment it was placed on the table. He was obviously ravenous. I was shifting my plate around, wondering where to start, waiting for my coffee to arrive.

Were they still picking the beans?

It was 10.40 a.m., and I couldn't put another morsel in my mouth without coffee. I also wanted a bite of the waffles, which I feared I was never going to taste, given the pace at which Ravi was polishing his plate. There were four pieces, and he had already eaten two of them.

I waved at the waiter and mouthed coffee when I noticed a familiar figure walking into the restaurant. He was a step or two behind a waitress, who appeared to be struggling with her footwear. The light was on him so I couldn't tell for sure, but the gait was Andrew's. The build was Andrew's. And so was the face.

What was he doing here? I was smiling; no, I wasn't.

Andrew spotted me almost as soon as I laid eyes on him and walked over. I tried to apprise Ravi of Andrew's arrival with my eyes, but he was so focused on his food, clanging cutlery on crockery, that nothing short of a full-throated yell, which would've invited the whole room to join the party, would've got his attention.

Fortunately for me, just before Andrew joined us at the table, my coffee arrived.

Ravi was quick with his appreciation, as always, glancing at my plate and adding, 'My girlfriend will finally eat something.' If I hadn't stopped breathing, I would've laughed out loud. He was so busy with his food, clumping the waffle with cream and syrup, I could've fainted and he wouldn't have known.

This was the first time he had positioned himself as my boyfriend in public.

Andrew, who was standing a little behind the waitress, had suddenly stopped smiling.

I picked up the cup and took a sip. I let the liquid trickle down my throat. I needed to take charge. Introductions were in order.

'Ravi, this is Andrew Brown, our political editor, and, Andrew, this is Ravi Rao.' This is where I should've stopped. Ravi had the advantage of knowing about Andrew, who he was, and even if only partially, what he had meant to me. Andrew had no idea about Ravi, who he was in my life, and that is not my problem. But my mouth was opening and closing on its own, speaking because it had to. 'He is Hari Rao's grandson,' I said.

'You two are dating?' Andrew asked, pointing at Ravi and me.

'Andy, is it?' Ravi asked, standing up to shake Andrew's hand.

'Andrew,' he returned. There was no smile to soften the correction.

Ravi's expression dimmed, and I wanted to dive under the table.

This wasn't about Ravi, despite how it appeared. Andrew had steadfastly refused to subscribe to shortening names, which was a pastime of sorts in Bengaluru. Like picnics and board games. Anita is Ani and Anil is Anu. It's that micro. I was Myra or Baby or Bubbs, to him, never 'Mai', which is what I'm called most times. I didn't protest the rechristening, but Andrew has always been vocal about it. I remember him cutting off a classmate when he called him AB. Even before the fellow was out of earshot, he was ranting, 'It's like people here don't have the bandwidth for more than two or three letters.'

'I'm pushing for an engagement,' Ravi said, placing his hand on mine.

Not only was the announcement unnecessary, but it was also against his grain. We hadn't spoken about keeping our relationship quiet only because that's what both of us wanted. At least until such time that it was formalized.

Andrew smiled.

Just as he opened his mouth to say something, another man, a politician type, tapped Andrew on the shoulder. Whatever else the dolled-in-yellow-metal political aspirant may or may not have been, he was the messiah of face-saving timing.

I was seated beside Andrew at a resto-bar some 10 hours later. The sound system was hurting my ears, a welcome distraction for a change.

I was getting ready to swipe out when Andrew asked if we could get a drink. I could've bought myself some much-needed time, saying I was meeting Chhaya or my dad or my kitchen counter at that particular hour, but I thought I owed it to him. Correction, I owed him nothing. But this was not how I had wanted him to find out about Ravi. I'd wanted to be the one to tell him.

It had been an awkward 10-minute walk from Morning Herald Towers. Our mute commute drowned out the deafening evening traffic.

Andrew disappeared to get us drinks as soon as we dropped our bags.

How had this day ended up the way it had? Even if it wasn't going to plan, the morning had been rescued somewhat when the coffee finally arrived on my table. But that was before my eyes clapped on Andrew Brown. Or was it a storm?

My phone pinged. It was Ravi. *Home?*

Office. I lied and dropped the phone into my bag.

I didn't have a clue where my personal life was headed. Only a few months ago, there was an order, which I may not have fully embraced but was beginning to accept. I was at peace, or so I thought.

There was a reason for this steadfast refusal to look at where Ravi stood in my life, what he meant to me. I was searching, digging, reaching, but try as I did, I couldn't go beyond friend.

Had it always been this way?

In the past, each time I felt a tug or was confronted with the question about Ravi, of where he stood in my life, I was sure it would pan out eventually. The candle I held for Andrew would die, and I would get on with my life.

Initially, when I was going to bed and waking up with thoughts of Andrew, bookending my days with the memories we had made, I let me be. It was understandable, given how things had ended or been left to dry. Some eight years later, when Andrew walked into my den, I told myself it was finally endgame. This wasn't closure though – far from it. This was stirring-to-life feelings, emotions that should've been dealt with and laid to rest long ago.

Why was I having a drink with a man who hadn't had the minimum decency to end what we shared before hooking up with my friend? Then, having gone right ahead and played that game, he hadn't bothered to tell me about it. I had to hear it from her.

My face must've looked a mess because Andrew raised his brow questioningly.

When my gaze met his, I saw a reflection of what had to be my own expression.

Andrew's smile was lugubrious. 'There's some stuff I need to tell you,' he said.

My back straightened, and I leaned forward. He wanted to talk about us!

'Noelene had been in a relationship with a man above her station.'

I blinked.

'She was 22, and he was 25, he couldn't marry her, he was always honest about that. Noelene was sure she would get him to change his mind.'

In journalism, I was taught that every story came with an intro. 'Who?' I asked. I meant, what.

'He married shortly after, and they continued to meet clandestinely. Noelene's lover was generous with money, and initially, his time, too. Then Noelene became pregnant,' Andrew said, pausing briefly. 'Their daughter, Sarah Ann, died 20 years later in childbirth.'

She was his mother! Sarah... Sarah something... Sarah Ann. Oh god! Andrew laid out the facts like it was the loose sketch of a film script.

He took a sip from his glass. I took a gulp.

I waited before asking, 'Have you met him, your biological grandfather?'

Andrew shook his head before taking another sip and placing the glass on the table.

'Does he still live in Bengaluru?'

Andrew shrugged before picking up the shakers.

Andrew had asked Noelene about his mother. She had told him that Sarah Ann had passed away when she was giving birth to him.

'I didn't like the sound of what I had heard. I remember that clearly,' Andrew said. 'I was just a boy, so I pressed. I asked if my father had been upset with me at the passing away of his wife.'

I was nodding, but I wanted to cry.

'Noelene told me my father didn't know that my mother was with a child,' he said. 'Much later, I understood that to mean that my mother didn't know who exactly the father of her child was.' There was a pause, a pronounced one, before he added, 'Maybe she didn't want to know, my mother was stubborn.'

'So unlike you, Andrew!'

Andrew laughed out loud.

At that moment, it occurred to me that Andrew's 'rejection' comment was linked to his roots.

I thought it was rejection that Andrew had told me on the evening he had caught me on my run.

'I want you to read something,' Andrew said, passing me his iPhone. He had been fiddling with it for a while.

I wondered briefly if it was the one Meena had bought him almost a decade ago.

I laughed. Sometimes, in the middle of a difficult discussion, I laugh. It's a release.

'What's funny?'

I flicked my hand at the testy bloke beside me, telling him there was something on my mind. He didn't ask me what it was but said, 'I have no dates. It must've been the early forties.'

I reached for a glass of water before seizing his phone. I was looking at a photograph; it was a handwritten paragraph on parchment paper.

I looked up at Andrew.

'This is a diary of a young girl. Her name is Bhumika Velu. I think she was a friend of my great-grandmother, Catherine.'

Bhumika Velu Me.

Em prety gril. Everybody sayed to me. Me appy gril. I no. Only I gril no englis in dis vilge.

Andrew reached for his phone, saying he'd read it out to me. 'It can screw your head,' he added.

I'm a pretty girl. Everybody said to me. Me happy girl. I'm the only girl who knows English in this village.

I moved closer to Andrew as he read. I wanted to see what this Bhumika had written. I liked her name.

Lots of rain in barracks one day. Water is like river go, go, go down. Red mud all place, on road, it's like mehendi design on my white leg. On my blue colour langa also came mud.

When I down, I walk in front of the Black Bridge and see the other side every time. Too much tree. I check to see if the bad board is there. 'Dogs and Indians not allowed beyond this point'. This board makes Bhumi very very angry.

Andrew's free hand was on the backrest. I let his fragrance envelop me. It felt good.

My appa is a school master. I can't go to school. Bhumi is a girl, so appa teach Bhumi in house.

Suddenly one day appa told me I'm getting married. I not have any amma, she dead. Bhumi 16 years, appa told me. My good father name Tilakanathan Velu Sir. He told me we have a proposal from white English Sir. White English Sir paying appa money. Englishman Sir not married. I was lot happy. I go to the other side of the bridge and break bad board.

The more Andrew read, the more I liked this woman. I looked at Andrew to ask how he had gotten hold of these pages.

'I found them when I was looking for papers of the house back when I was in school,' Andrew said, as if he had read my mind.

'Did you ask Noelene?'

'I asked her if Catherine was my great-grandmother,' Andrew said. 'She nodded and said it was all in the notes.'

On marriage day, the last one day of the weekend, me wearing langa white dresses, Bhumi never saw like this. Langa white dresses came in ship.

I met Englishman Sir husband one day before marriage day. He asked to Bhumi for marriage day to cut hair short. I likes long hair, but I cut it. I wear lots of many flowers on my hairs. Standing side to side with Englishman Sir husband on my wedding day, I smile big. No one else smiling. My appa no smile, my thangachi sisters, no one coming. Only I Bhumi in marriage and many other white peoples.

Catherine Brown wedding in garden in front of big house.

'They must've been good friends,' I said. This was giving me scary vibes. It was not making sense.

Before I come for marriage, my appa say, Bhumi Englishman Sir marry you, no one else. My friend having two kutti from another one Englishman Sir. He not her husband man Sir, no one her husband.

My appa say, my house. I say, Englishman Husband Sir house. The lawn I'm standing on is in front of the house, my favourite camanti pukkal flower on the side.

'Marigold?'

Andrew nodded.

I wanted to hug Bhumi tight.

I am writing after many time afterwards. My English is little bit improved. My Sir teaching me English. He better than my appa father. Many many time since I saw appa father.

I took a deep breath. I felt Andrew's eyes on me. He had stopped reading and was looking away.

'Seems to me that he fell in love with her beauty.'

Not the first man to love with his eyes.

My Sir came here many many years go. He went to Coorg and then very far away to Kolikata and then to my Coonoor village. My Sir love this place quiet and nice place. Yesterday when we walking I asked him if I pour paint on board, if he would let it be. Ronald Brown Sir asked Why loudly. Me got scare. 'You're not one of them any more,' he told, but he smile.

'Here she's talking about my great-grandfather,' Andrew said. His face was sphinx-like.

I felt Bhumi's victory and smiled, but I was also tearing up.

My Sir say he has sold house and garden, all the flowers the lawn and the marigold also. We are moving to another one place, in far way land. He told me, soldiers live there. I asked to him, with who we fight?

'Are you following?'

I nodded.

'They were shifting out of Coonoor.'

After my thangachi cousins stopped coming, in faraway place where soldiers live, children came. My appa never came to new big house. Not one time.

I make friends with white people, I not speak much but I listen lots. Sometimes I think of appa, where he is, my thangachis.

Are they marry? I ask My Sir about my father, he living? He answer all questions, not that one.

My Sir got smallpox. Catherine Brown also die. Bhumi alive.

'They must've been really close friends? Were they cousins?'

'I don't think so. Nana didn't say so.'

I took Andrew's phone from him and flipped the pictures back and forth a couple of times, reading from a photograph. I returned the phone to Andrew, who placed it on the table before getting up to get us another round of drinks.

Who was this Bhumi of the beautiful name?

I had so many questions about Andrew's family, though. Did Catherine see her grandchild, Sarah Ann, Andrew's mother?

Did she know about Noelene's affair?

Andrew had barely placed our drinks on the table than I grabbed mine. I didn't need it; I wanted it.

I wondered about his father, and then my focus shifted to Noelene.

Which mother doesn't ask her unwed, pregnant daughter that question? The one who had walked down a similar path, I guess.

I closed my eyes and settled into the settee.

My earliest memory of Andrew, which was from after I had adequately dealt with the attraction, was that of a man trapped in a boy's body. There was a sagacious stillness to him, which at that age was annoying. I was no more than a girl myself. Whatever the situation, wherever he was, he rarely lost his mind. He had an answer to every problem – big, small and exaggerated. He scythed through the smoke of my anger or fear and arrived at a solution that made me seem small. Almost everything I told him was met with an 'it's okay', when it was really not okay and it would never be okay for the next hour. Maybe.

Naturally, I'd rebuke it; he was belittling my issues. Embroidered or otherwise.

Sitting here beside him now, emptying my glass too quickly, his story played out before me. Catherine was his great-grandmother, whom he knew nothing about. Noelene was her daughter, who had raised her grandson single-handedly. Andrew had taken all that was tossed at him, every truth and unanswered question, and let it rest within. Until he smelted it into his inner steel.

'Since when have you been seeing the grandson?' Andrew asked, changing track like one who owned the road.

So, this is what it was all about. Andrew Brown's version of 'Truth or Dare'.

I shrugged off the thoughts in my head and focused on the question. I had the perfect antidote. I narrated how and when we had met. Ravi had been there for me at a very difficult stage in my life. I underlined it with a french fry.

I noticed Andrew twitch. I hadn't answered his question, only because I didn't really know the answer myself. I'm not sure Ravi knew it either. My response had few details. Which wasn't much unlike my relationship with the 'adopted grandson'.

Ravi and I were like a pair of well-worn footwear on irregular feet, comfortable, so not easy to put away.

'You met him the day of Auntie's accident?'

'Yes,' I said.

Thoughts of that day still filled me with a dread I cannot describe. I have spoken about it to my father, who told me that with the passage of time, he was able to appreciate what they shared, how fortunate he was, that we as a family were. I know I'm lucky to have had a mother like her, I was privileged, she took care of everything. But that feeling, a heavy fog that clogged the arteries, hasn't cleared over the years.

I looked up at Andrew. He was waiting for me to talk, finish what I was saying or what he wanted me to say, but I had said enough.

'When's the engagement?' Andrew asked, before adding, 'He's adopted; I hope you know that.' He shook his head just as soon as the words were out of his mouth. 'That's not what I meant.'

Andrew was taking aim at Ravi. I knew that.

'Any more modelling assignments?'

Andrew smiled. 'I was helping her out.'

'I know! You are very helpful.' I laughed.

'Sudha introduced me to her,' Andrew said. 'Pooja lives on the floor below mine. She's a persistent kid, and she just wouldn't take no for an answer.'

'I get all of that, Andrew,' I said, 'but polka dots?'

'What could I tell her?'

'I don't know! But I certainly wouldn't have said yes to polka dots if I were you.'

Andrew nodded.

'And bare-chested.' I was laughing. I just couldn't get that roll of cloth out of my head.

'Myraahh...'

He was calling me, cajoling me; he was trying to pick up the pieces. It was in his voice. Meena's name sat at the tip of my tongue.

'What are you going to do about your family?' I asked.

It was why he had come back. I could finally see that, and *Morning Herald* not only allowed him to return home, but he could also see if the medium worked for him.

Chapter 17

Chhaya was to meet me at Perky Grace, down the road from our respective offices, in an hour. Make that an hour and a half. And that would be my lucky day! #ChhayaStandardTime.

I couldn't be in office, though; I had to get out. I was struggling to stay away from Andrew. He was around somewhere. I had inhaled whiffs of him.

Even when I was horribly stretched on Thursday, I kept looking for reasons to chat him up.

Does this headline work, Andrew?

Caption with a kicker. Is that our style?

Piss poor, Myra! I know more about politics than the man will ever know about page-making.

Even though that last evening had almost ended with the 'the adopted grandson' counter, I rescued it somewhat when I asked him about Pooja. It was part alcohol, part that bare-chested image of Mr Wannabe Model posing beside that roll of cloth that set off a commotion of giggles on what had otherwise been a sobering evening.

I didn't know what to make of his family.

Noelene, his beloved Nana, only left him drabs of information. And some serious real estate.

He had a grandfather, who was perhaps living, but he had no idea who he was. Who does this?

His mother! Andrew would never know who his father was…

And who was Bhumika Velu?

I had a feeling those notes were a brain-teaser 3D wooden puzzle. It would take some getting used to.

I wanted his phone. I wanted to go through those notes, again and again, with an Americano for company.

Was it okay to ask him to send them to me?

The one time I came up with a suitable pretext to approach him, he wasn't in his seat. Mercifully. Friday was a whirlwind kind of day, where I was pulled in various directions.

I finally saw him on Saturday afternoon, at our end-of-week meeting. His rear actually. His full butt was right in front of my face before he sat down. It was a ripe few seconds, and just as well that he took his seat quickly.

I dropped a long-winding explanation about having to meet a source as I exited the editorial. It was for anyone who was listening just in case I was needed. I have a phone, but I was stepping out to fly a kite during work hours.

I walked out into a warm sun that embraced me instantly. I had 90 minutes to kill before I sat down with my friend. I contemplated walking down to the mall, a 10-minute jaunt, where I could pick up a much-needed running vest.

I was hyper about shoes. I changed them at the faintest hint of wear, never mind tear, but I was lazy about gear. I decided to buy some tees and vests and maybe even a pair of shorts or two. I always wore running tights, no particular reason why. That was about to change.

The display window of the Adidas store had more colours than a paint palette. I felt my smile as I walked into the flagship set-up.

I was looking at the vests when I heard a voice I recognized.

'Heeeeyyyyyy.'

I chose not to answer and stuck with the process of running through their collection. They had the racerback version in three colours – pink, blue and black. Maybe I needed to look at the half-sleeved option. That way, I'd get some protection from the sun that enjoyed colouring me in a deeper shade each time I stepped out to keep it company. Not that I'm complaining. Brown is bold. Chocolate. Scrumptious. Me.

The sound of stilettoes on sparkling tiles was getting louder. I was in my white sneakers.

I didn't want to meet Meena, not today. Not ever.

'Heeeyyyyyy,' she trilled again.

Another of Meena's USPs. Only people with power of one kind or another were addressed by their names; for the rest, it was simply 'hey'. It is my least-favourite reference. I have a beautiful name, my mother's choice. If you can't call me by that, then at least try the alphabetically challenged version of 'Mai'.

Hey is who? I'm not a feather duster.

'Are you ignoring me?' she asked, striking a pose as she tapped my shoulders. As I turned from the racks of soul-stirring colour, she pulled me into a hug.

This was the first time I was meeting or speaking to her since that forgettable evening more than three months ago.

'Hi!'

'Whaaaare havve you been?' she trilled.

To market, to market to buy a fat pig.

Had our friendship mattered to Meena, she'd have known where I'd been these last few weeks. Even if it was only to the corner shop to buy a bag of overpriced chips. This pseudo concern, much like that 'How-are-you? Not-that-I-really-care' kinda query comes from people who, for some opportune reason, have slipped into the fringes of your existence. That breathless, 'Whaaaare havve you been' opening is their attempt to gloss over the slush and make it appear like all would've been well had you kept in touch.

All would not.

If I had any idea that Meena Iyer was anywhere in the vicinity of this mall, I'd have sat put in office, making diabetic love to Andrew with my eyes.

Her perfume was all over me. I sniffed once more to make sure I wasn't imagining that stain of smell. 'Around,' I said, keeping with the smile that was already tiring. 'How about you?' What else can you say?

'Buying branded clothes, eh? Is it a gift from the good doctor?' She nudged my ribs, laughing, but pulled back quickly, like she'd got an electric shock.

I couldn't afford gear of my choice; I apparently needed my boyfriend's credit card. I laughed.

'All this running you are doing is good for your figure, but you are getting darker,' she said, patting my hands. 'That's not a smart thing, you know. Very little suits that shade.'

Distracted by the envy in her voice, my gaze dropped to her waistline. There was an extra layer around the middle I hadn't noticed before. Meena had been skinny in school, but after she shifted to the US, she gradually gained weight. She was still on the lighter side, and the extra pounds filled her out nicely, adding to her glow.

'Come, come,' she called, tugging at my sleeve. 'I'm sure this place has a coffee shop. Let's sit down for a bit. I've been meaning to call.'

Instead of saying I had to be in office in another five minutes or so and getting on with what I intended to do, I was thinking that this mall, with its high-street outlets, wasn't her kind of place.

'What are you doing here?'

I laughed as I asked her the question. It hadn't occurred to me before, but the nickname from our schooldays suited her. Summed her up. Meens.

'Never mind me and my boring life,' she said, standing at the entrance of the single outlet coffee shop tucked in the rear of the second floor of the mall.

How did she know about this place? She had obviously been here before with someone who knew the layout.

'You tell me about yours. Are you and Ravi engaged or not?'

She paid for the two cappuccinos that came with an almond biscotti each. 'So, are you engaged?' she repeated, joining me at the table.

'No,' I said. I wasn't engaged to Ravi. Much worse, I was beginning to think about this relationship more as a friendship, but I wasn't about to tell Meena that.

'Why?'

I shrugged.

'Like I was telling you the other day, snap him up. It isn't easy for someone like you to get a man as loaded as Ravi Rao is. Going by what you and Chhaya were saying the other night, he's into you. If I were you, I'd dump my complexes and get to the party. For some folks, looks are not so important. You're lucky.'

I wasn't sure if Meena had no filter or whether she chose to discard it on occasion. Was it possible to outgrow it like your fifth-grade uniform? She hadn't been this bad in school, but these days, she couldn't open her mouth without airing prejudices.

'He comes from great stock… heir to Karnataka literally.' Her pencilled eyes lit up dramatically.

Wow! I was pretty sure I hadn't mentioned who Ravi Rao was to Meena when we met, outside of him being a doctor. She and Chhaya weren't in touch; I knew that, too. It wasn't impossible to find out; all you needed to do was hit a button, but her mind didn't work that way unless she had examined the connection. Deliberately.

'Great catch, by the way!'

I yawned. I hadn't been sleeping well. 'How have you been?' I asked.

'Is that because you're not so into him?'

'What?'

'You're not excited by any mention of the man. I don't see any chemistry or life in the relationship.'

'Have you seen us together?'

'It's flat,' she said, picking up the biscotti and pointing it at me, to explain what flat meant perhaps. She placed it back on the saucer before breaking into a laugh. A shrill, piercing sound. It's funny how one doesn't notice these quirks, however jarring they may be, when it comes from someone close. It's camouflaged by an affection, perhaps, until you run out of it.

I shrugged. Why had she made it her business to know who Ravi was?

'Anyway, what are you doing with yourself these days?' she asked.

'The usual – work and home and all that stuff.' Why was I answering the questions while she turned everything on me?

'All work and no play makes Jill a dull girl. I can see that you're heading down that path. You need some excitement in your life, but of course, you need to work. I understand that.'

What she meant was she didn't need to work.

'What about you? What are you doing these days?' Outside of deleting other people's messages, that is.

Meena launched into an explanation of how she was chilling and going out every other evening. She had joined a book club, which Chhaya was also a part of. Chhaya never attended, and the ladies were planning to kick her out.

'Most of the women are older, late 30s, 40s. You know, it generally takes people that long to get into these circles,' she said, rubbing her index finger and thumb, suggesting money. 'Unless, of course, you are born to it. So Chhaya, if and when she actually attends, and I, are the youngest.'

Chhaya hadn't told me about this book club.

'I'm thinking of going back to the US,' Meena said. 'I want to get back to work, not for the money. Though I have to say the pocket money was good. I loved managing the art gallery. You meet the right kind of people there. I think I'll go back for a short trip in September and look around. Hopefully, I'll find something there and stay on.'

The same gallery where she reconnected with Andrew? Maybe he'd follow her, and they could rediscover each other all over again.

'That's a good idea,' I said dully.

She might've been particularly good at artfully managing the men who walked into the gallery and arranging them in her life.

I was still reeling from that first 'hey'. It had cast a gloom on my morning. Besides, I didn't know where to take this conversation. I had questions she would not answer, but other than that, I had nothing to say to her.

'The weather is great these days in Bengaluru,' I said to no one in particular.

Then, just like how she had picked me up at the Adidas store, literally with the snap of her fingers, she dropped me.

She rang for her driver and told me she had to rush to an urgent meeting. Her cappuccino was untouched.

I sat put for a while, watching her leave the bare setting of the café before I picked up my coffee and the unsavoury subject of our friendship. If you could call it that.

Had I taught her how to treat me?

When it suited Meena, or when she had the time for me or anybody she associated with, you became her project. It wasn't barter with Meena; it was always about her. I doubt if it had even registered on her that I did her homework every day in school.

I decided to get those running vests and shorts and anything more I might need. I had to rid myself of the taste of milky cappuccino. It was offensive.

'Myra!' my father called.

He didn't give me time to respond before knocking on my bedroom door.

My father is never loud, but he has a booming voice, which he's not really aware of. He's not an introvert, not much of a talker either, but when he decides to say something, his voice is bouncing off the walls, like it was today.

I was changing into my tracksuit, getting ready for our Sunday evening walk, which had become our tradition. A father–daughter thing.

The knocking intensified until it stopped. 'Are you okay, Myra?' I heard him ask.

I was ready outside of slathering my face and arms with sunblock when I yanked open the door.

My father was dressed in Adidas joggers and a collared Climacool tee. He was in black, save for the charcoal-grey Cloudfoam shoes. Perfectly coordinated, including a smile that stretched ear to ear.

My father never bought himself anything, not even a pair of socks. My mother had done all his shopping. After Mummy passed, I made sure all his essentials were bought and replaced at regular intervals – day clothes and night suits. He'd wear frayed or faded clothes, oblivious of their condition, had I missed putting them in the recycle bag. Just as well that distress was a look people strived for at this time.

Activewear was something we hadn't invested in as a family back in the day. Mummy wore a salwar-kameez set, including a dupatta, for her Sunday evening walks with her husband. My father wore his day clothes but didn't tuck his shirt in. They had Bata shoes, which I think they changed every leap year.

I had abandoned the idea of running vests for myself when I returned to the Adidas store two days ago. I had walked over to the men's section when a pair of walking shoes caught my eye. My father needed shoes, but he needed gear more.

'We are matching,' my father told me, tugging at my sleeve. Indeed! We were twinning in black.

'Ready?' he asked as I patted his chest.

Fitness was alien territory to my father. The concept of working up a sweat was never introduced to him. He moseys.

I'm like my mother, quick of step. Today, suitably kitted, my father was walking faster than I have ever seen him do. He was out of the door at such speed that he had forgotten the house keys.

Sunday evening walks at Cubbon Park were my parents' thing. They usually left around 5 p.m. and only returned at sundown, a couple of hours later. I knew of their routine only because of my dad's lower-back issue; bending was always tricky for him. As a kid, I would be required to dive under every sofa or rack in the house on Sunday evening, looking for his walking shoes.

A couple of months after my mother passed away, I fished out my father's shoes one Sunday evening. I slipped into my mother's keds. That's how my father left the house for the first time since we had laid Mummy to rest. Thereafter, Dad and I went for a walk every Sunday in the second half. We left earlier than my parents did. We were out by about 4.30 and back by 6 p.m.

Today we were a little late. It was almost 5 p.m. when we left the house, but we were bounding along, making up for the time we had lost in sprucing up for the adventure.

I was a couple of steps behind when I noticed a missed call from Chhaya. My father had stopped by a rocky outcrop with a thick copse of trees. It was a compelling sight; everything was dark except for the evening light. We stood against the fence, peering inside.

'We never came here,' my father said. He was talking about my mother.

I must've run past this rock formation innumerable times, but I hadn't known it existed. 'We meant to,' my father said. 'We thought we'll come here and sit and listen to the birds.'

'Sitting was whose idea, Papa?'

My father grinned.

There was no way my mother would decide to go for a walk and then abandon the activity midway so that she could birdwatch.

'Do you want to go in?' I asked.

I walked around the fencing, looking for a way in, when my father caught up with me and steered me across the road. He wanted to walk along the library.

Usually, we were quiet on our walks, but today, my father was giving me a tutorial as we walked past the silver oaks and the mighty gulmohar, with its bright orange carpet around it.

'Your mother loved the gulmohar,' he said, pointing at a family that had spread out a bed sheet and opened a picnic basket.

I knew that the gulmohar was her favourite; mine was the tabebuia. He picked up a pink tabebuia petal and gave it to me.

My dad knew all about the exotic botanical species found in the park. He had a friend in the horticulture department who briefed him about every petal and pond on the 300 acres, which was then duly reported to my mother. He then rattled on about the nearly 6,000 plants and trees in the park. I felt the wind caress my cheeks.

'Myra,' he said just after we had crossed one of the motorways in the park, 'to be able to forgive is a wonderful thing.'

I nodded. But where had that come from?

'I learnt that from your mother – to let go and live freely.'

My mother travelled light. She didn't do baggage.

We walked along the araucarias and beds of canna lilies, red and yellow stalks swaying in the evening breeze. We passed the compelling colonial construction of the library and made our way towards Hudson Circle.

This was my running path, and suddenly, I was itching to run. I turned to my father. He was smiling; his head was in the sky.

'I'm going to run a little bit.'

He looked at me and blinked. 'Let me try,' he said, and without warning, one foot in front of the other, he was moving faster than he ever had.

'Let's go, Daddy.' And we were moving again, father and daughter.

When I was a kid, I once called my father 'Poppy'. He was overjoyed that I had a melange of expressions for him. 'Myra has so many names for me,' he told his wife. It was his chest of treasures.

We ran about a kilometre, stopping at the peanut vendor just outside the grounds, where we packed boiled peanuts for ₹50.

My parents always picked up boiled peanuts on their Sunday walks. They had some of it on their way back, and whatever was remaining was tossed into a salad; they called it the 'Cubbon Park salad'. Mummy added finely chopped onion, half a tomato, one green chilli, the juice of half a lime, salt to taste, and no points for guessing, turmeric. The hors d'oeuvre with their evening drinks.

As we turned to walk back home, I decided to rustle up the same salad for the evening.

I was considering a fresh lime with tonic water and a dash of ginger when I heard my father call me. We were almost home, and I reached for the keys.

'How is Andrew?' he asked.

I wondered for a moment if Andrew had got in touch with him. Is that where the forgiveness advice had come from?

They were quite fond of each other, but I would've known had Andrew reached out to him. He would've told me.

Andrew was not a subject I wanted to engage in with my father. One-way traffic. Elvis has left the building.

'He must be okay, Papa,' I said. I wasn't lying.

I didn't turn to look at him but instead had a question of my own. 'Will you run again?'

'A little bit, yes! Today we ran too much.'

Today we made progress.

Chapter 18

My big thing in college was to go on a trek. At least once. Everyone I knew had walked and climbed great distances. I liked the sound of it, the sense of adventure it entailed.

I mentioned it to Andrew one weekend. The following morning, we were headed to Ramanagara of the seven-hills elevation, where one of Bollywood's iconic films was shot some four decades ago.

It was a staggering sight. An imposing 3,000 feet above ground level, it was home to a few temples and the bald-headed eagle. The town sat on Bengaluru's fringes.

I was in baggy tracks and sports sandals; I didn't own a pair of sneakers then. My backpack had a packet of biscuits and tissues; Andrew had thrown a bottle of water into it. That's how prepared we were.

Had we registered for the trek, we'd have known that in the last decade, there had only been night treks in the summer, but we didn't want to spend the ₹1,000 each that would've taken care of the guide and refreshments. Instead, we decided to go on our own.

It was blistering hot – the hottest day in March in 40 years. We were not the only barmy souls on the trail though, but the only ones without caps, and as far as I could see, I was the only girl around.

We climbed several hundred steps – not steep uphill, but it was hard work – before we hit the trail. A narrow path that led to the clouds, it was an extraordinary sight. I'd have enjoyed the grey and green collage a little more had it not been 10 a.m. with a sharp sun beating down on us. I could feel the beginnings of a headache. Andrew was engrossed in clicking photographs and suggested we should walk some more and stop at a stall where they served refreshments. The more we walked, the denser the foliage around us became, but there was no shed or shelter in sight. We heard the voices of people though, which kept us going. Maybe there was something in the next 100 yards. A wine store and a nail bar, too!

We had walked for almost half an hour when we saw a group of guys. They told us they were headed back as they hadn't carried enough water with them. The regular vendors weren't there either because, in the summer, there were only night-time treks.

We turned back, too.

Andrew was sweating profusely, a steady stream; the front of his tee was wet, and the back was in a similar soaked state. He sweats buckets anyway, but this was way off even for him.

My head felt like it was splintering.

'You need to hydrate,' he said, suggesting we stop and replenish.

I dunked half the bottle of water and gave him the rest. He opened the biscuits I had carried and gave me two. I ate one and then threw up everything I had ingested. What a waste. We had just one bottle of water. Andrew forced me to drink the rest of it, saying we'd find some shop or the other at the base, where we had parked. I was sobbing. I'd never known physical pain that bad.

I don't know how, but we managed to get to the end of the trail. I remember seeing the steps, painted a garish blue, before I passed out.

When I came around, I was in a moving vehicle. My father's. Andrew had blasted the aircon and was singing with the radio, something he never does. I was lying down in an almost-flattened seat; he was driving like a rally driver.

'What happened?' I asked. It felt like I had missed half the highway chase.

'We're going home.' He was loud.

'Lower the volume, you won't need to shout.'

'No,' he shouted. 'I need it to get us home.' He was singing again; he had cranked up the decibel level. He patted me with his left hand; it was wet.

'How did I get here?' I didn't think he had heard me.

'I carried you.'

'Down the 300 steps?'

He continued to sing. The nineties chart-toppers were playing on a bad stereo, and Andrew was driving like a man possessed.

The view from my position – I was on my back – was lovely. It looked like Bengaluru was a tree-lined avenue. My mother had told me that was the city she had grown up in during the seventies. Was this some kind of a time-warp race we were in?

I spotted my backpack in the far corner and pulled out the biscuit packet. I offered it to Andrew, but he preferred to sing.

'Don't get up, Myraah,' he screamed, 'just rest.'

I wasn't trying to get up.

'What a crazy trip,' I said, not trying to match his decibel level.

He didn't respond, and I shut my eyes and dozed again, thinking we'd be home soon.

I opened my eyes when the car came to a jerky halt. After a brief struggle with the door, Andrew crawled out of his seat and threw himself under the gulmohar tree. I stared at him confused. We were supposed to go to my house, but here we were, at Andrew's.

'Get me water quickly, bubbs,' he shouted as he rolled to his side, curling up like a baby, clutching himself.

Something was wrong. I rushed to his side, asking him what had happened. 'Cramps,' he shouted.

I ran into his house, using the back door, which was always open during the day, and grabbed a few bottles of water from the kitchen counter. Andrew gulped them down. I was massaging his calf muscles, his shoulders and finally his head as he lay shirtless on the fiery orange carpet. He was moaning. That's when I realized that he needed more than water. I rushed out and got him sugarcane juice from a street vendor, which is what I think finally did the trick of restoring his electrolyte balance.

'Has this happened before?'

When he was in school, after a game of hockey, he had suffered similarly. He started carrying water everywhere he went thereafter. He had another episode, but he didn't elaborate on the when and why of it.

The Browns, typically, hadn't consulted a physician but had clicked on Dr Google and come to the conclusion that the both of them had hyperhidrosis.

'Why did you make me drink all the water?'

Andrew was on his back now, and his bony hand was on my cheek, trying to pinch it. His face was wearing a tired smile.

'Why didn't we go to Ramanagara town? We'd have found some shop or supermarket selling water. We'd have been okay.'

Andrew tugged me, and I fell on his chest. We lay there for I don't know how long. I drifted off to sleep, and I suspect, so did he. When I opened my eyes, he was on his side, pushing my hair back.

Andrew had gambled with some decisions. Had we gone into Ramanagara town, we could've bought ourselves all the water we needed, but had he stopped, he wouldn't have been in a position to drive for at least another five to six hours. It would've taken his body that long to get control. He wasn't sure if I was okay to hold on for that long, given that I wasn't keeping anything inside me. I had apparently puked my second ingestion of water, too. He decided to drive us back, willing himself, using the music as a distraction.

He put me before him, and I did the same. It was our signature.

Chapter 19

I don't see much of my father during the week. I return late in the evenings and tiptoe around the house because he's already asleep. He's a morning person, but after my mother passed away, he started calling it a day at the meekest of hours – 7 p.m. I coaxed him out of that kindergarten roster, and he grudgingly pushed it back by a couple of hours.

So, to find him sipping a can of cola on Friday night when I arrived home well past 9 p.m. was a pleasant surprise.

'Papa!' I exhaled.

'You're early,' he said, returning my ear-to-ear smile.

I arranged my paraphernalia on the dining table where he was seated. A half-filled whisky glass sat next to the can my father was holding.

My parents sipped their drinks together, from hot beverages to alcoholic portions, unless Mummy was at work. So much so that their weekday evening fare was had after she returned from work, which was anywhere between 6 and 7 p.m. On weekends, the kettle was whistling by 4 p.m. They had their Sunday walk at 5 p.m., remember!

As far as I knew, my father hadn't had a drink in more than eight years. Each time he allowed himself an aerated treat, he laid out an extra glass, which I suspect he finished later.

I picked up the glass and joined him. I didn't ask who it was for. I was breathing heavily.

'Did you run?' my father asked, pointing at my flash black trousers and my disquieted cast.

'No!' I said, forcing a smile.

I hadn't told my father about Andrew joining *Morning Herald*. I had hardly spoken to my father about Andrew since he left for the United States. He asked me once, years ago, how Andrew was doing. I recounted his professional success, and that was that.

My father didn't pry; he was a remarkably non-curious creature.

When he'd enquired about Andrew on Sunday, my answer was indefinite. I had deliberately let the question hang on a distant, disconnected peg.

My life with Andrew was in the past, and this most wonderful man sitting before me would find it hard to understand that.

All that my father knew about Ravi's presence in my life was that of a good Samaritan, who was now my close friend. Blame that on the way we communicate with each other.

A little after he had questioned me about Andrew, he hesitantly enquired if I had a boyfriend, after which he broached the subject of marriage.

I mentioned Ravi then. It was a vague reference, something to the tune of, 'I think he likes me, but I don't know.' It was an awkward conversation, and we were both glad it was over in less time than it took to make a cup of instant whatever.

I took a sip of the Coke and told my father about *Morning Herald*'s most high-profile hiring ever. I spoke for three minutes, giving him the details of Andrew Brown's entry into No. 7 MG Road. His face was glowing with what I thought was pride. But it was hope, a ray of light.

My father was on his feet. He went to the fridge and brought out another can of soda, half of which he poured into the glass I was drinking from.

'I knew it!' he said. 'I knew something was happening. You are dressing differently; your lipstick is darker.'

'Poppy! My lipstick is old.'

He was shaking his head. He was right.

'I'm so happy,' he said when he finally found his voice, raising the can, 'that he has returned. This is where he should be – by your side.'

Welcome back to the eighties. It floats around our home – sentences, songs, sentiments. The segue to Whitney Houston's 'Saving All My Love for You'.

Then he laughed, a whole-hearted sound that resonated through the late-evening air. It was ages since I had heard my father laugh.

My glass was on the table. I refused to respond. This was not a time for kindness.

'No, no, Papa,' I said. I couldn't let him think we were a couple or were ever going to be a couple. 'He's going to be the editor of *Morning Herald* shortly, my boss. But yes, I guess we'll always be friends.'

'Yes,' he said, still smiling and wiping a stray tear, 'that's one part of the story. The professional side.'

'There is only the professional side, Papa.'

Shocked was a scarce summation of my father's reaction. His eyes were wide, and his mouth was half-open. Understandable, coming as it did from a man who had known love and embraced it. My father was sensitive enough to recognize that he couldn't let the expression play for much longer and so compromised with a quick nod.

He wouldn't allow himself the question of 'what about all those days and months', but it was plastered across his face.

'Andrew is going on Hari Rao's campaign trail on Monday and Tuesday.' My father was still recovering from the body blow. 'He asked me to go with him. I'm planning to go.'

The smile returned to his face quicker than it had disappeared. He was shuffling in his seat, and I heard the controlled strains of the laughter that had sung in my ears only minutes ago. 'Is he married?' he asked, as if he were checking my temperature.

'No, Papa, he isn't.'

He clamped his lips. He was trying to keep the laughter down, but he couldn't help himself. He took a swig in a bid to hide the delight. 'Of course, you will go with him. He will be there to take care of you,' he said, his eyes on a photograph of Mummy on the mantlepiece.

'Daddy!'

'I know you don't need him to take care of you and that you are a big girl, but it is always nice to have someone around. Someone to talk to,' he said, shaking his head. 'You'll be going to rural areas, and these places are not always safe for women to be on their own.'

I was shaking my head when I realized I hadn't told Ravi about going on Hari Rao's campaign trail with Andrew. He had surprised me with the offer. Andrew had come around to my desk and asked if I would go with him just as I was winding up for the day.

'Mr Kumar mentioned that you might be interested,' he'd said.

I had told my editor well before we hired Andrew Brown that I would be interested in writing a colour piece on the canvassing leading elections. I was happy to go with any of the beat reporters, feel the pulse and note the nuances.

I think I nodded. My mouth was dry, and I was out of words.

He would drive, and a photographer might or might not join us for part of the journey. We were going to Malavalli, Maddur, Mandya and then on to Mysuru, which was Hari Rao's constituency, from where he last contested and won more than a decade ago. He wasn't sure if we would be returning to Bengaluru for the night and asked me to carry an extra set of clothes and toiletries in case we decided to stay back.

My heart was in a race with Usain Bolt. An overnight road trip, with Andrew driving.

'Are you up for it?' he asked. He was leaning against my desk.

I nodded. 'Are we leaving in the morning or the day after?'

'No, early Monday.'

'Should I prepare an extra breakfast for Andrew?' my father asked.

I took a deep breath as I got up from my chair and stood next to my father. I dropped a kiss on his balding pate. Someone had to be a responsible adult.

'Andrew and I are not dating any more, Papa, and no, you don't need to make breakfast for him or me.'

'You both will have breakfast together then.'

'We're on assignment, Papa. This is not a road trip.' I said it because I needed to hear it more than my old man.

His eyes were on my mother's photograph, and he was smiling. A sweet, shitty mess.

We were cruising. Andrew's fragrance filled the vehicle, and I inhaled it. It was like sitting in an oxygen cylinder. I felt the stain of healthy colour each time I took a breath.

He was shifting between speeds of 60 and 100 kmph, which was fast for NH 275 with its patches of civilization every 10–20 kilometres. Back-breakers posing as speed checks forced drivers to pause before they hit the accelerator again. A sprinkling of shops and stalls dotted the highway. For the rest, it was great expanses of green paddy fields, sugarcane cultivations and sunflowers eyeing the rising sun. Karnataka had suffered a drought for the second successive year, but who could tell.

Outside of 'Good morning' and 'All set?', Andrew hadn't said much since he picked me up from home at the crack of dawn. I replied but didn't ask any questions myself.

I had offered to take the wheel any time he wanted a break.

He'd nodded.

This time of day wasn't for words, even in the best of times. More so when he was driving, eyes on the road and focus on the assembly election.

Karnataka was going to polls next month, and six months later, India would vote, because of which this exercise assumed greater significance.

It was all about Rao, Karnataka's longest-serving chief minister, who was in office for three successive terms before he walked away from politics. The 74-year-old had decided to roll the political dice again, returning to lead his party, KANNADA, in the upcoming fixture.

Theories, fuelled by rumours, were doing the rounds as to why Rao had decided to re-enter the cauldron.

Since his reign, which was a game changer for the state economically, his party had been all but wiped out from the region in the last decade. Late last year, when Rao took to public life again, making appearances at social gatherings, the party headquarters in Bengaluru came alive suddenly. A three-line announcement of Rao's return to politics followed shortly after.

It said the party would contest all 224 seats after contesting in under 50 in the last two elections, bagging just a handful of victories.

It was believed, even if it wasn't definitively reported, that Rao was reviving the party to hand it over to Ravi, who was apparently developing an appetite for politics. There was talk of Rao's yearning for a national role. He had made a few trips to Delhi since November. I had been meaning to ask Ravi if the national role was for him, but he had shown no political curiosity whatsoever. Not even when I had raised the topic of Rao's return to the stage. If anything, Ravi wasn't pleased by the move.

The first thing I had done when I left my father on Friday evening was to call Ravi and tell him that I was joining Andrew on Hari Rao's campaign trail.

'Why Andrew?' Ravi asked. 'I can take you if you want.'

'I want to go as a journalist, not as your girlfriend.'

Ravi laughed. He wasn't happy. 'You are my girlfriend, and you are a journalist, but you don't cover politics.'

'No! But I'm a writer, Ravi, and we don't have boundaries.'

He might've nodded, but he wasn't convinced.

I get Ravi. This is a difficult profession for anyone to understand, more so if you've never had a job. It was different from holding a position in a leadership team or simply signing papers. They may have assembled to a greater ideal, but the order was different.

Andrew pulled up at a weather-beaten stall in front of which tables and benches had been laid out haphazardly. He told me they served thatte idlis besides tea and coffee. It was, as the name suggested, idlis cooked in a different vessel, a flatter plate, giving it a sleeker texture. It was popular in this region. There were no other options. I preferred dosas, but no one asked me.

Andrew picked up two glasses of filter coffee, handing me one, before engaging with the lorry drivers and cleaners who had parked alongside us. He had found a spot on the bench beside an older driver, who saw Hari Rao's campaign as a last-ditch fight for regional expression in Karnataka.

Andrew's full lips opened and closed, stretched and rounded as he spoke. His Kannada was flawless – not even a hint of a twang. 'What do you think?' he finished with a question.

'We need a leader from here, who has partaken of this soil. We need it more than any other state in India,' Shivanna, 54, pronounced while reclaiming the key to his vehicle with his left hand.

Shivanna went on to bestow the title of the most accommodative Indian on Kannadigas, who went out of their way to welcome everyone. 'Not just that,' he said, his saliva augmenting his argument, 'we will speak to every migrant in their language, even if we barely know it.'

Andrew took the steel tumbler from me, replacing it with the empty one he had just finished, punctuating the act with a smile.

'Sir, you and your wife,' Shivanna said, 'stopped your vehicle here at a time when there are Kannada-speaking drivers.'

Shivanna's words had come like a theatrical cue.

I leaned into Andrew, who dropped his left hand on my denim-clad knee. I felt a current spark through my spine. Andrew's eyes were on my cheeks. I made a conscious effort to breathe, shifting in my seat. I didn't quite know why at that point, but I understood that we were putting on a show for these people.

'So, you think Hari Rao will win?'

There was a smile, a nod. A general waddle. 'It is hard to predict what will happen in an election, sir. Nobody will say who they are voting for,' Shivanna said.

Andrew nodded.

A little after, following another round of tea, the motley crowd dispersed.

The tea stall owner sidled up and informed us that this was the lull before the next lot of lorries arrived in an hour, or a few hours, depending on the weather, he said, looking up at the sky, which was without a dark cloud.

It was an open, brilliantly lit landscape that the tea stall owner stood against. A page that was waiting to be filled.

There was no telling how long they'd take, he continued.

Like Shivanna and the cleaners, who were on their way now, he expressed hope about Hari Rao's return, saying that it would be good for Karnataka, but he wondered if Hari Rao would spend the money that swings elections these days. Like a good businessman, he gave some and asked for more.

'What is your business, sir?'

What kind of a question is that? I wondered.

'I'm working, but we are on our way to Mysuru to visit family.'

I ensured that my smile was all about familial contentment while I cheered Andrew on. He was prepared with his lines.

This was why we were posing as a couple. Lesson No. 1 on campaign duty: Do not disclose your identity. People, especially in the hinterland, are wary of media personnel.

'IT?'

What else? Everyone in Bengaluru is a techie!

Andrew nodded.

'Which office?'

What? Were we expected to write code now?

'Wipro.'

I quickly gave my posture a techie order. A casual expression, a calculated stance.

Once we got back on the road, Andrew made a phone call to determine where exactly Hari Rao was. After a couple of exchanges with the personal assistant, we learnt that they were only a little ahead of us, by a couple of kilometres perhaps. I looked at my watch. We had spent more than an hour at the tea stall.

Just then, a television van overtook us, and Andrew decided to follow them. 'They'll be headed in the right direction,' he said.

I nodded. I was still trying to read into the conversation at the stall. Would they vote for Hari Rao or not?

'Your first time at an election campaign, Rai?' Andrew asked. I nodded, determined not to be annoyed by his using my second name.

'You did well out there at the stall.'

'I'm glad I have your approval, Brown.'

This wasn't anything like what I had seen in the movies. An ocean of humanity moving in unison like waves that jostled for space to feel the sun. Picture perfect. And then the din, where voices were heard but not the words. It was into that setting that the politician, invariably cast as the villain, arrived, stepping on a carpet of slogan shouting before the speeches took over.

As removed as reel is from real, I could tell it was beginning to boil, going by the chase Andrew was involved in. Another press vehicle was honking annoyingly behind us, but Andrew wasn't relenting. I was not sure he should be driving. I thought he'd have been better off taking notes, planning his moves or whatever it was political reporters do at such times. We should've taken the office car. Anonymity be damned.

'Do you want me to drive?' I heard the squeaky trill in my voice.

'No. Why?' A smile punctuated his question.

I shrugged. I just asked. A different why was playing on my mind though.

Why had Andrew asked me to join him on this campaign trail? It was the editor's nudge obviously, but he could've shrugged aside the suggestion.

Was it because of the pressure he was supposedly under to get the Hari Rao interview?

I could hardly ask my almost-fiancé for a favour for my ex-lover.

Not only did Andrew know me better than that, but he was also a thorough professional. He took the direct approach; going through someone or everyone was not his style. If there was a way, he'd find it himself.

So why had Andrew knocked on my door then?

Why had he shown me that diary, belonging to whoever this Bhumika Velu was – his great-grandmother's friend maybe – after all these years?

It's not something he had chanced upon last week; he'd had it before he left for the United States. I had meant to ask, but we were caught in a different tango in the aftermath.

I had spent a sleepless night wondering why he had read it out to me. But there was something more; those notes just didn't fold. They were filed away but only momentarily. They kept coming back to me like some sort of endless hide-and-seek game.

My mind was ticking in myriad directions, and my emotions were all over the place.

There was Andrew and there was Ravi. I couldn't have one, and I didn't want the other, not in the way he wanted me in his life at least. That was why my heart was tap dancing when Andrew asked me if I wanted to join him.

I told my father it was an opportunity for me.

Bollocks, as Chhaya would've said.

Andrew parked just around the corner from the village temple in Malavalli and walked in the direction of an open estate truck that was carrying Hari Rao. He was smiling and waving at the crowds, but he looked old and frail.

'Rao's PA told me he's expecting me. So when he gets off the truck and walks to the car, I could approach him for an interview,' Andrew whispered in my ear. Not that anyone would've heard, even if he shouted.

The entire village had gathered, it appeared. There were children as young as two and three years of age, screaming and dancing alongside the youth. Then there were the middle-aged and old folks, who were finding it difficult to put one foot in front of the other but standing there resolute. If this was a show of solidarity, it resonated serious muscle.

I wondered how Andrew could get close enough to Hari Rao given the number of people around the man. It was far more civilized in the world of feature writing; we didn't accost people. We set up interviews and sat down for them with a cuppa maybe.

'The whole village is here', the PA told me after we had somehow managed to fall behind the truck that carried the mountain of a politician. We were moseying with the crowd. 'We go this way for two kilometres,' he said, pointing at the mud road, 'and then stop at every house.'

I watched as Hari Rao descended from the vehicle. He looked a little fuller than from a distance. Andrew approached him as he headed towards a waiting SUV.

There was an exchange of greetings, I think, and as I moved closer, I heard Hari Rao tell Andrew, 'I know who you are, Mr Brown.' Both men smiled at each other. Andrew's expression was a little forced.

After Hari Rao got into his four-wheel drive, Andrew tried to extricate himself from the crowd. Oily-haired boys and girls tugged at his arm, asking if he was a 'fillam actor'. Andrew lowered his frame down to their little lengths and held court before he came around and found me.

'What happened?'

'He didn't want to speak to me,' he said as we got back into the car and followed Hari Rao's cavalcade.

I chewed on Andrew's response until he stopped in front of a house Hari Rao had just entered.

'You can try again,' I told Andrew, whose eyes were fixed on the elderly man's back.

As Hari Rao exited the house, Andrew got out of the car and walked behind the politician, who repeated the exercise in 15 such thatched dwellings. He spoke to the men and women, asking for their trust to finish the work he had started in taking Karnataka forward.

The tableau played out across habitats in other hamlets in the district. Andrew didn't say much, even during the drives when we were joined by the *Morning Herald*'s chief photographer in Mysuru, who more than compensated for the laconic word count.

He had clicked about a dozen pictures of Andrew and Hari Rao, which he kept thrusting in my direction. 'Myra ma'am, see this picture of Andrew sir and sir,' he said. Andrew finally told him to take pictures of Hari Rao with the people and leave him out of the frame or the paper wouldn't be able to use any of his photographs.

He laughed and wagged his head.

'Anyway, Andrew sir,' the photographer said, inching forward and sticking his head between our seats like a five-year-old asking for a treat, 'I don't think Hari Rao will win this election. There is too much money doing the rounds in the other camp. This election is a bought election, sir. If you have money, you can buy. My vote is for KANNADA, my language, my people.'

Andrew nodded.

'You think Hari Rao won't win?' I asked the photographer, turning in my seat.

'I'm not so sure he won't win,' Andrew said.

'Why, sir?'

'People here vote with their heart. He *will* win. I'm not sure if the party will get a simple majority though.'

Hari Rao looked regal in a Mysore peta (a dressy turban), standing atop an estate truck. The sun came down on Pandavapura, lending colour to a compelling picture. The beloved monarch and his milling subjects. People had lined the thoroughfare, waving party flags and cheering as his vehicle inched through the main road.

I had read that the power of Hari Rao's campaign lay in the person-to-person exercise. He not only went to houses, especially in small villages, which had two or three hutments at most, but he also met with every resident. He carried sweets for children, whom he engaged with, and took the blessings of the elderly. It was easy to see why he was once known as the 'people's chief minister'. He was a mass leader.

By the time Hari Rao was done, it was almost 7 p.m. The photographer said he was heading back to Mysuru and would join us the following morning.

'What do you want to do?' Andrew asked as we made our way to his car, which he had parked at the bus stand.

I wanted a cup of coffee, any damn coffee at this point, because I hadn't had a sip all day.

'I'm sorry, Myraah, I was meaning to stop at a café on the highway,' Andrew said, bringing his hands together in apology. 'We'll do that now, on our way back.'

'Back?' I had the beginnings of a headache.

'Yeah,' Andrew said. 'I think we still have time to get back to Bengaluru and start early tomorrow and maybe catch them here and go forward.'

We were an hour from Mysuru, maybe a little more than that. So, what sense was there in driving all the way back to Bengaluru only to return here in the morning?

'I thought you'd want to go to the party office or wherever it is these peeps hang out once their day is done,' I said. Why? That would add more colour to my copy?

'Hari Rao and his PA are going back to Bengaluru. Apparently, he always does that. He'll start early tomorrow.'

I was looking forward to a late-evening gin and tonic with Andrew.

'Oh! Okay.' It made sense for Hari Rao, who wasn't getting younger. But for me, who had no plans of geriatric care for another 50 years, it was a party spoiler.

'There's no point in us staying here. We're better off trailing him, even if it's by a fair distance.'

The question was in my expression.

'I don't want him drawing conclusions, Rai.'

The surname again! What conclusions? About Andrew and me? That we were a couple?

'I hope he's not unwell or something.'

'I think he likes what we all like – to sleep on our own beds. It's more the case as you get older, I suspect.'

'You were born old; you'd know, Brown! I think if he sees you around long enough, he'll give you the interview.'

Andrew shook his head. 'I don't want him thinking we are tailing him.'

This was a disjointed conversation, like after a few gin and tonics down. Questions that never got asked were answered minutes later.

'Even if that's exactly what we are doing, Brown!' I said, joining the party. I saw him wince!

Not once during the day had Andrew asked me to contact Ravi to find out anything about Hari Rao. Not even something as lame as cross-checking his plans for the day. Ravi talked a lot about Hari Rao and Kamini but never about politics.

I called my father to let him know I'd be back for the night. He wanted to know if Andrew would be around for breakfast. I cut the call and messaged him. *No. Not Andrew not me for breakfast.*

A pair of blue ticks was the reply I got.

The moment Andrew heard that Hari Rao had started back for Bengaluru and that he would pass the café we were seated at in 15 minutes, he was on his feet. I paid for the coffees and sandwiches and rushed back to the car. Andrew had already fired the engine.

We had some time before Hari Rao's cars caught up with us. 'They are usually five minutes or so behind the time they give us,' he said, when five black SUVs overtook us.

'That would have to be Hari Rao's,' I said, 'but why does he need five of them, especially when, as he claims, he's working with a shoestring budget?'

'My guess is he's in the third,' Andrew said, dismissing my question. It was apparently unworthy of a novice even.

'Five black Toyota SUVs, one behind the other. How conspicuous.'

Andrew shrugged.

I wondered aloud if Hari Rao was hyper about safety after the air crash that destroyed his family. 'I can't imagine how that would've been for him,' I said.

Andrew nodded.

'It can't be easy for Ravi either, sole heir of this staggering legacy, which he doesn't even want,' I said without thinking. I had been conscious not to mention Ravi with Andrew all day, but with caffeine in my veins, my mouth was moving on its own.

'Not sole,' he said.

I was so engrossed in my thoughts that I hadn't grasped how quickly Andrew's face had changed colour.

'What do you mean?'

Andrew didn't answer my question. He honked, something he doesn't do very often.

'Oookaaay! He's not technically the grandson,' I said, rolling my eyes. But he was the sole heir.

A tempo truck was on the wrong side. It was swerving all over the place. Andrew was quick on the brake, pulling off the road before getting back on it.

Chapter 20

Andrew pulled up at Maddur and parked about 100 yards from the railway station. The sky was blue, and the clouds were white. The morning sun was a bashful stream of light.

Andrew was behind me; I could feel his eyes on my back.

I settled down at the first empty table I spotted in what was a tin shed that abutted the railway station. The place was filling up quickly with anxious commuters, fieldworkers, wailing children, men shouting into their mobile phones and women managing browbeating spouses and cranky kids.

'It's popular,' Andrew said, looking around him. I think he meant loud.

We were at the very stall where the Maddur vada was first formulated. A lip-smacking consequence of a late start to the day. Legend has it that the cook, an hour or so behind schedule, rustled up these delicious discs as an apology for not being ready with a full breakfast. Sliced onions, curry leaves and grated coconut were never put to better use.

This place was my choice. I had sold it to Andrew for much of our way here. He might not have known what to expect, but the moment he bit into the first of the vadas, I knew I had called right.

'This is so good, Rai!'

This sonnet of surnames was beginning to annoy me. It was more a reaction, I could tell, but it might've increased after he ran into Ravi and me.

Andrew took a second bite and closed his eyes. It was fresh and crisp like the morning air.

I had three vadas, enjoying every bite. Each was the size of my not-so-considerable palm. I had two with chutney and one plain. I could've had a couple more easily, but Andrew forced me to stop. There was excess edible oil in my system already for a whole week.

I wanted chutney for the last bite of my vada, but the steel bowl on my plate was wiped clean. Andrew had eaten my share of chutney, too.

He was on his feet to get us an extra portion, but I told him not to bother. I was going to savour the flavour.

'You had five!' He was smiling, sparking the sun.

'Two,' I said, keeping a straight face. That raw, early-morning contour had soothed into quiet certitude. It was inviting. 'You should've asked your fashion-blogger friend to come along, Andrew.'

He was suddenly engaged with picking the crumbs on his steel plate.

'Three can be company,' I said.

Andrew looked around him. I think he was looking for a waiter to either call for the bill or have him walk me out of this busy location.

I opened my phone to Pooja's Instagram page and found that she was online. 'And she's an early riser.'

'How do you know?' Andrew asked, hawking the tired look.

I flashed the page at him. Andrew looked away.

'You should've worn a polka-dotted shirt.' I giggled. It was that kind of a morning.

Andrew smiled; his face coloured.

'Hari Rao would've been impressed.'

I had crossed a line, I could tell, by the way his eyes hardened. I'd done the polka dots to death. Maybe.

'Why would I want to impress him?'

'Because…' I said, tilting my face up to his. Our lips were not in line.

I was craving coffee, black and bitter. I raised my hand to signal for one, and Andrew, who was seated opposite me, took my hand loosely in his.

'Not here,' he mouthed.

I returned his smile, brighter and warmer.

'They don't do black coffee here, Myraah,' he said.

I should've known; I was the local girl. I had done this road a million times growing up.

I took my hand back and let him keep the smile as we exited the stall.

Some 10 minutes later, Hari Rao's convoy passed us. I couldn't help but throw a glance at Andrew. His foot slammed the accelerator; we were back at work. On the campaign trail, en route to Mysuru.

We drove through a couple of villages before stopping at a two-lane expanse, which had some five homes. Mud and brick constructions, never touched by a paintbrush. Hari Rao stepped into each of the shelters and interacted with the adults. The villagers from the seemingly better-placed settlements that we had driven past had been transported to the remote Chittakayanakoplu. Hari Rao wanted to bring this hardy commune into public consciousness. If he went there, especially in the lead-up to the elections, the media would follow and train their lenses on local issues like housing and electricity. More people, even if they were just in the backdrop, would lend to the voice of the people.

I followed Andrew into the first house. I hooked my fingers into the belt loop of his carpenter jeans to keep up with him. He turned once to check if I was okay before returning to the action.

Hari Rao had spent between 10 and 20 minutes in each house, addressing their problems, which were basically the drought and its impact. He listened to their woes and came up with easy, inexpensive solutions.

Like every politician, he finished with the promise that he would take care of them if he came to power. Unlike most of his ilk, though, he appeared to mean what he said. Either that or he was a bloody good actor. There have been a fair few of those, too.

His hair was thin, his kurta was thick and the lines on his face were readable.

I wondered why Ravi hadn't joined him, just to support him. Maybe he was scared that his presence would endorse what Hari Rao wanted – that he'd eventually get into politics.

Some six months from an election verdict, I could see that there was no happy resolution here. The old man was trying to get his party rolling one more time for the grandson, who didn't want the stage. Still, I thought, Ravi should've been here for his grandfather. There were a lot of people around Hari Rao, but they were not family.

It was late afternoon when we arrived at the once-capital city of the kingdom of Mysore. I love Mysuru because it's the picture of what Bengaluru once was. The air is fair, the temperament soft and the surroundings clean.

We had lunch close to the state guest house, where Hari Rao and his team had halted. I settled in my seat quickly, dropping my handbag on the floor so that I could dig into my dosa freely. I had taken the first bite of my ghee-soaked Mysuru masala dosa when Andrew's phone rang. Hari Rao was unwell; he was returning to Bengaluru immediately.

I sat in my seat for a whole minute wondering if I should pack the dosa. No shit!

Hari Rao had looked fine, and I was famished.

Andrew was at the cash counter already.

It was early evening by the time we were back in Bengaluru. We decided to go to office, but we both wanted coffee before that. Andrew met me at Perky Grace after he parked his car.

He had been quiet for most of the drive back. I was annoyed at having to leave my dosa uneaten. *Mostly* uneaten. I had shovelled two giant bites into my mouth.

I had ordered coffee and a couple of sandwiches by the time Andrew joined me.

'There's something I need to say to you,' he said just as he was sitting down.

About? I wondered.

Our food and coffee arrived as soon as he was seated.

'You remember Nana, Noelene,' he said. It wasn't a question; it was a nervous introduction to a subject dear to him. 'Do you remember her watch?'

I nodded. I didn't really remember; no, I did. It wasn't exceptional. 'It was steel.'

'She always wore it.'

I took a deep breath. Something was wrong.

The only piece of jewellery Noelene owned was a stainless-steel HMT watch. Broad strap, thick white dial. Noelene returned it to a black plastic case at the end of each day. The box had long come apart and was held together by a rubber band. Andrew had taken the watch and the box with him to the United States.

'You've lost it!'

Andrew's eyes were misty.

'Two days ago, when was I tidying stuff around my house,' Andrew paused, 'I opened the box. I wanted to check the watch. It had obviously stopped ticking. I pulled it out and rubbed it. That's when I noticed a notepaper at the base of the case.'

Andrew fished out a thick, rectangular box from the side pockets of his cargoes and placed it on the table. He rolled off the rubber band. The notepaper was laid out like a carpet in a dollhouse.

'Okay!' I said.

Andrew picked out the paper. It contained a signature. Four letters.

'Who gave it to Noelene?'

Andrew passed me the slip. 'Hari' was scrawled across it.

'That's not Nana's handwriting.'

'Who is this?' I asked. I was panicking.

'When Noelene dropped those hints about my grandfather, she was fiddling with the watch. Moving it up and down on her wrist. She was smiling.'

Coy was the word Andrew wasn't using.

This was harsh, but I had to ask. 'Do you remember that conversation with Noelene?'

'She only said, "Your grandfather is someone famous."'

Sometimes Andrew is so slow when he speaks, I could bake an apple crumble between sentences.

'I asked her, "How famous? Shah Rukh Khan famous?"'

'Is he an actor?' Where in god's name was this going?

That had been Andrew's question, too, after Noelene told him that his grandfather wasn't as famous as Shah Rukh Khan.

'She knew him because she had worked for him as his secretary. At that point, I thought he was money, he was a businessman. But no.'

I was feeling faint, but Andrew sat before me, straight back and square shoulders. His face was pale. There was a similitude somewhere, though the writing was not in the features.

While Noelene hadn't named her lover, only giving her grandson a broad outline of the situation, she had emphasized that it was only her version of events. It was how she saw things. There was no drama in the revelations.

Andrew didn't have to say it, but it was obvious that Noelene had lived much of her adult life with a broken heart. She had told Andrew that she had known all along that her boyfriend wasn't going to marry her and that she, and she alone, was to blame for the situation she found herself in.

That, I thought, said more about Noelene than what may have transpired between the paramours.

Andrew cleared his throat. 'Last evening, I checked it again, just to see if I had read it wrong.'

I nodded.

'He knows, and that was the only confirmation I needed.'

Andrew returned the case to his cargoes and crossed his hands across his chest. 'Ravi was adopted; I wasn't accepted.' He shrugged.

I wanted to reach across the table of untouched food but picked up my coffee instead. 'Why?' I mouthed. I was a journalist; there had to be a question.

Andrew shook his head.

'No!' was all I could manage. I had meant yes, but not that it mattered. Yes, what? I had no idea.

So, Noelene's lover was Hari Rao. The doe-eyed Noelene, frail but not fragile. Not a strand of grey in that fall of brown that touched her waist on the rare occasions she let her hair down. They had a child, a daughter, who died when giving birth to a baby boy, who was now the man sitting across the table from me.

Andrew Brown was Hari Rao's grandson. By blood.

Andrew looked a lot like his grandmother. He definitely had her eyes. His grandfather's mark wasn't as distinct. Like with Ravi.

Andrew was on his feet. 'I'm going back to the office,' he said.

To lose himself in his work, I thought.

I leaned back in my chair and watched him disappear into the evening crowd that was swarming all over Church Street.

There was the odd horn that blared, the sound of motorbikes coming to a screeching halt. The road was an ill-tempered space.

There was a general buzz in the air, but you rarely heard words or caught a conversation from the next table. Perky Grace was that kind of a place.

And Bengaluru was that kind of a city – where grace and disgrace were hard to separate.

I wondered if Hari Rao had lured Noelene with the promise of marriage and then backtracked on it.

Would Noelene have a yen for someone so above her station and have his child without some kind of exchange?

Why was Andrew chasing Hari Rao for an interview?

Were his reasons professional or personal?

Is this why Andrew left the life he had made for himself in the US and returned home?

What did he want from the man?

The Browns had clearly lost more than they had gained in this business of love. They had tasted it, embraced it and lost it. Lost at it. They'd been pursued. Catherine Brown.

My mind went back to those notes; it kept going back to the notes. It was a puzzle I needed to fix. Five thousand strains of grey.

In the end, Catherine had to pay, perhaps just like Bhumika. As did Noelene.

Maybe more than they had bargained for.

I thought of Andrew. To carry that burden, your family's history, and yet walk so lightly, as if nothing was weighing you down, was quite something. I might've checked into an asylum.

Later that evening, I messaged Ravi, telling him I wanted to meet him. He asked about my trip with Andrew, adding that people had asked him what *his* girl was doing with Andrew Brown. He wanted to know if my story was coming out tomorrow. It was scheduled for later in the month.

That piece of information was met with a question mark I ignored.

We decided to meet at our usual coffee shop at 2 p.m. on Saturday. *Morning Herald*'s weekend meeting had been pushed back to 5 p.m. Ravi wanted to pick me up, but I told him I'd see him there.

After the logistics were taken care of, I slipped my phone into my bag and got to my feet. I decided to walk home.

I thought about Ravi and what we shared. We had done well to build a relationship on barely existing common ground, coexisting with our differences. We were mindful never to cross lines, the both of us. Never ask questions the answers to which you had a right to know as a couple.

The details of our lives were lost on each other, and curiously, that was where the balance came from. The blank pages. Together, yet alone.

It was late in the afternoon; the office was a relaxed space. Almost the weekend, even though that didn't really apply to us. Cut that smirk, remember the Sunday morning paper.

I caught one of the photographers yawning as I walked over to Andrew's cabin.

I stopped mid-stride. Andrew was on his feet talking to Sudha. The door was closed. I swivelled around and almost bumped into Soor.

'Andrew is busy, eh,' he said, waving a freshly minted page at me.

I yawned.

Andrew was moving his hands animatedly. His black tee was crumpled, but his proclamation was crisp. I could tell from his expression.

It was an impressive turnaround from a couple of days ago. Our eyes met. Andrew lowered his gaze and disappeared from my vision.

I returned to my cabin and settled heavily into my seat. There was so much on my mind, it felt like a sumo wrestler's torso.

I pulled my hair back, and along with it, those thoughts that I didn't want to deal with. I preferred instead to dwell on Andrew Brown's family tree.

I opened a new mail and typed his address in.

Hey. Too casual.

Hello. Too formal.

Hi. Third-grader.

Brown, I want to read Bhumika's notes. Thanks in advance.

I read my 10-word email admiringly, revelling in its precision, before hitting the send button. I was so absorbed in my genius that I hadn't considered what Andrew's reaction might be. Two minutes later, I got a reply, and shortly after, a WhatsApp notification.

Check your WhatsApp, Myra, was the reply.

I opened my phone and saved the images of the notes he had sent me.

I read them carefully, one by one. I read them again; it was quite an exercise.

I only had one question to ask Andrew. What were the similarities in Bhumika Velu and Catherine Brown's life stories?

He needed to put that down on paper. Black ink on white paper.

I closed my eyes and rested my hand on my knuckles.

Ravi and Andrew, cousins? If there was another in that blend, I'd marry that one maybe. Those with the bashful backstories.

Karnataka's former chief minister and his biological grandson, a crack-shot political analyst, who was perhaps the only one betting that Hari Rao would pull off this ambitious gambit.

The more I looked at the two men, the more I could see the physical resemblance. It's not obvious. They had narrow foreheads and stubby fingers. It was the gait, the upright fashion in which they carried themselves. Shoulders square, back straight, an animal-like edge to their stride.

Ravi was nothing like his grandfather, not even in manner. I sighed. I didn't want to, but I was arriving at a decision. We couldn't continue.

I could taste the tears.

I wish I had restricted our relationship to a friendship. That was how it began. It should've stayed that way. An easy alliance, a seamless coalition, neither making demands on the other. I should've paused, dwelt on the emotions and seen it for what it was instead of just coasting. It was my call to make.

Our first kiss should've alerted me. Vanilla had more to it.

Ravi had initiated it when he dropped me back from an evening out. We had gone out for drinks with a few of his friends, and I was a little high by the time we were done. Ravi had stopped at a Patiala peg, maybe because I was on a free run. He parked his car and followed me into my apartment complex. We were in the elevator, an old, rattling booth, when his lips met mine full. I leaned against the controls for support. My hand or back hit the pause button, suspending us somewhere between floors. I was so chuffed that it was me who had stalled this cubicle that I wanted to explain it to the man who was all over me. Whatever came out of my mouth sounded like moans and groans. Suitably encouraged, Ravi's hands were on my waist, stroking it. It was a long kiss. Too long.

So delighted was Ravi by my reaction that it became a reference point for him. To me, it was an invitation I hadn't expected or accepted. I may have been present, but I wasn't a participant.

All that I didn't verbalize. When you express it, you wrestle with the words, and in doing so, deal with it, even if only at a surface level.

It wasn't because I didn't want to be alone. I'm an only child. Alone is me.

Another first followed, not long after. This one was a gift.

He'd got me a pair of gold earrings for my birthday. To say I was stunned was putting it mildly.

What was this? Our 25th wedding anniversary?

I put away the gift somewhere safe, I presume, and forgot all about it. How else could I have lived with it? I have no recollection of what it looks like, except for thinking that it was too big and ornate for me. In subsequent years, I got more of the yellow metal. I accepted it, even if it annoyed me. I wasn't even wearing the stuff. Couldn't he tell? Unless he was asking his PA to buy me gifts.

I finally told him I'd prefer a book or a library or his Netflix password.

Last year, he gave me a watch, I only take it off when I shower or sleep. I love it, but I never told him that. I didn't need to. Which, in a way, was us: we never exchanged a rude word, we didn't try to control or attempt to change the other.

I could see Andrew move across the editorial floor from my perch. My chin was resting on my right hand, and my eyes were following him. Quick, light steps. He was carrying some pages; maybe he was checking the edition. Wasn't it too early for that?

When I spoke to Chhaya a couple of days ago about my feelings for Ravi, the lack of chemistry given that we were almost engaged, she asked, 'What if Andrew hadn't returned?'

The only reason Ravi was in my life was because Andrew had exited it. And it was because of him that I had refused to look at my relationship with Ravi. Andrew was always around – in a coffee cup, an inkless pen – even when we were living on different continents.

Chhaya and I had walked to our usual table at Perky Grace after picking up our steaming beverages when she posed the question. I almost poured the coffee on myself.

'Maybe I'd have made this relationship work, continued to live in this disconnected fashion.' I had practice.

Chhaya was quiet.

'That's not to say that I'm falling into Andrew's arms.'

'In a way you had stopped living because of Andrew, stopped feeling. You would've gone along with anything and everything.'

'Ravi is not anything and everything; it is a nice friendship.' That was not the point she was making, I knew that.

'Nice, yeah, like a scenery.'

My heart was thudding, sticks on drumheads.

'You were hiding behind Ravi.'

She was right. It was a safe place to hide, even if the space itself was a tad lonely.

'I always had this feeling that you guys were tiptoeing around each other.'

It was the truth. Walls, hedges and a little light. Eight years ago, it was what I needed.

'There were places in his life he didn't want you to go, and you didn't.'

And vice versa.

I walked over to Andrew's cabin, shutting the door behind me.

I inhaled his scent.

Andrew nodded; his eyes were on me.

I let the silence envelop us. I felt the activity around the room. We were approaching 9 p.m.; it was edition time. That's when the editorial floor came alive, like a Deepavali evening.

Andrew took a deep breath. 'I have a feeling it didn't end well between them. Hari Rao's reaction to me has something to do with that,' he said.

Had Noelene tried to blackmail Hari Rao, to maybe get him back in her life?

'It is what it is. I can't change what happened between the two of them. Two adults who brought a child into this world. One of them looked after that child, the other walked away. Still, both of them are to blame.'

I nodded. 'Acceptance is revenge,' Andrew said. He was smiling.

There was a new equilibrium to Andrew. His face wasn't blank, it was calm. *It must be liberating,* I thought as I rose from the spare chair.

I wanted to ask him about Bhumika Velu and Catherine Brown, but that carefully phrased question walked out with me like an invisible clock I had draped around my arm.

Chapter 21

I was anxious. I reached the coffee shop almost half an hour in advance. A first in our association.

I'm punctual, but you can't set the clock by me. If and when I'm late, it's by a few minutes. Ravi is always ahead of schedule. If he was picking me up at 11.15, he was there at 11. That showed me as slack perhaps, when in actuality, he was early. It was a little like our relationship.

I had decided to call it off with Ravi. I didn't want to break his heart... Not that I had the power to do that.

The orphan boy... Was he even that? I had always wanted to ask him that question. It had slipped out of my mouth once, but Ravi chose not to answer it. I hoped at least he knew whose son he was. Was he the godson who became the grandson?

This is hard to believe, I know, coming from one who has made a living from posing them, but I hate questions.

Like Andrew, Ravi was a loner of sorts, too. He had some friends, fitness freaks like him, who met for a drink from time to time, but while he was good with the group, he kept them at arm's length. It was his family ties, possibly, that made him wary, he had said.

That reserve didn't extend to me; still, there were invisible walls I couldn't scale, not for a lack of trying.

We were close and closed at the same time.

Ravi walked in some 10 minutes later, looking dapper in a khaki shirt. Our regular waiter was doing cartwheels around him.

'Ma'am is already here, sir. She came very early, sir.'

I wished he'd shut up and make himself scarce, I had a headache already. But he was so bent on impressing Ravi that he sent a dessert plate crashing to the floor, and with it, a slice of the chocolate ganache cake he was carrying. Ravi was his gentle self, telling him to be careful the next time.

I wondered if Ravi had trained himself to be this way, as a quasi-public figure. His actions a reaction to his status. Measured. Hari Rao wouldn't have entertained headlines like 'Grandson in a Tiff', 'Drunk Grandson in the Gutter', or like the tabloids might say, 'GrandDope'. He was so relaxed about most things, it was near impossible to get a reaction out of him. Maybe that's why I was on the edge. What I had to say could cause him to explode – that carefully cultivated image blowing up and falling around us.

'So, how did the campaign trail go? Your first one, right?'

I nodded. I didn't have an answer to the first part of the question. 'How come you weren't there?' I asked.

'Where?' he asked, sitting back in his chair.

In Malavalli. In Mandya. In Maddur. In Mysuru. My query had surprised him.

'Campaigning with your grandfather, rallying the troops,' I said, not sure why I had chosen this moment to take it to him. 'He's old; he could've done with some help maybe.' I couldn't stop myself.

Our coffees arrived without us having ordered. They came with a large serving of orange and dark chocolate cookies that looked like bird droppings. I reached for one. I was hungry; I hadn't eaten during whatever part of the day I had already seen.

'If he wanted me there, he'd have told me.'

'And you'd be there?'

'To support him? Yeah, sure.'

So the only reason he wasn't with his 70-something grandfather in the midst of an election campaign was because he hadn't asked him to be there. I chewed on the cookie; it tasted better than it looked.

It bothered me that Ravi wasn't with his grandfather in Mysuru. I tried to brush it aside, but it found a way to surface. Maybe it was because of what I shared with my parents, and now with my father. I know all relationships are not the same and not everybody is as fortunate as I am with the DNA lottery, but caring is a choice.

'How is he? All okay health-wise?'

'Yeah.' It was a dry response.

Andrew didn't like talking about his family, and neither did Ravi. If the men I mingled with were to be categorized, it was guys with ambiguous ancestry.

'Did you enjoy yourself?' Ravi asked. 'He drove? You went with him?'

That was a fair comeback. Caring or not, I had crossed lines.

But how did he know I had driven with Andrew? I had told him I was going with Andrew, but we may have taken an office car, more of our colleagues could've been around, even driven us.

'My grandfather told me.'

Ravi had told me that he had spoken to his grandfather about us. He had shown him pictures, too, obviously. How much of Andrew and me had Hari Rao noticed?

This was pointless. It was not why I had asked Ravi to meet me today. I was playing for time I didn't need.

'Ravi,' I said abruptly, 'we need to talk about us.' I was looking down at the tiles. I felt a chill in my bones.

'My favourite topic,' he said.

I took a sip from my cup. I held it for a bit. I was comforted by its warmth. 'I want out.' I heard my voice shake. My heart was hammering My pulse was exploding.

I could've said, 'I love you, but I am not sure if I'm in love with you.' Or, 'I feel for you as a friend and not a boyfriend.' Both of these were true, but I pulled out the scissor instead.

'Want out?' Ravi barked. His eyes were all over me, and his mouth was open.

'Yeah,' I said weakly.

'Why?' He exhaled.

I held his gaze.

'You have developed feelings for this Andrew?' His tone was stone cold.

'No!' I wasn't in love with Ravi. This wasn't about Andrew; I was clear about that.

He shrugged. 'The way he looked at you when we met. I am not sure if you noticed, but I did.'

'How did he look at me?' I heard myself exhale.

'He was surprised when I said you were my girlfriend.'

'He had no idea we were dating.'

Ravi shook his head. 'He didn't like that we were dating.'

I couldn't refute that.

'Sympathy, is it?' Ravi asked.

What was he talking about? If I was feeling bad for Ravi, which I was, it's not a crutch I would walk out on. Then I realized he was talking about Andrew and not himself.

'Why would I be sympathetic towards him?'

'My grandfather told me about Noelene. His grandmother and my grandfather had a relationship. There was a child from that, his mother.'

Oh my god! Oh my god! Oh my god! There was a head-on collision in my upper storey. I felt it just as I did the coffee that had spilled on my white denims. The cup was sitting on my lap.

When I returned some 5, 10 or 15 minutes later, there was a dark stain on my trousers, but I was smiling.

'That shocked you,' Ravi said. 'You're always so correct, so careful, Myra. Everything in its place. Just like me. I've never seen you like this. You're shocked.' He was laughing now.

I'm effortlessly clumsy.

'Sorry,' I said slowly, settling into a clean chair.

'I have to apologize. I shocked you.'

'How do you know?' I asked.

'My grandfather told me. I thought you knew. That Andrew might've told you.'

I ignored the second part of the sentence. 'Why did he tell you that?' What kind of a question was that? Hari Rao's reasons for telling Ravi about his biological grandson were obvious. I was blabbering even after I had the time to pull myself together.

Ravi smiled. 'I guess he wanted me to know. Didn't want me to be surprised by any revelations in case Andrew confronted me.'

I shrugged. Was Ravi testing waters with his *Andrew might've told you* line? How much of his family's history had Andrew trusted me with?

'We don't know. We have to be prepared for everything,' Ravi said.

However carefully the man may have worded his explanation, there was no escaping there was a child from that relationship. *A child*. Hari Rao had cheated on the grandmother Ravi worshipped, and he was powdering his nose.

When had Hari Rao dropped the bomb? I swallowed the question in the nick of time. My stomach felt bloated with all the questions I'd been swallowing.

'This has nothing to do with Andrew, Ravi. This is about you and me. And again, it's nothing to do with you; it's me.'

Ravi moved forward in his seat and took my hands in his. He told me I was going through a lot, most of it work-related. He said I looked troubled and moody lately. He told me to chill, think it through and then decide.

I shook my head. However much this was going to hurt him or me, I wasn't going back on it. I already felt lighter having told him about it.

We didn't say a word to each other for another five to ten minutes, both of us staring in different directions.

'Take your time,' he urged again.

I shook my head.

'So you want to end it right here? Just like that?'

'Ah, ah.' I nodded.

'What's the reason for this, Myra?'

'It's me, it's my fault, Ravi. I think of you as a friend. I can't think of you as more than a friend.' I had tried, god knows.

'So what? That's where the best of love stories begin.'

I shook my head.

He sat back in his chair and wrapped his hands across his chest; he did that when he needed a moment to think. 'You know, in your position, life is not easy. I can help you,' he said, pausing before adding, 'We're good together. Everything else we can work out later.'

So this was what it was all about? The great rescue act. Myra Rai needed help. My eyes burned. So, all the times he'd said I was beautiful and strong and that he loved me inside out…

'No,' I said. I was fighting back tears. 'It's not enough, Ravi. You deserve love, for the woman you marry to be in love with you.'

He was looking down, at his hands or feet probably, for a while, and then suddenly, without a word, he picked up his car key and exited the restaurant.

I sat there for a few seconds, immobilized. Then I followed him out a little after settling the bill. This was the only time he hadn't paid when we had gone out.

As I exited the coffee shop, I noticed a familiar frame. Her back was to me; she had just turned. Thank goodness. The last thing I needed at this moment was to run into Meena Iyer.

I walked back to office, a 10–12-minute trek, tears rolling down my cheeks. I was sad yet relieved.

This was a relationship that had steered me through my darkest days. Ravi had facilitated bringing my mother home on her last journey; he had made it as painless as possible. He was with me when I had no friends. He met me at short notice, filling in the blanks without realizing he was doing it. He was there when I missed Mummy, he was there when Andrew was out of my life, he was there when I was just starting out as a professional. Had he not thrown the power card at me today, it may have remained a cut that never healed.

Chapter 22

I was in a white salwar kurta. I don't know why I had chosen white for a jail visit. My rust-brown dupatta was lying on the desk like an exotic decoration. I was leaving for Parappana Agrahara (Bangalore Central Jail) in an hour. I had kicked off my slippers and drawn my left knee to my chest. I was feeling heavy. I exhaled.

You know, in your position, life is not easy. I can help you.

I don't know why I was allowing this remark or was it an offer – more like a confession actually – to colour what I had shared with Ravi. He's right. *We are good together. We* were *good together*. Even if it came as an afterthought that Saturday afternoon.

Ravi had called a couple of days later. He wanted to meet for coffee.

'I'd love that,' I said. 'I'd love for us to meet as friends.' As equals.

He was quiet for a while. I was tired. I rested my hand on my desk, holding the phone to my ear. The silence was increasingly uncomfortable.

'That's okay then,' he said and disconnected.

A week or so later, I called to check if he was okay. Not that I expected him to be drowning his sorrows in single malt, but I wanted to reach out. He didn't answer my call. He sent me a WhatsApp message the following morning. It was one of those send-this-to-10-people kind of thing. Ravi scarcely forwarded stuff to me, much less anything like this.

It bothered me that I hadn't salvaged anything from what I had shared with Ravi. As yet, I reminded myself. Maybe years on, we could meet and chat. Until then, he'd probably no more than acknowledge me in public. If that, even.

It was that loss of exchange with Ravi that made me more determined to re-establish my friendship with Andrew.

The foundation we laid a decade ago was solid. The monsoon evenings spent squatting on the footpath debating current affairs. We'd stay there until a bonda cart or two rolled out, devouring the first of the savoury delights that were also treated to the leaves and twigs that dropped on the kerosene stove.

Andrew understood the complex strain of my seemingly straightforward existence. The way I sometimes dragged my feet through it, in protest, preferring to laugh at myself instead of letting the confusion surface in a sob. Then, after having had no contact for eight years, he picked up my determination, my new-found zeal for life and living at our first meeting. We had the comfort of history.

I was going to Parappana Agrahara to interview a family of serial killers who had left a trail of 21 dead across the country. It was for 'Crime 3.0'.

The Sharmas – husband, wife and adult son – slit the throat of their landlord, an octogenarian, when he knocked on their door to collect rent. This happened 12 years ago. They had occupied the two-storey house in a pricey but relatively new layout in the city and hadn't cleared their dues for two years.

News reports of the time said the wife had attacked the old man with a kitchen knife when he refused to sign the house over to them. The father–son duo then smothered him with a pillow. They drove almost 100 kilometres to the Tamil Nadu border in the dead of night to dispose of the body.

I had a memory of this story. My mother and I had read the paper together. It was one of those crimes that had happened when Bengaluru was moving from sleepy bean town to IT Capital. It held the city captive.

It took me all my contacts in the police department to locate the fourth and youngest member of the Sharma family. He's 26 now and works as a food and beverage manager at a four-star hotel just off MG Road. He agreed to speak to me on condition of anonymity.

I met him at his workplace, in a room crowded by multiple shelves of crockery and cutlery. We sat in the centre; there was a table between us. He started on his story even before I turned on my recorder. It was like he was waiting for me.

He had woken up to his nightmare at 2 a.m. – sounds of pushing and shoving, doors opening and muffled voices. He reached for his older brother, but his side of the bed was empty. He called out to his mother, and she asked him to go back to bed. From the window in his room, he saw his family crowding around the boot of their car. He returned to bed.

A couple of days later, the crime branch of the city police connected the dots between a missing-person complaint and a body that was burnt in an open field in Tamil Nadu. The octogenarian's identity card was in his back pocket and was only partially burnt. Not everything dies.

The cops apprehended the Sharmas as they were preparing to flee the city. A constable let the 14-year-old escape. He made his way to the house of his domestic help at the crack of dawn, after spending the night in a bus shelter. The lightless morning was his invisibility cloak. He later burnt the blue denim and saffron-coloured tee he had worn that day, torching an identity.

He called her Mother, and she named him Pradeep. She was a spinster, living in a one-room lodging, and she ensured he completed his education.

This piece was going to be different from the others I had written for 'Crime 3.0'. I wanted to write two stories, the first a profile of the boy who was now a man and juxtapose it with a portrait of the family. The Sharmas' blood trail, spanning 11 years, saw them hoodwinking the police by changing identities and addresses.

I went alone for most of my 'Crime 3.0' pieces. On occasion, I had company, a junior in the team, tagging along for the thrill of coming face to face with a criminal. Only a couple of stories in the series were done by other reporters and that was in the early days. It was a monthly feature, and Mr Kumar was increasingly looking to me to carry it forward.

I hadn't informed my editor that I was going to Parappana Agrahara today. That was the one thing that was sure to annoy Mr Kumar. He liked to know where his team was during work hours. He took great pride in it even if it was borderline intrusive. I thought of messaging, then I looked at the intercom before walking over.

'Myra,' he said when I was about to knock.

I was telling Mr Kumar about my proposed Parappana Agrahara visit when the political editor joined us. I'm not sure if he was listening to me summarizing the story, but all eyes were definitely on me.

For some reason, I was reluctant to go to Parappana Agrahara on my own this time. It wasn't that I would have to speak to the three Sharmas at the same time. It would be on the same day, of course, but in different sittings. My palms were wet, and I could feel sweat beads on my upper lip. I didn't convey my nervousness to my editor, but as I prepared to exit his space, he enquired if I wanted company on the assignment.

I told him I was good.

Andrew followed me out of Mr Kumar's cabin. 'Rai,' he called. This second-name business was infuriating. I paused, but I didn't turn. 'I would ask for an army to go with me if I were you, or I would just ask Brown to drive over.'

I could feel myself tear up. *Get your act together, Myra.* I took my time turning around. 'Please be my driver today,' I said with a laugh that wasn't forced.

'At your service.'

Andrew had waited until we were out of earshot from Mr Kumar's cabin before he offered to go with me.

I had missed this friendship, and I was damned if I was letting it go again.

Andrew shadowed me as we walked past the iron gates and through the grim construction of Parappana Agrahara, spread across 40 acres with almost 5,000 inmates. The bare walls of the quadrangle echoed the stench of oppression. Or was it vomit? At a distance were the barracks. If you listened carefully, you could hear groans and shouts, the shuffle of chained feet.

Each time I walked through these spaces, I felt like I was in a movie set.

'Feels like a reality show,' Andrew said over me.

I giggled only because I needed to.

The meeting room, a separate one for media, far removed from where the undertrials met with family, had a distinctly corporate feel to it. A roll call of Inspectors-General of Police adorned the wall. An empty vase and two bottles of mineral water were on the table. There was an intangible coldness to the room. I felt a shiver go down my back.

I spoke to the mother first. She was a remorseless killer; her eyes blanketed her face. They remained unmoved even when she laughed, and she laughed a lot. A soft, hissing sound. Then they brought the son, a strapping man, now approaching middle age. The parents had got life imprisonment; the landlord's family had asked for the death penalty. The son had got 15 years. Unlike the parents, there was regret in every word he spoke.

None of them brought up the youngest member of their family.

'I think the older boy wanted to know about his sibling,' I told Andrew.

'I thought so, too, but why,' he said, steering his car through the traffic as we headed back to office.

'Maybe he genuinely cares, maybe he was not part of those previous murders. He was 23 when they struck in Bengaluru.'

'He may have known about a couple of them, advanced help to his parents... remotely, perhaps.'

'His affection could be sincere, or he may just want to piggyback on him when he's out of prison, which is in a maximum of three years. He could get out for good behaviour before that even.'

'Or both.'

Andrew had melted into the background, waiting patiently for me to complete my job. The chair next to me was empty, but he had positioned himself behind me, at a considerable distance.

'Were you comfortable speaking to the younger boy?'

I nodded. 'He's lucky in that he was allowed to grow into his own person,' I said. 'The lady he now calls his mother shifted from Koramangala to Kengeri less than a year after he went to live with her. That helped him establish a mental distance from that time in his life.'

She had gained employment as a housekeeper in a farmhouse, some 40 kilometres from where she first lived. It was a whole new environment for the boy.

'Is he aware that his brother could be released from prison soon?'

I nodded, making a mental note to task the graphic artist with an imaginative sketch of the boy. We had file pictures of the parents.

'Are you going to say he lives somewhere else in your story?'

'I'll make him a techie living in Kuala Lumpur maybe, out of the country for sure.'

'Crime fiction!'

I laughed. No, I had snorted.

Silent tears flowed from my eyes. I didn't want Andrew to know; I didn't want anyone to know.

I clenched my hands tight and shut my eyes, willing the tears to stop. I forced myself to breathe quietly. It was at that moment Andrew turned on the radio. I couldn't have been more grateful. I sank back in my seat, and this time, I closed my eyes and let the tears dry.

The volume of words coming at you for almost three hours, your mind taking in all that is being said and not being said, registering the reactions and deciphering content. It's intense and exhausting. This time, though, it was more than the experience of a couple of hours ago; it was the weight of the last couple of weeks. I felt Andrew's gaze on me. We had stopped at a signal maybe.

'That was some show, Myraah Rai. You were doing such an amazing job in there, I wished I were you.'

When I opened my eyes and turned to him, we had already parked. My face was still moist, but he didn't reach out to dry my tears.

I must've been bloody fucking good, I thought. Then I smiled a real smile.

It was Wednesday morning, five days after I had been to Parappana Agrahara.

I was missing my midweek coffee, where I'd have poured out the story to Ravi, repeating details, underlining them. Ravi let me run. He didn't interrupt or ask me questions, but more than once, he had tried to talk me out of writing this series.

These meetings, listening to the recordings, the emotions that were stirred by recreating the crime, typing out nuances that weren't in the recorder, were getting me into a state from which I took a while getting out of. I had nightmares after some of these encounters, and in the less gruesome cases, a gloom settled on me in the days that followed. I swung between talking non-stop and going into reclusive mode. It took me a few days, a week even, to shake off the experience.

This time, I didn't have an outlet. I spoke to my dad and Chhaya, but I wasn't able to spill out as much as I would've with Ravi. Chhaya attempted to steer the conversation to sunnier shores, trying to help me escape the despair. My father was constantly interrupting, getting up to get something or the other. Still, despite not having a significant conduit, I was more in control of the situation.

Maybe because Andrew had accompanied me for the assignment and I had unconsciously drawn comfort from the company.

Though my spirit was still sore and the air around me was heavy, I was able to get on with my day, live my life without constantly going back to that beastly greed that cost an innocent man his life, leaving his visually impaired wife to grieve.

I had finished writing the two stories, 5,000-odd words, including additional intel that could be used for graphics. I forwarded it to my editor, who decided we should jump the queue and carry the piece this week, ahead of some of the other pieces I had banked.

I needed an out. I would've loved to go for a run at that very moment. This office needed to invest in a gym. I considered telling Mr Kumar that but thought my time would be better served in getting a coffee.

I was headed in the direction of Perky Grace and was walking past another of the coffee chains when polka dots, black on mustard, caught my eye. It was her I saw before I spotted Andrew, and I wanted to giggle.

Andrew was on the edge of his seat, elbows resting on his knees, desperately trying to make a point.

She was wearing a dress only a little longer than a top. One of her hands was trying to hold the skirt down and the other was disciplining the hair. The wind was harsh, and they were a spectacle. An aesthetically enchanting one.

I had stopped walking and was openly gaping when Pooja let go of the skirt of her dress and reached for her coffee. The dress ballooned in the wind, and Andrew was all over himself trying to keep it down. If that wasn't enough, Pooja turned the mug on herself.

Start walking, I told myself.

I had barely finished ordering my coffee when Andrew messaged. *Make that two, Rai.*

I considered spitting into the second one. That whole production to protect her modesty.

I watched Andrew saunter up Church Street. I love his walk; Beethoven was playing.

I wasn't going to bring up the chaotic scenes I had just witnessed; it had been entertainment. Even though I felt a twinge when he lurched forward for her skirt.

Andrew settled into the opposite seat. Were his eyes on my lips? Honey drizzle on warm bread. I smiled.

'I saw you,' he said.

'I know. I saw your message and ordered for you, too! Duh! You have a phone, check it!'

'When I was with Pooja just now.' Was that a blush?

The takeaway coffees arrived and so did my laughter. I just couldn't stop. I wasn't being mean; I was feeling bad for the kid. I promise.

Andrew picked up his coffee and leaned against the seat. He was waiting for me to finish.

When the hysteria finally subsided, I asked Andrew what that was all about.

'She's going through a difficult break-up, Myraah, and I'm just trying to help her.'

I stuck the steaming coffee to my lips. I could not laugh again, hysteria or not. I was on my feet.

I took a second sip of my coffee.

'I was telling her I couldn't see her much more because of the elections.'

'Was that when she poured the coffee on herself?' Because she couldn't see more of you.

'It was the wind!' He looked away; his eyes were on the cashier.

'Of course!'

'How are you feeling?' he asked as we headed back to office.

'Better now,' I said with a smile. I was able to establish some kind of a distance between the jail visit and my emotions.

We were out on MG Road, and the sun was shining. Just like an old acquaintance.

Andrew wondered if the younger son knew more about his family's misdeeds than he was letting on.

We conjectured if he would leave Bengaluru, whether it was actually safe for us to run the piece on Pradeep. What if his older sibling came after him?

Pradeep wanted his story out. It was his call. I had asked him why, and he said it was important to his mother. I didn't need to ask which one.

'Happy to chauffeur you every time, Rai,' Andrew said. We had paused and were looking at each other.

My neck felt warm.

'I don't think I'm going to do the next one in a hurry. We have three or four pieces in the bank.'

'Whenever you plan to do it.'

'Why?'

We had stopped walking; we were in front of Chhaya's office building, facing each other. Andrew was smiling.

'It's not because you're a woman and you need protection in an environment like what we were in the other day. No one, man or woman, should do this alone.'

My mouth was salty again. I bit my teeth and stopped the tears.

'Unless the adopted grandson has already offered?'

I smiled. I hadn't told Andrew about Ravi yet. 'You are better than that,' I said.

He nodded. His gaze dropped to my lips before turning away hastily.

'This is too dark a line for a reporter to pursue on their own in the regularity with which you do it. It's literally your column now. Editor Uncle doesn't want anyone else to contribute, which is fair. You own it. But don't go on these assignments alone. I'll go with you every time I can. Let's try and work the meetings at a time when it is convenient for me, too, to accompany you. Let me know what you're pursuing, how and when, and I'll try and keep myself free around that time.'

This was the Andrew I knew. Once my pillar.

'And nobody needs to know about this arrangement, Myraah. It's just between you and me.'

I shut my eyes, and for the first time that evening, I felt calm.

'I'm sorry to interrupt this.'

I heard Chhaya's voice from behind me; she was laughing. Andrew, who was generally alert in public spaces, had completely missed my friend, whom he was facing.

I hugged Chhaya and told her we had just picked up coffee.

'Buy me tea,' she asked Andrew.

Chhaya motioned to the security officer of her building and told him she'd be back for her car in 10 minutes. I corrected her and told him it would be an hour at least. She laughed and fell in step with us. This was the first time Chhaya was seeing Andrew since after school.

'You're looking wonderful,' she said.

Andrew smiled. 'You, too,' he replied.

'I don't know how you guys haven't run into each other all these months, given that our offices are so close.'

'I think I saw you at a distance once. It was a little after I returned to Bengaluru,' Andrew said. 'You both were having coffee.'

His eyes shifted from Chhaya to me.

Like old friends, which they were not, Chhaya and Andrew quickly lost me, updating each other on their lives. I interrupted only because they were dismissive of their respective successes. I spelt them out. They returned to schooldays every now and then, recalling an incident or a teacher, but steered clear of Meena Iyer.

They were enjoying each other's company so much that I asked them to sit down and went to collect Chhaya's drink.

'You, too?' Andrew asked as I sat down.

I had no idea what they were talking about. 'I'm sorry,' I said, looking at Chhaya and then at Andrew.

'Apparently, everyone in school thought I was a snob.'

'Ah, ah…' I didn't know; I couldn't be sure. Did I think he was a snob? I had the hots for him.

I don't remember much of Andrew in school, outside of the poster pinned in my head. Maybe it was a time I had unconsciously blocked out after we started seeing each other in college. I wanted to remember only our time together. It might have something to do with Meena and his affection for her or the fact that I didn't really know him back then. It was more an image I had of him.

'Snob?' I asked. The moment the question was out of my mouth, I realized that I wasn't in with the talk in Bangalore Scottish. I wasn't one of the StyleStahs. Maybe they had thought of Andrew that way.

'Yeah, yeah, that was the general opinion,' Chhaya said, filling me in on what I didn't know.

He referred to me as 'she' and 'her', not by my name, like an old couple who didn't need an address.

Was it that easy for him to give me up? I wondered even as I returned the sunny disposition to both of them.

What we shared was tossed aside for what? Hot sex and an iPhone. I didn't realize – but I don't think anyone else at the table had either – I was shaking my head. Maybe they hadn't discussed me, Meena and Andrew. She wouldn't have wanted to bring me up for whatever reason, and Andrew was adroit at controlling his emotions.

'Finished writing?' Chhaya turned to me and asked about my 'Crime 3.0' piece.

I nodded.

'And she's done a darn good job of it,' Andrew said.

Our eyes met, and I nodded before a smile took over my countenance.

Andrew and I walked back to drop Chhaya, and just before we entered *Morning Herald*'s premises, I patted Andrew's arm. He was walking ahead of me.

'Meena and you were a thing, I know.'

'Myraahh!'

I turned on my heel and waded into MG Road, but before I walked away, I asked Andrew not to follow. The air was heavy, and the footpath was busy. The peanut vendor was working up an aroma. My tears were salty.

Chapter 23

I had spent most of the first half of Monday running around bookshops in the CBD.

I don't know if any city in the world (not that I had the stamps on my passport that would qualify me to make that comment) had a collection of bookstores like two parallel streets in the heart of Bengaluru did. The city's intellectual compass.

There were the old names – Premier (Mummy's favourite; she loved it so much, she took it with her perhaps. It shut shop the year she passed away.), Gangarams, Sapna, Higginbothams. And then there were those that sprouted at the turn of the millennium – Blossom, Bookworm, and more recently, Bookhive. Therapy on rickety shelves.

I was looking for a rom-com to lift my mood, and I was at Blossom, not for the first time in the morning. I had settled on the floor and had a pile of pre-owned books on my lap when I knew Andrew was in the room. I felt him in the air.

I was between two racks of books that touched the ceiling; if the timber trembled, I'd be buried in this pile of romantic dialogue. The lighting was dull, and when I looked up, I was looking at the CCTV camera beside which Andrew was standing. He was wearing an uncertain smile, jeans that looked like they needed a washing machine cycle and an olive-green tee that had been perfectly ironed. I always envied the way he ironed his tees… when he ironed them.

Andrew got down on his haunches. His back was slightly bent, and his shoulders had collapsed around him.

I inhaled his scent. His eyes were a storm. Had he followed me?

'Hi,' I said, with a dull wave that was an ache.

I'm not sure if he mentioned her name first or if he just started talking. '...was working in an art gallery in Boston; that's where she went to college,' Andrew said.

He was talking to my head now; I was looking at a book.

'I went to the gallery a couple of times. I sought her out but as a friend.'

I felt a weight fall on my shoulders. Was it a book? Were the shelves collapsing?

The gallery was a 15-minute drive from Cambridge, Massachusetts, where Andrew was stationed.

'That's why I went to see her,' he said as my eyes met his. 'All I wanted at the time was friendship.' His eyes pleaded.

I understood. Even if I struggled to swallow it. 'I want to talk to you; I've been trying to talk to you, Myraah.'

'How did you know I was here?'

He shrugged. 'I was looking through the old books, and then I strolled up here. I wanted to go to the children's section.'

'Why?' I meant why children's books.

He exhaled, rattled rhonchi. 'Maybe I was looking for you.'

He turned his head, to fix his thoughts, perhaps.

'Like you, she had it all – the comfort of home and family. I just wanted something, anyone. I was searching for the familiar.'

He was shaking his head.

'You didn't want anything to do with me... I called, I messaged.' Andrew raised his hand, perhaps to stroke my cheek, but quickly pulled back.

I held his gaze.

'Why didn't you reply to my messages?' he asked.

What was left to say?

Andrew's eyes were moist. 'Meena and I were friends. It was she who wanted more than friendship. Yes, I finally gave in, but that's not why I had reached out to her.'

I laughed. The sound never left my mouth.

'I had the hots for her in school.'

I was without air, I was suffocating.

After what seemed like an eternity, Andrew said, 'Then I met you, and you were it.'

That's where a good story ends, I thought.

'I didn't hear from you, but you were chatting with Meena.'

It was one, two or three, maybe four conversations at the most.

'Why didn't you respond to my messages or calls?' Andrew asked again. He was looking down, his fingers locked in a tight clasp.

I did, eventually, I thought.

I heard whispers of conversations around us – people discussing books, what to take home.

'No, wait, I know I was wrong to leave; I should've stayed.' He was looking at me now.

Those were my words. I recognized them, but I had also admitted to being unreasonable. I'd told him to go, but I'd wanted him to stay. Just a tiny bit longer. Meena had obviously done some convenient editing before delivering my words to Andrew.

'I was happy to have met her at first. I thought I had someone in my corner,' Andrew said.

There were questions burning inside me, reducing my vocal cords to a cinder. I just couldn't speak.

'It was a physical thing.'

'How long were you together?' My tone was gruff.

He shrugged. 'Not long.'

'You didn't want to call, get in touch? Afterwards.'

'There were others.'

This was unravelling expressly, like substandard timber.

'Nothing serious, nothing that meant anything.'

'I wouldn't have understood it even if it was love.'

'It was just physical,' he said.

There was a question in his eyes; I could read it.

'I'm sorry.'

I stared at him; my face was a blank canvas.

Then he shrugged, an involuntary reaction, before getting back on his feet. He stood there for a moment longer, perhaps to get his balance back before walking away.

My head was spinning, and I desperately needed to focus on something or I would kill this man. I wanted to throw up on the pile of rom-coms sitting on my lap. The bitter aftertaste of a cancelled love story.

Our paths didn't cross for most of the week following our bookshop meeting.

We were both in office. I knew he was around, and I'm sure he caught glimpses of me, too, but we hadn't sought each other out.

I was stinging from the *It was just physical*, and I'm sure he was wondering when and how I had found out about Meena and him. He hadn't run into Meena in Bengaluru.

It was Friday afternoon when he knocked on my cabin door.

'May I?' Andrew asked. His digits were hard on the doorknob.

I nodded. What now? Did he want to discuss rom-coms?

'A couple of my National Law School mates are in town from London,' Andrew said. 'I'm having a get-together at my place tomorrow evening.'

'Tomorrow?'

'It's short notice, I know, but I just found out today.'

I nodded before running through my socially robust Saturday mentally. It was a blank page.

'I would like you guys to finally meet.'

I laughed because I may have caught Chhaya's laughing bug, but he read too much into it.

'I would've extended the invite to Ravi Rao, too,' he said, 'but this is a really small crowd.'

Then I laughed because this was funny.

Andrew had caught on to the difference in the cadence, and he wasn't smiling.

'I'm getting a plus one.'

Andrew was on his feet and at the door.

'Andrew,' I said just as he was about to yank the door out of its hinges, 'you haven't met my father.'

He spun right around, and he was smiling that smile that he saves for Thanksgiving each year. 'I haven't,' he said, knowing exactly what I meant by plus one.

Saturday was a particularly severe monsoon evening. Dad and I were the last to arrive. I was delayed by work first and then the Bengaluru traffic, which is difficult anyway but unravels into a cheerless safari when it rains.

As soon as we entered, I heard a voice in the mix say that the space sorely needed a woman's touch. My dad's face lit up while my step slackened, and my eyes met Andrew's. It was all a little too much for me. It was not just my first time in Andrew's apartment, but I hadn't met his friends before, save for random introductions.

You're Andrew's friend now, Myra, I reminded myself. *It's okay to be walking into your friend's apartment for the first time. There's always a first.*

Andrew had told me it was a four-bedroom unit, which he secured as part of a sizeable monetary deal when he signed off the property. This was seriously big, though; it had acres of space, twice the size of my place. Maybe it looked bigger than it was because of the walls; they were bare.

I thought of Meena. That was a girl who'd have made her mark on the decor, brought in shades of blues and browns, matching dainty lines with robust, earthy hues. She'd have turned it into a multi-star retreat in the middle of town. A perfect picture you might or might not want to own, depending on who you are.

I was not sure, though, if the place needed a woman at all. The walls may have been plain, but there was something intrinsically Andrew about it.

Andrew is essentially a social soul. He doesn't gravitate towards any one person in his rather wide circle of friends but is there for everyone. In school, he shared strong bonds with a lot of boys, different groups of people – the hockey players, student union mates, the science group and the debate and drama club. It was the same in college; his social calendar was always full.

Ashish, Neha and Andrew were a trio in law school. Ashish was a barrister now, and Neha had done corporate law; she was working with a pharma company.

While Ashish's folks lived in Bengaluru, Neha was back in the city for the first time since she graduated. Andrew had been in touch with her off and on over the years. A year ago, she had married a UK-based doctor.

I experienced a side of Andrew that I may have suspected but hadn't seen. That of the charming host.

Andrew had apparently done a lot of entertaining in the United States. Neha would vouch for it, he said. She had stayed with him a few times when she was in New York, and he would have people over on the weekends for what he called 'cocktails and crumbs'.

As I worked my way around, taking my father along with me, I saw that the interiors weren't yet completed. In two bedrooms, the wardrobes had been half-done – in one the polishing was yet to be completed, while in the other, the sliding doors had been lined up against the wall, waiting to be assembled. The carpenter, an alcoholic pal of Andrew's from school, had taken ill. He was waiting for his friend to recover and complete the job.

That was Andrew. He could wait forever.

The furniture was teakwood, chunky in design, no-fuss pieces, no carvings, few intricacies, perfectly functional. The bar counter was massive, with no particular design element to it save for the space it stood on.

He'd have needed a crane to shift this stuff.

In his bedroom, I noticed the original movie poster of *Invictus*; it had been framed but not mounted. Beside it was a blown-up autographed photograph of Lionel Messi on the move.

'I had gone to Camp Nou with a friend, and I got it autographed,' Andrew, who was standing a little behind me, said. 'He looks much bigger on television. It's the way he plays maybe. You tend to look up at the skill rather than the physical specimen, but it's different when you are face to face.'

I nodded.

It was possible that Andrew would decorate the walls in time with a piece or two he had picked up during his travels. I was sure he would put up some pictures of his family, maybe arrange them on a table in an intimate nook of the house. In his bedroom, perhaps, away from the prying eyes of every guest who walked through the door. Not to shroud but to save in memory.

Slowly, he would turn the place around from house to home, not just for him, but for all the Browns before him. A place where love lived. And died.

Bhumika Velu. Catherine Brown. Those names crossed my mind for the first time in a few days. Their stories. An analogy.

There was an antique showcase in a corner of the sitting area. I wasn't 100 per cent sure, but this piece may have been there in the old bungalow. Refurbished and brought up to date perhaps. Its four shelves now had little knick-knacks arranged on them – spoons, snow globes, plates, stuff he had collected from different parts of the world, besides certificates and awards. There was a hardbound copy of his first book, which he had co-authored – *India*: *She'll Unmask You* – on the bottom shelf.

I was standing beside my father, scanning the stuff, when my eyes touched on a spoon that I had seen in a sugar pot not far from where I was standing. There was a ruby-coloured stone attached to the thread. I turned to my father, meeting his moist eyes.

My mother had given Andrew the spoon; it was a silver spoon used in the sugar pot. Every time Andrew was home, he'd insist on using it to stir the sugar in his coffee. If Mummy changed the spoon for whatever reason, he'd go looking for it. So much so that she stopped keeping a spoon on the saucer for him; he'd take the one from the pot anyway. No one knew why he was so attached to the spoon. It was beautiful, but so were a few others that Mummy had. We joked at his obsession, which he shrugged off with, 'It's sweet.' Finally, my mother gifted him the spoon.

My father walked away, joining a couple of older men who were talking cricket. I watched him nod and laugh even though he had little interest in cricket. I turned to join him when I felt

Andrew's arm on my shoulder. I hadn't noticed that Ashish was also standing by the showcase.

'My oldest and dearest friend,' Andrew said.

'We were in school together,' I said.

'I know of you, Myra Rai,' Ashish said, his smile exploding at his dimples. 'My brother here used to empty bottles of Davidoff on himself when he'd leave the campus to meet you. My mother wondered if I was drinking perfume.'

Andrew laughed.

'Andrew was telling us about your crime column. Bloody is how I like my steak, eh?'

I smiled. What else had he told them about me?

'Did you live in the US, too?' Ashish asked.

Was he confusing me with Meena?

Just then, the doorbell went off. I turned to look at Andrew, who was excusing himself again. Our eyes met and we held the gaze for a few seconds before he signalled to me that the food had arrived.

He collected a gigantic hot box of mutton biryani and another modest-sized container of capsicum rice and headed to the kitchen, where Ashish and I joined him.

'You don't cook these days, bro?' Ashish asked, telling me that Andrew made the best vindaloo he had ever eaten. He was a regular in the kitchen in college apparently.

'Only occasionally. I have a lady coming in most evenings for the daily stuff,' he said. 'The hours in journalism are not very different from law, but they are more definite in the second half of the day, so I'd rather she's here when I'm not.'

'No one to cook for?' Ashish asked, winking at me.

'He's really good,' Neha said, joining us. 'I've eaten plenty of his cooking,' she continued, pointing at her generous frame.

Neha had settled herself on the counter and was filling her plate with the biryani. 'Just checking to see if everything is pukka,' she said, winking at her friend.

I headed to the dining room with table mats, leaving the friends to their banter.

My father was on the balcony with one of the older men. It was 11.30 p.m., well past his bedtime, and though he may not have been particularly hungry, it was better he ate something sooner than later.

The view from the seventh floor was exhilarating, the better part of Bengaluru at a time when she flowed easily. The skies, like the roads, had cleared. I could see my office even.

I stayed there for a few minutes after my father walked back to the party, promising to eat. When I turned to check if he had helped himself, I saw him on the sofa with a sparsely filled plate. Neha had joined him.

Andrew walked across the long, rectangular room to me. 'Do you like it?' he asked. His eyes were bright with hope.

'Like home,' I said.

The old place, even in that shabby state, had possessed a living, breathing quality. A sagacity that comes with having seen life. It was dented, not bowed. Maybe it was the showcase or the bare walls or the trees on the grounds that hadn't been uprooted. Andrew had managed to dispel the darkness but retain the essential character of the house he was born in.

'I love it, too,' he said.

We were both looking out, watching the gentle ebb and flow of a rain-soaked Bengaluru.

'I had asked for the gulmohars to be retained,' he said. We had spent many a Saturday afternoon on its fiery orange carpet. Not playing chess.

I nodded.

My father was walking towards us; we spotted him together.

'It was a mistake,' Andrew said. 'My life's biggest regret.' Even in the dullness of the lighting, I could read the regret on that beautiful face. It was etched on the just-forming lines.

'Andrew,' my father said, patting him on his back. Andrew's arms went around my father's shoulders, it was halfway to a hug.

It was then that the question popped into my head. *What exactly did Andrew Brown regret? His affair with Meena for what it had done to him or what it had cost us?*

Chapter 21

I was marching, shoulders square, arms swinging, across the CBD, unconscious of its sweep and fall, high streets and winding alleys. I had been at it for over an hour. The sun was beating down, but I was in no mood to let the road outlast me. I was stampeding it, on my way to an Olympic record on block heels.

I was cogitating Andrew's *regret*, the why of it.

It was I who had brought up Meena, not Andrew. Would he have told me about their relationship had I not found out?

Was the contrition courtesy the affair gone wrong, or was it because of what it cost us?

I had asked myself, *Why should it matter?*

It was the way we were, putting the other above ourselves. It is the only way I knew us.

I was walking fast, and I swallowed something; it wasn't spit.

The pace had dropped as I wandered in the direction of the five-star coffee shop that I had frequented with Ravi. The tabebuias were in bloom, pink and yellow. It was three months since I had last been to this end of the city centre. I didn't miss the coffee, but I was longing for the privacy a monstrous place like this offers. The coffee shop was spread over 1,200 square feet, only marginally smaller than my house.

Xavier, the waiter who sang and danced to Ravi's every look and nod, was at the door. His white shirt sparkled. It was either freshly laundered or I had been in the sun for too long. He was in conversation with two tall, heavily built men, dressed in black, shirt to shoe. Heavy boots, big belts.

I waved at Xavier, who lifted his hand in response. His expression was strained. I had caught him at a busy time perhaps. He disengaged himself from the boys in black and was standing a foot or two away from me now. Was it shock I saw in his eyes? Or was it confusion? I couldn't tell.

It must've been me; I was sweating profusely. Xavier had never seen me in this state.

'Ma'am,' he said, straightening his back. 'Sir?' he asked panic-stricken, his gaze shifting to the coffee shop.

I hadn't factored in the curiosity Ravi's absence would create when I decided to get myself tepid five-star coffee. There was a fair chance I would run into Xavier if it wasn't his day off, and he was likely to bring up Ravi.

I missed Ravi, in an organic fashion. Like a scenic sponge painting I may have replaced with a portrait. It was a seamless affiliation. I don't remember second-guessing Ravi. What would he say? How would he react? I thought there was mutual respect; maybe there was, but it was also about how Ravi saw things – my life and where he fitted in it.

My knight in shining armour. No one had asked me if I needed one of those.

'I want a coffee; usual, please, Xavier.' I placed my order and walked towards an empty table.

I should've asked Xavier how he was doing; it had been a while since I had seen him. Ravi had never gone beyond the customary, 'How is your family?', which, of course, he knew nothing about. Xavier was a middle-aged man, so I assumed with wife and child. I was wary, though, of starting a conversation I would have no control over. I didn't know what I wanted to say to a virtual stranger like this waiter, who, funnily enough, was one of the few people who knew about us.

I fixed myself on the first available piece of furniture. It was behind a pillar and a fair distance from the spot Ravi and I preferred. I chose not to occupy that table because it was symbolic of a time when I was in a relationship. Sweaty and torn apart but definitely single.

Xavier had my coffee ready in record time, denting the character of a production that functioned in slow motion.

It's like they pick the Robusta cherries after you call for a cuppa. Xavier had even got my order right. He had brought the brew along with the hot water and milk on the side without prompting. For some reason, the Long Black, as they call it in this hotel – Americano to the world – was much stronger here than in any other place I have it. The pot of hot water was to save my innards.

I sipped my Long Black, which was more long brown now, slowly, allowing the blast from the air conditioning to dry my skin before opening my phone and tapping the Kindle app. I had stalled at 80 per cent of a book on how India had won her freedom. It was a bruising read. I'm not sure if this is what I should've been reading now, but there's no good time for literature of this nature.

I had gone through a couple of pages, sipping my coffee, munching on the complimentary cookie, when I thought I heard Meena's voice. Was that her? It was a shrill laugh. My head snapped back in recognition; my gaze shifted from the phone. I looked around me. It was all quiet save for a hollow echo. It was her voice unless I was imagining it. Then I heard a murmur; it came from across the room. What if it was her over here? I looked down at my lap. She was the last person in the world I wanted to meet. I contemplated calling Xavier, paying the bill and running out before I ran into her. But was that really her? Was I conjuring it, or did I really hear her?

I hadn't sighted any other guests on my way in, but I could tell from the rumpus that I wasn't the only person in the restaurant. There were more people around. I forced myself to read. My eyes went over the lines on my phone, but my mind wasn't registering what I was reading. I swiped quickly, backwards and forwards, trying to look busy. Salt Satyagraha. I wondered what that was. Who did that? Why? When? I love salt. I feast on savouries. I was eating a cookie. I was panicking. I put the phone down and closed my eyes.

That's when I caught the strain again, a low, hissing sound this time. It was coming from somewhere behind me. The laugh followed the click of stilettos. I clenched my hands to stop myself from shaking. Then, slowly, the sharp sound of heels on granite faded, as did the scent, which was familiar yet not quite. I inhaled and exhaled quickly.

It was Meena. I could tell even though I hadn't seen her, and she wasn't alone. She was with a man. I couldn't be sure, but the whiff I had caught wasn't her perfume. It was *pour homme* as the French might say. Was she with Andrew? Before I knew it, I had unseated myself and walked out of the restaurant and into the lobby, from where I spotted her and the man she was with. I caught their rears; they were the same height. She with the advantage of her footwear, and he with his slick formal shoes. He was Ravi Rao.

I took a couple of steps back into the restaurant. That's when I noticed that the two men dressed in black, who were positioned at the entrance when I had walked in, weren't there either. I turned and walked back into the lobby. My eyes scouted the place; they were behind Ravi.

I checked to see if I had my phone. I briefly debated if I should go back to the restaurant or simply exit the place. I wasn't sure I wanted to see Xavier.

That I wasn't aware of whatever this was that was playing out before me made me anxious. Maybe it's the reporter in me. I didn't know that my ex (of a few months) was meeting my one-time friend, dating her even, maybe.

My phone buzzed. Andrew was calling.

'Hello,' I said. I had decided I was not returning to the restaurant. I would go back at some point and pay for the coffee.

'All okay?'

'I was meeting a source for a story.'

Why did I lie? Why didn't I want Andrew to know what I had just seen? Who I had seen?

'Oh, sorry. Do you want me to call you back later?'

'No, no, that's fine. What's up?'

'I have some news, Myraah.'

As if on cue, my head stopped turning and focused on what Andrew was saying. 'Ravi Rao might contest these elections.' There was a pause, and then he continued. 'I'm not calling to confirm the news. I just wanted to tell you what I had heard.'

I managed a laugh. A weak one.

I hung up and dialled Chhaya. I wanted to vomit it out. All that I had seen and heard. I wanted someone to take it in and call it for me. Meena was with Ravi. They were together, but there was no physical contact. I repeated it in my head as I waited for my friend to pick up her phone.

'Babe.' That was Chhaya. The equanimity of her character resonated in her voice. It calmed me instantly. What could be so wrong?

I took a deep breath and spoke slowly. Told her everything I had seen and heard, every little sound and note, the size of her heels and the starch of his shirt. I also told her about Andrew's call and my little lie about where I was and what I was doing. I spoke quickly, whispering, throwing a glance around me every now and then, like I was giving her details of a heist I had just fumbled through.

I heard my friend's smile.

Seeing Meena and Ravi together was a kick in the gut. I didn't tell Chhaya that. He had not only dismissed my offer of friendship, but had also moved on. And with a woman who had played hide-and-seek with my emotions.

'So she's been stalking him.'

'Who?'

'She.'

'Who she? What are you talking about?'

'What do you think Meena was doing at the café the last time you met Ravi?'

Chhaya spoke slowly, slower than usual. I checked my watch; it was about midday. Had she started drinking early?

'You spotted Meena at the same café when you broke up with him. Remember?'

'Oh, come on! She hardly knew I was breaking up with the man!'

'Of course, she didn't, but when has that stopped her?'

I despised the way this woman saw things so clearly; it was almost plain.

'I can't remember who said this; maybe I read it somewhere, "When someone shows you who they are, believe them the first time."'

If I was in any other place, other than this city I call home, I'd have squatted on the footpath and shut my eyes so tight they would've hit the back of my skull. My head was turning, my shoulders weighed a ton and my legs felt heavy. I knew far too many people here. I'm not 18 any more, and while I'm not famous, this is home. At home, everyone knows everyone. Even if not by name. I turned to my right, and I saw a phone cover vendor, who had spread his wares on the ground. 'Salaam,' he said. I nodded. I see him every other day. He didn't know me, but he recognized me.

'What are you scared of?' Chhaya asked.

'I don't care if they are seeing each other. I don't care if they are already sleeping together. I don't give a fuck.'

'You are bummed. You should be, even though your heart is with another man. They're two different things.'

My breathing was heavy. I could hear it.

'If you weren't, I would've had to rush over and check your pulse.'

I was almost running, and the rumble in my heart was finding expression in my respiratory tract.

'That relationship meant a lot to you. It didn't go where you thought it might. Maybe it had run its course, maybe Andrew returned, and you realized the depth of your feelings for him. But this is not either/or; it never is in matters such as this, darling.'

I felt tears running down my cheeks. 'This is ridiculous.'

'These are feelings.'

Even if it felt like a storm.

Seeing Ravi and Meena together was bothering me; it roughed up my spirit. Meena was on cue, Ravi had moved on, and my own life was unravelling like a badly bound book, pages fluttering in the wind before finding the floor.

I wiped my tears and took a deep breath.

I moved the phone away from my ear and felt a breeze fan my face, whistle past my ears.

'The reason why seeing them together has distressed you so is because of where your own life is. Your refusal to take things forward with Andrew. That's not to say you're not feeling bad about Ravi and Meena, an ex-boyfriend and a friend, but...' Chhaya paused for breath, 'you shouldn't want to engage with Andrew because these two have maybe found each other. Andrew and you, Myra, have what everybody wants.'

We knew everything about each other, Andrew and I. From how we mixed our drinks to when he smoked his cigarettes and how much water I drank every morning. When I dialled his number and he didn't pick up, I knew where he was and vice versa.

'Are you scared to commit, Myra?'

'To whom?'

'Brad Pitt.'

I laughed at myself, at my state of disarray.

'Do you love him?'

'Yes.'

'Then?'

'I brought up Meena with Andrew.'

I felt Chhaya nod.

'Would he have even told me had I not found out?'

'Maybe not.'

'Something is broken, but I can't fix it. I can't make it whole again, and god knows I want to.'

What was Andrew regretting – the affair itself or what it had done to us?

Only at home can you drop your guard. So what if cart pushers and hawkers, stray dogs and pedestrians, recognized you? I sank down on the dirty footpath where men had peed and women had spat. The ground beneath was solid and strong.

I managed to pick myself up and drag myself back to my cabin. I had seen enough for the day.

Just before I rested my forehead on my forearms, I exchanged smiles with my mother. That picture was from that day.

Despite having denoted a boundary in the life of her only offspring a moment ago, 'Limit the physical to touching. Nothing more,' she had said, interrupting me as I sequenced Andrew's loveliness. That was the only tenet I had to play by.

Andrew of the dysfunctional lineage, however, had no idea about the limits cautioned to me.

Venturing into forbidden territory was the trigger for my collapsing into Andrew's arms one November afternoon, less than two months into our relationship.

If ever a line was meant to be crossed, this was it. We were the perfect fit, a seamless sentence. As if our 20 and 20-something years were lived to eventuate in this – exquisite bliss. Whole and full.

Later, seated before a television set, I knotted my hands. His hair was a mess, and his tee was askew. He looked so vulnerable. I wanted to reach out, but I didn't. I didn't want the dream to end.

I didn't call him after I got home that evening. He called some 24 hours later.

'Home?'

A tear had rolled down my cheek a decade ago.

Today, I was clearing a deluge with the back of my hand. The sights of a day. I let it flow, then it stopped and dried, and somewhere during that process, I must've drifted off to sleep.

There was a knock. I think I heard a knock. The door opened just as I raised my head.

'I knocked,' Andrew said.

My face was a mess. It had to be.

'Was that a good rest?' Andrew asked, picking up a pen that had dried.

I nodded, smiling. Everything was in place mercifully. Kajal, mascara, hair.

'It doesn't matter, Myraah, that you didn't know Ravi might contest these elections,' Andrew said, returning the pen to the holder.

I nodded. I was smiling. I had pulled back in my seat; my arms were crossed. I was the picture of dignity and command, I assured myself. Andrew's eyes seconded that.

'This is my line of work, that's why I heard first.' Andrew's voice was so soft and soothing, it was as if he was wary of volume, that it might stoke an unnecessary emotion.

'I want to go to Coonoor for the weekend,' Andrew announced, breaking a comfortable silence.

'Why?' I had been staring at him, and there was a trace of colour on his cheeks.

'My great-grandmother… Maybe there's more to those notes.'

'I think–'

'You want to go, too?' he asked before I could finish. Our eyes met like old friends on a familiar street.

I reached for the pen Andrew had just returned to the holder. 'I would love to, Andrew.'

'Great!'

'Two rooms.'

'Of course.'

As Andrew left the room, I picked up my phone and opened the camera, turning it to selfie mode. My face, like my emotions, was in disarray. *Was.* I winked, and then smiled at my reflection, a sexy slant of the lips. A better look definitely.

Chapter 25

Andrew and I hadn't done road trips together until we trailed Hari Rao latterly. That would hardly count as a jaunt, but we were on the road for about eight hours on each of those two days.

Andrew's eyes were on the road. He fiddled with the music system every now and then, changing stations and increasing and reducing the volume. Apologizing every now and then, too loud or soft. I was taking in everything my eyes clapped on – the dark sky, the green earth, a barking dog, a cycle parked at the side of the road. *Whose wheels were they? Where had he gone?*

At some point, I settled deeper into the seat, my shoulders relaxed, and my eyes caressed Andrew's profile. His body language had tempered, too.

We stopped for breakfast a couple of hours into our journey. Andrew had swerved into a place earlier but quickly steered us back on the road. 'The dosas aren't good here,' he said.

I nodded. I didn't really care what we ate and where; it was too early for food for me.

Andrew's smile was warm when we stopped 20 minutes later; my expression was puzzled. I had been flicking through Bhumika Velu's notes.

'What do you know about Catherine Brown?' I asked, seated opposite him.

Andrew had eaten his dosa and was finishing mine when I tossed the question at him. His face wore a quizzical expression when he looked up. 'She's my great-grandmother – Noelene's mother.'

'I know,' I said, smiling. 'What's her life story? Where did she grow up?'

Andrew laughed. It had a nervous ring to it.

We were almost done with the food.

'You should eat something. I've eaten two dosas; you barely took a bite.'

'Maybe later.'

I felt Andrew's palm on my back as we approached the cashier. We paid less than 100 bucks for two dosas and two sugary coffees.

'She's an only child, I think. Her mother passed away early, and her father didn't remarry,' Andrew said as he got us back on the highway.

'Her father was a teacher.'

'She was married off to Ronald Brown. They moved to Bengaluru; they were from Coonoor obviously…'

Andrew stopped talking. He drove some distance, 10 minutes or maybe 20, before pulling up. He was breathing heavily.

'Bhumika Velu is Catherine Brown, right?' He was looking at me, into me, like the answer was written somewhere inside of me.

I was nodding. 'I think so.'

He pulled out his phone and started going through the texts one by one. 'Ronald Brown contracted smallpox and died. They moved to Bengaluru, too??'

He was cross-checking their stories.

'It's so obvious. How could I have not known? The notes all but spelt it out for me.'

Andrew's hands were gripping mine tight; they were pale almost. He apologized and let out that intensity on the steering wheel. His knuckles were white.

'Bhumika never saw her father again.'

That really bothered me. How could he claim to love her and not let her father visit them or she visit her father? Love? A prisoner in your palace.

Andrew's face was taut.

After a while, he asked, 'When did you find out?'

'The first time you read it to me, I thought something was amiss.'

Andrew nodded.

'I must've read those notes some three or four times when I discovered them,' he said. 'It was those notes that brought me back to India because even though I didn't think it was my great-grandmother's then, it gave me a starting point from where I could begin my search.'

Andrew wanted to walk around the place, know it and understand Catherine Brown's life. No… Bhumika Velu's. 'I have been here twice as a child, for a wedding and something else. I can't quite remember what that was.'

I could hear him breathe.

'With Noelene?'

He nodded.

I wanted to say something funny to lighten the mood, but I couldn't come up with anything.

'She's Bhumika to you?' I was addressing him, he who doesn't shorten names.

Andrew nodded.

'I'm guessing Noelene didn't think of her as Bhumika, more as Catherine.' It wasn't a question.

'She only referred to her as "mother".'

Obviously. Those turns had slowed my mind down to a crawl.

'I think,' I said, patting his arm, 'she thought you'd finally get it...'

'More like she wanted me to figure it out.'

I laughed. It was timorous.

'It's not the kind of life you want to talk about, not that she didn't own her choices, but the uncertainties that it brought kind of destroyed her.'

That was a choice, I thought. A harsh truth.

'I think she trusted I'd arrive at the truth.'

That was a bit heartless. My hand reached halfway to his shoulder before returning to my lap.

'The only thing she told me about the notes was, "It's all in there." And that's why, when you had me focus on her life story, I could connect the dots.' Andrew was laughing now. 'About time, don't you think?'

My heart was bleeding for the boy tasked with figuring out his family tree.

'Do you know where she lived?'

Andrew had made some enquiries about Catherine Brown after he returned to Bengaluru.

While there were people who knew of the Browns, no one seemed to know of Catherine Brown's antecedents. There was one gentleman who had told him that Noelene had two younger sisters, both of whom had died early. Andrew thought that was a possibility going by the size of the house; he could've had a different bedroom for every day of the week if he wanted.

On the way up, we stopped at a stall selling fresh carrots and cucumbers. Andrew enquired after the Velus, a schoolteacher named Tilakanathan Velu, whose daughter, Bhumika, had married an Englishman. The last part of the sentence was met with a flicker of recognition. Something heard, something learnt. A story that had come down from grandparents.

Andrew's Tamil wasn't as fluent as his Kannada, but he could get by.

'Maybe we could walk around the barracks area, talk to people,' I said.

The last hour of the almost eight hours on the road to Coonoor was a journey mapped in hell – 36 hairpin bends.

'I wish Noelene had spoken to me about Hari Rao,' Andrew said as he approached the first of the hairpin bends. 'What happened and why it ended the way it did.'

I looked at him, surprised at the announcement; we were talking about his great-grandmother. Earlier, he had said he understood why Noelene hadn't wanted to talk about it.

'She was cold in her grave by the time I switched to media, but I was always interested in politics,' he said. He was talking slowly, just like how he was driving. 'I was living in Bengaluru. I might have run into the man.'

Even though Andrew had always planned on going abroad to pursue his education, there was the off chance he would return. Noelene should've sat the boy down and spoken to him. He had a right to know. Maybe she expected to be pushed, asked for the answer... but she should've known that the question would haunt him when there was no one to give him answers.

'I have a feeling she wasn't proud of something she had said or done to him,' Andrew said.

I looked at him.

'I have no evidence; it's just a feeling. It's because of how she relayed it to me, her tone maybe. There was regret, and it stood out like a column against the sadness that swirled around her when she spoke about him. She was distraught that he didn't acknowledge her or their daughter, but there was more. They might have had something good, and she may have broken it with something she said or did. I don't know,' he said, slamming his palm on the steering wheel.

'Are you mad at her?'

'This half-knowledge is killing me.'

'Is this because he recognized you?'

'I don't think it was me; it was my name. I don't know of any other Browns living in Bengaluru.'

I nodded.

He loved his Nana and she him. They spoke a lot to each other, not that there was anyone else to talk to. But on the most important subject of his life, his roots, he and his beloved grandmother had steered clear of hard truths. She had held on to all that she had lived through, letting nothing show, and he, not wanting to cause her more pain than he thought she had already inflicted on herself, had stayed silent.

His father? How could Andrew not want to know who the man was? It was burning me. My eyes were on his fingers which were on the steering wheel. Then it hit me. My stomach tightened, to the size of a golf ball maybe and my eyes shut. Of course he wanted to know, but how? Who could he ask?

'I should've spoken to Nana on some stuff,' he said, as if he had read my mind.

And she should've asked her daughter who the father of her child was, I thought. What if Noelene had and Sarah Ann returned the question to her mother? If there was a prettier mess in all the world, I didn't know it.

'Especially after I discovered the diary. It's just old paper, but imagine, I was holding something Bhumika had also touched... I didn't know it then.'

I loved how he had ditched Catherine Brown for Bhumika Velu.

'I wanted to come here, come here with you, and walk these roads,' he said, pointing at the newly tarred surface of the barracks we were crawling up on before the GPS announced, 'Your destination is on the right.'

I wanted to ask, 'Why me?', but we were on our feet and fishing out baggage.

We read Bhumi's notes again after we checked into the hotel. We tried to visualize everything she had written about.

We were in my cottage; it was almost double the size of his. It had a garden with rose bushes. We were on the sofa. Andrew's feet were on the table and my legs were crossed. I closed my eyes and took deep breaths.

I'm not sure if I dozed off, but it seemed like a good half hour had passed when Andrew tapped me on my shoulder. Then, together, we walked down the road she may have walked a century ago in the early evening light. The air was fresh, and it wrapped around me like a coat.

We went to Coonoor town and chatted up a few people. We tossed the 'Velu' name around and then the 'Brown' question but were met with blank looks. On our way back, we stopped at a café that sat on a hillock. It was like we were seated at the edge of this fabulous landscape and some 30–40 metres away, you could see the mighty Nilgiris drop in a majestic sweep.

My fingers bit into Andrew's forearm. A gust of wind could blow our seats, and with us on it, into those endless woods. His palm was on my fingers. He was looking at me, telling me we were fine and that it was only a matter of time before I got used to our setting.

The coffee was great and the view, as terrifying as my thoughts were, was even better.

A couple seated at the table next to ours ordered walnut and blueberry waffles. We pointed at their order and told the waiter we wanted the same along with another round of coffee.

'Would you have told me about Meena had I not brought it up?'

I have no idea why I had brought up Meena, but it seemed like she was never far from my thoughts when I was around Andrew.

Andrew shook his head. 'I have no clear answer on that,' he said.

My eyes met his.

'If you were single, I would definitely have told you. But you are almost engaged to Ravi Rao… I'm not sure.'

I nodded.

'I don't think I would've mentioned anything if you and Meena were still close.'

He was moving his hands as he spoke, trying to define close perhaps.

'I wouldn't have wanted to ruin a friendship. I had already ruined what we had.'

Thoughtful. Was it considerate? Another adjective?

'I was not thinking then, Myraah.' Andrew's hand was on my shoulder. 'I was alone…'

I nodded. He had consistently tossed the word 'alone' at me. As if it were a frisbee I was meant to catch in a flying disc game we were playing on some sunny beach.

A gust of wind washed over us, my tee rode up and my hair swept across my face. Andrew's hands were on me, pulling down my tee and straightening my hair.

'For my mother, I would've done anything, given everything. I loved her beyond reason, Andrew.' My curls were in my mouth.

Andrew's eyes clouded. After what seemed like an eternity, he said, 'That's what you felt for me…' He was nodding, his eyes hollow.

I looked out at the scenery. The words that were going through my mind were deep, thick, intense and dark. Words that finished like the strokes of a brush.

Andrew was on his phone, and then suddenly, his eyes were on me.

'Did you know he was contesting?'

I didn't respond to the question, not because the answer was no but because I didn't want to let him in on the status of that relationship. It was not his business.

That was the moment the waffles arrived. They were smelling of a world beyond the skies, a sweet paradise maybe.

Suddenly, Andrew was on his feet, his hands clutching my wrist. I turned, and before us was this big house. From where we were standing, it appeared to be sprawled out across the lawns.

Andrew was walking, and I followed him.

The server started walking with us. He was worried that we were going to complain about the order that had taken some time to come. He was explaining to Andrew that it was a homestay and that the café was attached to it and that sometimes, orders got delayed when all the rooms in the house were taken up, like now.

Andrew told the waiter he was only interested in the house. We had no problem with the service.

The man nodded, but he wasn't sure.

'Who are the owners?'

'Raju from Bengaluru.'

One side of the house was lined with french windows, giving it a period silhouette.

The manicured lawn was edged with marigolds. Both of us noticed the flowers at the same time. Andrew's hand clutched mine so tightly that I thought he might crush it.

As we walked up the walkway towards the tastefully enclosed porch, I noticed that on the rear wall was a line of pictures. Most of them were wedding pictures, and all of them were black and white.

Andrew's hand was around my shoulder as he steered me back to our table.

'That's another thing; we don't have any pictures.'

'Your mother's?'

Andrew shook his head. *Noelene didn't have a picture of her only child?*

It's like the Browns wanted no record of their existence.

Andrew paid for the coffees and the untouched waffles, and we walked back to our cottage wordlessly.

We had skipped the dinner Andrew had prepaid for and drank from the bottles we had smuggled into the room.

'Where did you stay when you came here as a child?' I asked.

'At a house; it was huge.'

'Whose place was it?'

He shrugged.

I wanted to ask if it had a lawn edged with marigolds.

'It had a garden with marigolds.' With that, he shut his eyes and let the tears flow.

Andrew was in my room to drop off my bags; he didn't knock.

His hands were full with his backpack and duffle bag. His biceps strained against the weight he was carrying. These were arms that knew load.

The lighting in the room was annoyingly dim, and the acacia-wood furniture merged into the backcloth. I realized then that he'd taken off his hoodie.

I was by the door. The image of that house we had walked into uninvited kept coming back to me. I wanted to tell Andrew we should've hung around the place, waited a little.

He dropped the bags and turned to me. I took a step towards him.

Somewhere in that movement, I lost that imposing piece of real estate that had occupied my thoughts.

I inhaled Andrew's scent, a zesty olfactory sensation.

His left hand took my right, and his lips full brushed against mine. They were rough, like my breathing.

I felt him and he felt me.

Our tongues explored in turn, revelling in comforting tastes, cigarettes and citrus, his joy and my keep-me-awake chewing gum. He was giving, I was taking. We stilled suddenly, but our bodies hummed, telling each other things that words couldn't quite articulate.

A boy. A girl. Heat.

I felt a smile warm my cheeks. However the day had panned, this is how it was supposed to end. I'm not sure if that was a thought or if that's what I was telling myself. Maybe it was both.

My nails dug into his warm palms.

I exhaled, Andrew inhaled. In sync, like ballroom dancers. Eyes locked, smoking fire. We repeated the exercise, revelling in the notes our bodies hit.

My eyes toured the length of his arms before returning to his full lips.

'Your skin,' he said, 'smoother than single malt.'

I laughed.

A half-smile flashed across his face. Those lips were meant for kissing.

My heart was racing. Ferrari engine.

Andrew drew me to his full height. He was carrying me, my legs were locked around his waist, and I wriggled my way into him, nearer, closing the non-existent gap between us.

I heard a cry. Was it me?

My nervous fingers stroked his jawline; my tongue was discovering flavours. I heard a moan. I love the sounds he makes.

Andrew was swaying to an inner beat, maybe, and I was being rocked from side to side. My hand was in his tee, and my mouth shifted to his clavicle. I took a bite of the bone before leaving a trail of love bites. A bright blush against his pale skin.

He groaned.

I kissed his neck.

Andrew's right hand was deep inside my denims; he was stroking me. I squealed. Andrew put me down gently.

'I'm going crazy,' he said. I thought it was me.

I worked off his jeans, tossed them aside and knelt before him, taking him in my mouth. I stroked him with my tongue, long, slow strokes, a playful brush of the glans.

A shiver ran through Andrew. I felt it; he shook. His fingers were in my hair. Tangled. He tugged, I hurt.

'Myraaahhhh.' It had been ages since I had heard him call out to me that way. A cry that came from deep within him.

I intensified the stroking; my fingers roamed his rump, then kneaded his quadriceps.

'Aaahhh,' he shouted and pushed my arms aside. Andrew joined me on the carpet; he was kneeling before me.

He rolled off my tee. The lacy ombre bralette followed.

Andrew's eyes were bright; it was a light I hadn't seen before.

He let the back of his hands brush my breast. My nipples were so hard they hurt.

I wanted Andrew, and I could see he wanted me.

We were back on our feet again. Andrew eased off my jeans. I rolled my head. I was caught in a hypnotic spell of scent and heat. I went down on my knees and took him in my mouth again.

'Myraaahhhh,' he shouted. I mewled. This was crazy ridiculous.

He flooded my mouth, and I swallowed before collapsing on my back... Andrew was on me, covering me like a blanket.

I lay on his denims, and his phone poked my shoulder. I tried to move his trousers away unsuccessfully.

'What?' he asked, smiling into my eyes. I pointed at his jeans.

Andrew tossed them aside.

Andrew's phone fell on the carpeted floor. It had opened to an Instagram page, which had a picture of Meena and Ravi.

My eyes stayed on the phone screen, just to confirm what I had seen.

Andrew was on his feet, and I joined him.

'This has nothing to do with that,' he said, bending to pick up his phone. 'I saw this just now, an hour ago maybe, when we were at the café.'

I nodded.

I knew just when he had seen it; it was in his expression.

'I wanted to show it to you right then, but that's when I saw the house.'

I hadn't told him I had broken up with Ravi.

Andrew probably sensed it at that very juncture, that same evening, but he hadn't brought it up. In our profession, the deity was in the details, but when it was personal, Andrew tread lightly. It suited him.

'I knew this,' I said, pointing to his phone. 'I saw them together.' I moved my head dramatically. We were on the sofa, not a stitch of clothing on either of us.

'I am okay,' I said, turning to face him.

He nodded. Andrew didn't need me to say it.

'He didn't need much time,' I said, laughing.

'And neither did you, Rai.' His thumb was stroking my cheek. I could still taste him.

We had brought a couple of bottles with us. I had asked for Chardonnay. I was suddenly only drinking white wine.

Andrew had poured out a couple of glasses, something dark for himself.

I pulled on his tee, and he was bare-chested.

We were quiet to begin with, sipping our drinks. I was considering the day, the miles we had driven, Bhumika's notes, all the people we had met and everything we had learnt.

Then Andrew spoke about his family. It was just little titbits he was dropping, about Hari Rao, the campaigning. He asked me if there was a physical resemblance. Alcohol had freed his tongue.

I told him there was nothing he had of his grandfather looks wise, but there was the other stuff, like their walk.

I mimicked Andrew's walk and that of his biological grandfather, like some burlesque dancer, and ended up on the sofa, laughing.

I opened my eyes and tried to look around me. It was early. I tried to lift my head, but it hurt. It was like someone had filled it with boulders that shifted when I moved.

I was wasted. I had no idea how much I had tanked the previous evening. A whole bottle of Chardonnay, 750 ml? Maybe more? From where I lay, I could see a capless bottle, empty glasses, some nuts scattered on the table.

I was parched. I reached for a bottle of water and downed it before drifting off to sleep. My last thought was that I was in a water body. Swimming.

I woke up hours later, feeling marginally lighter. I managed to pull myself up. I was leaning against the four-poster cot. The sun had found gaps between the curtains and strayed into the room.

Yesterday had been a frustrating day. The steps we thought were taking us somewhere saw us arrive at crossroads without leads. My fitness app showed I had walked 12 kilometres, but in the only way it mattered, we hadn't moved. We were on the road to nowhere.

We had walked up and down the barracks, roamed around Waterloo Road, we stopped at five different tea shops, a grocery store and a medical shop, looking for leads on the Velus and the Browns.

We had evening tea with an elderly receptionist from a guest house, but outside of the fresh cucumber sandwiches, that came to naught.

There was a schoolteacher in his eighties, called Dorai, who said he had known the Velus. He couldn't recall any more than that the widower had lived in the area. He repeated that about 10 times over lunch. Andrew might've told him that actually.

We returned to the room late in the evening, sufficiently spent.

I couldn't recall much of the evening expect that we poured out glasses and glasses of wine and the brown stuff. My guess is we didn't say very much. Andrew was lost in his thoughts.

'I didn't think I would find all my answers in one trip,' Andrew had said more than once in the last couple of days. Last evening, the conjunction followed. 'But I expected something, anything.'

He wanted to hear it all – the whole truth, every last detail. It was his life. I wanted it for him, too.

My eyes strained in the direction of my watch on my bedside table. It was the same one Ravi had gifted me. It was almost noon. Andrew and I should've been on our way to Bengaluru by now.

I jumped out of bed, grabbed some clothes and rushed into the shower.

When I returned to the room, the bed was made, not neatly, but there was an order to it.

It wasn't the service staff.

As I walked up to the kettle to get it ready, the door opened behind me. In the mirror to the right, I noticed Andrew walk in. He apologized for not asking to come in.

My smile, like the afternoon sun, was bright.

Andrew dropped a kiss on my cheek. My knees buckled. Andrew's hand was on my elbow, steadying me.

His phone was beside the kettle. Both the phone and kettle lit up at the same time.

One gurgled, the other said: *I miss you.* Andrew had a message from Pooja. *Thank you for letting me lean on you.* The second line was punctuated with a red heart.

Andrew had turned to pick up the coffee mugs. He hadn't seen the message.

My heart hit the floor of my stomach. It fell with a thud. I turned to look at Andrew. Had he heard the fall?

Andrew poured us the coffee and took quick sips. 'Let's not make it very late, Rai,' he said, dropping a kiss on the top of my head.

The coffee wasn't going down my throat. My eyes were moist.

'Drink up,' he said, patting my arms before reaching for my bags.

I went to the loo and poured the coffee into the sink. I was panicking. My legs were shaking, and my stomach felt like jelly. Sweat beads had formed on my forehand. I splashed water on my face and dabbed it off with a towel. I repeated it. Thrice.

When I returned to the room, I saw that Andrew had taken our luggage to the car. His phone was gone, too.

It was four hours later that we stopped for lunch. That was when Andrew saw Pooja's messages.

'Okay,' he said, 'this is why you are so quiet.' He smiled as he showed me Pooja's messages. 'Please check the messages. There is nothing from me before this.'

My eyes flicked across his screen briefly. Clearly, only Pooja was messaging. I laughed. Hysterically.

'I'm not responsible for this,' Andrew said. His eyes were on me. 'I haven't encouraged this. She sends me random messages like this from time to time. It doesn't mean anything.'

The sambhar was hot and spicy. I felt sick.

I turned away.

'I just read it,' he said.

He may not have engaged with Pooja, but they definitely shared something. No one talks to a wall, not even a 22-year-old.

'She does this all the time.' His eyes were dark. We were back in the car.

How can I trust you again? I didn't ask that question, but it was my companion for the better part of that nearly eight-hour journey.

Chapter 26

I had to shut the door on Andrew Brown – lover, friend and colleague. All of it.

I miss you.

Thank you for letting me lean on you.

Both messages were punctuated, the second line with a red heart.

Independently, they meant nothing, but I'd be a fool to treat them in isolation. Pooja didn't threaten me; she only reminded me of a wretched probability.

Meena Iyer. Past. Present. Future.

It was happening all over again.

I couldn't be around him again. I needed time. Months or years maybe. If we were in the same cloud space, I wouldn't be able to keep him out of my life. When around him, everything passes, the load lightens, and the road beckons. I'd want to take walks, get coffee, go on campaign trails, road trips…

During the day, doubts hovered over me like a threatening nimbostratus. At night, it made for a hard pillow.

Who breaks up with the love of her life just because he had an affair? With her best friend? People mess around; it's what they do. It was just once. It started with one woman, then there was a chain reaction.

I don't know when that became 'just'. I must've read it somewhere, in one of those pathetic self-help pieces, or I may've heard it in a song. A tune that stayed and words that stung. A magnitude of 9.5 on the Richter scale. Just?

I could flip it, too. *Just* because he had admitted to the transgression and apologized? *Just* because he regretted the affair with Meena. Those two messages shone the torch on all those questions that needed answers.

The toing-and-froing in my head had woken me up at the crack of dawn after two hours of sleep. Just two hours.

I had directed myself to stay in bed. That's not much of a struggle usually, but this morning, I wanted to be out. I was itching to run. When I run, I often race away from things that need to be dealt with. Rejoice in the morning air, the early sun and the irregular carpet of flowers. It's a beautiful time of day. I hear the hum of traffic at a distance. It reassures me that I'm still in the city and not kidnapped and locked up at some half-cooked resort they call one with nature.

I'll look at it after another kilometre. It's my favourite hiding place.

The time for dwelling on matters was over. I needed to commit.

There was a seed of an idea in my head. I rolled to my left, stayed in that position for a few minutes, then over to my right. It was almost 8 a.m. I could afford to go to work late. I had no assignments, and my diary was empty, too. No calls to make, no dots to connect.

I pulled myself up and sat square on the bed. My phone was charging on my overcrowded side table. I reached for it, dropping a couple of books in the process. I didn't know how I was going to go about it, so I simply got started. People looked for jobs all the time.

Some folks get offers, but it's not like they aren't tapping sources. Sudha was constantly being romanced for jobs, but

I'm sure she was laying it out there that she was looking for something more, a change. Maybe.

I've never been faced with the delightful dilemma of a job offer in all these years. I don't recall ever having got a mail or message, much less a phone call from whomsoever these folks are who cast the net for these mighty media houses. It's not like I'm not good at what I do. I have a decent reputation, some 10,066 followers on Instagram (the last time I checked) despite sporadic effort. You'd think people knew I existed, and someone would call and say, 'Hey, Myra Rai, look out of your window; you'll find a jet waiting to pick you up. We have an offer you can't refuse.'

I'd love the jet.

Maybe it's the business guys, political heavyweights, people like Sudha and Andrew, who are the ones in demand. Who'd be interested in storytellers in a culture steered by commerce?

The only place I've worked at is *Morning Herald*. I was one of those odd journalists of my generation who didn't jump jobs with the frequency of two-wheelers switching lanes on a Bengaluru road. It wasn't a case of landing the perfect job first up, if there's any such thing as a perfect job, but living here, I couldn't have asked for much more. I made decent money; I got my raises and promotions even before I asked for them.

People with my capability in Delhi and Mumbai earned much more; I was aware of that. Not that I needed a heftier bank balance, but it would've been nice to take my father on a trip.

I was still to celebrate my 30th birthday, but I was already heading a department, which wasn't common in traditional media houses. I wasn't a favourite, but I wasn't disliked either. I got by. What I liked about *Morning Herald* is that I had the freedom to function. I had floated the crime column; yes, my editor did sit on it for a month or two, but he gave me all the support I needed once we were off the blocks. It was the most-talked-about feature of the paper, and I got due credit.

So, where was I going to go looking for a suitable opening? Bengaluru wouldn't do. I couldn't live in the same city as Andrew. Persistence is powered by proximity. It would be too easy for him to knock on my door and for my treacherous heart to relent.

Sudha had told me a year or two ago that she had been asked if I was looking to switch jobs. People apparently thought I wasn't willing to shift base because of my family situation.

'Surely I'm not the only single woman with a parent to care for in journalism.'

'No,' she had agreed. 'But sometimes, just by being ourselves, we lend to a reputation that precedes us.'

The patriarchy, maybe. Could be geography, too. A Bengaluru thing, a South thing.

I briefly considered one of *MH*'s bureau offices, perhaps in Mumbai or Delhi. I dismissed the thought swiftly. If Andrew was editor, which he would be soon enough, I would have to deal with him on a daily basis. Besides, the organization would do everything possible to talk me out of shifting cities. I couldn't leave the door half-open. I had to move out.

Did I want to live anywhere else?

I loved Bengaluru, all of it. It's unruly traffic and pot-holed streets, lined by sturdy gulmohars. The honking taxis and swerving two-wheelers, pedestrians who walked on roads and spat on pavements, the Kannadiga who'll speak to an outsider in Hindi even if he couldn't string two words in the language. The city may have long traded its fair-weather charm of the eighties, yet, for me, there was no place quite its equal. I loved the weather despite the wear of climate change. The summer heat is sharp but never oppressive, maybe because of the gentle breeze that rustles through your hemline and wipes your face.

Home is where your family is, your best friend resides, the only place on the planet where the positives go over the negatives even if they outweigh them. I had to leave it, though; there was no other way.

I had to leave Dad. I had to leave Chhaya. I had to leave this bed.

I scrolled through my phone, up and down and back again. I looked at every outstation number I had on it. I considered the ones I thought were a possibility. Would they be safe to ping?

Over the years, I had made contacts all over the country – journalists whom I travelled with on assignments and junkets, bonds I had made over wine and dinner and cemented when I travelled to Mumbai or Delhi or the tier-two towns on work. I made a list of seven people, all senior in the profession, whom I could reach out to, let them know I was in the market. I would request them to be discreet. I couldn't afford for *Morning Herald* to hear about this.

I shot each of the editors carefully worded messages, finishing with a request for a time to have a chat.

My head was in charge now. If I so much as asked myself how I would feel about leaving not just *Morning Herald* but Bengaluru, too, I couldn't go through with it.

Chapter 27

I got my first offer two weeks after I sent out feelers. The money was good; it could pay for that holiday I wanted to take my dad on, but I was unsure of how the place functioned. I would be the features editor and report to an associate editor, whom I didn't know, not even by reputation.

I would be managing a raw team in a city where I would be starting from scratch. It would take me years. Mumbai, the country's commercial capital, was so removed from Bengaluru culturally that I could've relocated to Moscow.

I parked my car in Andrew's basement and messaged him. I told him that I wanted to see him. I waited until he replied, which, as always, was immediately, even before I rang his doorbell.

Andrew opened the door, wearing his welcoming smile. His red shorts, which I remembered from our trip to Coonoor, were partially hidden by the door, and his left hand waved me in.

I focused on the room. It was bright; he had drawn the curtains. He did that for a couple of hours each day to let the sun in. His fragrance was all over the sitting area. Did he dunk it on himself the moment he woke up or was it just before I entered? I placed my bag down carefully and sat next to it. We hadn't said a word to each other, but the smile had disappeared from his face. I had been avoiding him in office these last few days, which he had noticed but hadn't brought up.

'I'm quitting,' I said after squeezing out every strain of emotion that threatened to tinge my declaration in ambiguity.

Andrew's brow shot up. 'Those messages–'

'Have nothing to do with my decision.' I completed the sentence for him.

Andrew was seated at the end of the long divan at the head of which I sat. I could tell he was uncomfortable. I rested my back against the only arm it had. He shifted to the leather sofa and dropped his elbows on his knees.

I told him I was moving to Mumbai in three months; that was the notice period. I was joining the online portal 'The Full Story'. I would put in my papers at *Morning Herald* in the next half hour, hopefully. I had already typed out the six-line letter. It was sitting in my drafts.

'Why?' he asked. If I wasn't putting in my papers because of Pooja's messages, then what was it? He wanted the reason.

Andrew stood up and crossed his arms. His bare legs looked like they belonged to an athlete, but I don't think Andrew had stepped into a pair of sports shoes since he left college.

How can I ever trust you? 'As features editor,' I said.

'If you want a promotion, don't worry about it. We'll take care of that.' His eyes were dark, unlike the room we were seated in.

A sliver of a shiver went down my spine, erupting in my core. I wanted to punch his pea-sized, narcissistic heart. He thought I was chasing a title that he could toss at me like an extra biscuit? That I would leave my mother's home, my father, my dearest friend, the city I loved, a job I valued, for a position. A danged label.

How had I ever thought this man knew me, got me?

I stood up slowly. I'd be damned if I was going to let him tower over me. I had worn heels. I felt like Beyoncé with a day job.

A steely calm dropped over me. I exhaled. I smiled. I did all those things I had practised.

'Actually,' I said, my voice, a cool spring drift, 'it's the money. They've doubled what I'm getting here.' I couldn't even say *Morning Herald*, not that he noticed.

'We'll match that.' He was so quick with his offer that it came back to me as I finished my sentence.

I walked the breadth of the room, stopping at the wood-panelled glass doors that led to the balcony. They were closed as I assumed they were most days at this hour as he prepared to leave for office. A coffee mug sat on the bar counter and beside it was a crime thriller, which was bookmarked at the halfway point.

'What do you regret, Andrew?' I didn't need a gun; I had already shot myself.

'Meena.'

'What about the Meena episode do you regret?'

'My biggest mistake.'

Why couldn't I just hear the man? He was speaking clearly; he had done that over and over again. He regretted the Meena episode of his life for what it had done to HIM, for the havoc she had caused in HIS life. In that period, I was incidental.

'It's for the better.' My voice was hopelessly frayed. 'The split.'

'I returned home to know my family's past, to find you...' His voice shook.

'And you thought I'd be waiting?' Bookmarked at where you disappeared.

He exhaled.

'Eight years, Andrew. Eight years.' And that wasn't even the point.

'We've moved past that,' Andrew said.

I wanted to laugh.

Maybe it was the burden of his family's complicated past or that time in his life when he was alone and splashing around with no shore in sight or that he was simply lust-sided. He just didn't get what his tone-deaf rumba had done to me.

'Why?' he asked.

I wondered if this was the reporter in him or the lawyer, armed with that right to question. Even if it was lawless.

'It doesn't feel the same any more, and at times, I get the feeling it's the same for you.'

'What doesn't feel the same? You're holding back, not always, sometimes. I can see that.'

That he had ignored the second half of the sentence wasn't lost on me. The wary prosecutor.

I turned so that I could face him. Andrew's hands were knotted across his chest, his knuckles were white. I met his gaze.

'I don't think I can feel for you or anyone else what I once felt for you… It covered the earth and the seas; it scaled the mountains and kissed the skies.' I paused. What I didn't say was, *There was no place for doubt*. 'This, what we shared these last months, would've been enough with anyone else. With you, I want everything.'

'Myraah!' He was shaking his head. 'I hold back at times, too, you're right,' he said, taking a step towards me. 'I wrecked what we had.'

Among other things, I thought.

'What is everything?' he asked, after forever and a day.

The accomplished Mr Brown didn't know; he needed me to decode it.

'We had it once.' The way we were.

'The only way we can put that behind us is if we work together.'

'You took something out of me and gave it away. I can't get it back,' I said and stopped to take a breath. I was not pausing for time but to swallow the words I wanted to say to him. *Only you can get it back. Only you, Andrew.* 'I told you earlier that I wouldn't have understood Meena and you even if it was love, but if I had to lose you to anything, it might as well have been love...'

'Is Meena more important than me?'

This was Andrew throwing everything he had at me. Reporters do that when they fear a story that they had pictured as the page one lead was suddenly going nowhere. Then you tossed everything, including the kitchen sink, at the object of your attention, hoping to get the response that would make your report. Take it out of the dustbin and restore it to a place just below the masthead.

'Nobody is more important than you, nobody was. Outside of my mother, that is.'

'Are you punishing me?'

'It's everything to do with Meena, and yet nothing to do with her. It's right here,' I said, pointing at my heart.

Andrew shook his head. His eyes were moist.

'I tried, Andrew... I tried because I wanted it, needed it.'

'Slowly,' he said, taking my hands in his, 'step by step, we'll make it happen. We need to give it time.' I let the warmth of his fragrance envelop me for a full moment.

'As much as I wish it is, it's not an exercise, Andrew. You either feel it or you don't. The politics of love...'

'What's missing?' His breath was spiced with confusion.

'Us, like we were. Myra and Andrew, just kids with hearts. Nothing was wrong with us, Andrew. There wasn't even a hint of a crack.'

'You're making a mistake. You're giving up on us for something so small.'

That did it. The dam burst. Tears tipped down my cheeks. I was sobbing, but I wanted to scream, *It's not small; it's what I feel for you. It's everything I am. EVERYTHING.*

He was kissing my tears, drop by drop, tasting them. An old ache and a new anger.

His fingers were in my hair; mine were stroking the back of his neck.

'A mistake,' I said as his lips took mine in a hypnotic embrace I wholly returned. It wasn't the mistake, it was the complete lack of empathy.

I wanted to break away from this man, but I couldn't. My fingers were on his shirt… This is why I had to change cities.

His fingers were underneath my top, which he had freed from the waistband of my trousers, and were stroking my bare back in an up-and-down motion. I shifted into him, feeling his hardness. I was kissing his chest. Little wisps of love.

Andrew unhooked my strapless bra, and the only reason it didn't hit the floor was because we were breathing each other. He pulled me closer, and I did the same.

An alarm went off in my bag; it came as a warning. I pulled back and fastened my bra.

I picked up my bag and walked to the front door.

'Myraah,' he called.

I don't know why I turned. It was a reaction perhaps.

He was at the entrance to his bedroom, his shorts askew on his spare frame.

My eyes shifted from him to the bar counter. I took four steps into the room and swung my bag at the coffee mug. It went crashing to the floor along with the crime thriller that was now divested of its marking.

Chapter 28

I had put in my papers at *Morning Herald* a month ago; the intervening four weeks had flown.

I had met with my editor right after I left Andrew's apartment. It was a difficult conversation. I told him I was looking for a change, that I wanted to move to a digital platform, which was no longer the future. I couldn't tell him the truth, but I wasn't lying either.

He was shocked. 'Why, Myra? Why so suddenly?'

I told him I had been thinking about it for a while. 'If I don't take the plunge now, I probably never will,' I said. 'I don't want to regret not having taken a chance.'

Mr Kumar told me *Morning Herald* had plans to ramp up its digital space, which was why Andrew Brown was hired. He added that the management's laid-back attitude was beginning to wear on Andrew, too, but they both knew that it would happen sooner than later.

As long as the advertising revenue of the organization kept swelling, we both knew that going digital was a distant dream. Rightly so, maybe.

Andrew, I expect, knew what he was signing up for.

Andrew Brown.

That left-handed strike with my pocketbook bag that sent the keepsake coffee mug crashing to the floor wasn't my proudest moment, but I liked the result. Maybe that's why the image of the broken pieces of china kept nudging me. It felt like my heart. Broken.

My eyes had met Andrew's before I exited his apartment. My stare was unapologetic while his face had crumpled.

I will apologize to Andrew for the damage to physical property, I know that now. A month ago, I wasn't so sure.

I had floated the idea of moving cities with my father a little after I sent out feelers. He greeted the news enthusiastically, much to my surprise. Not only was he willing to move with me, but he was actually looking forward to the shift. He thought it would be good for the both of us. He asked me why I had waited so long.

When speaking to Mr Kumar, I had weaved that in, too. I said my father would benefit from the move.

I don't know if it was something I said, in which case I don't know what exactly it was, but my editor seemed to think this decision to relocate was stirred by my father.

My mother's death had been reported in *Morning Herald*; it was a page-one story. It was a horrific accident. If I'm not wrong, *MH* even carried a picture of my father sobbing at the crime scene. Quite a few of the senior staff knew how badly my father had taken the loss.

Dad may be the reason why my editor accepted my notice without the spectacle that accompanies a shock resignation.

'These doors are always open for you, Myra, should you change your mind at any time,' he had said.

As the weeks rolled by, my father's enthusiasm seemed to deflate. He was like a punctured tyre now. At first, he suggested that we rent out our place for a year or two. He even started looking for apartments in Andheri and Vile Parle, which he passed up for a better location in Prabhadevi. Then, early one morning, he walked into my room to tell me he didn't want to rent our house. I understood that because if we leased our place and Mumbai didn't work for us, or even one of us, reclaiming our home would be a hassle. He briefly considered letting it out short term – there would be takers given the location – but he backtracked from that, too, saying people would spoil the furniture Amma had bought.

Finally, he said, it didn't make sense to lock up the house; it wasn't safe either. He would come with me for a couple of weeks, maybe a month, help me move and then return. That way, I would still have our home every time I was in Bengaluru.

'Don't worry about me,' he said. 'Andrew is also here. I can call him if I need anything.'

I was sure that once we were in Mumbai, I could convince him to stay longer. An extra month, a year.

I hadn't told Chhaya that I had quit *Morning Herald* and was shifting cities. We hadn't met or spoken in over a month. When I made my decision, she was in Delhi, after which her brother had taken ill. Though we messaged every day, it was mostly me asking about Chetan's condition and her giving me updates.

I didn't want to debate my decision to quit *Morning Herald* with Chhaya. All I needed to stay put was an excuse, and she could facilitate more than one.

I was in my cabin, working on my last weekend edition as *Morning Herald*'s features in-charge. I had a piece in it, too. I took a deep breath, exhaling laboriously. The following week, I would begin handing over charge of the eight-page magazine, which I had given a new look and more weight in my almost seven years in the organization. So much so that it was the most complete weekend section in the country. I had spent weeks and months conceptualizing, planning, finding ways to make an already good product better. *Morning Herald* sold 30 per cent more on the weekend than our closest rivals. That's the kind of popularity the pull-out enjoyed. I take great pride in that the graph kept rising with me at the helm.

I noticed Andrew walking across the editorial floor. He had tried to talk to me twice in office after I had been to his house. The first time I was on a call, the second time I pretended to be on a call when I was actually listening to music on my phone. He had been coming into work early these last couple of weeks. He might've wanted to talk, but he hadn't messaged, and I wasn't meeting his gaze.

Maybe all he wanted was an apology.

I pulled out my phone on impulse and messaged Chhaya. I typed, *When're we going to meet, Bae?*

The answer came back before my screen locked. *Like right now? You won't believe it, Bae. I was just thinking of asking if you are free for a tea break just now.*

I was on my feet in a flash. I reached for my phone and typed, *In Perky Grace in 5. For a COFFEE break.*

Meeting your bestie after a longish gap is like changing into clean undies.

We're not the physically embracing kind, but we hugged this time. Real tight. She had gone through a tough, tough time. I could only imagine what it was like for her, but unknown to her, I had fought a ragged bout, too.

'How come you haven't ordered our drinks and found a table?' she asked after sashaying in only 10 minutes late. She must've missed me.

'You must be craving a cup of tea,' I said. 'In the excitement of seeing you, I arrived with only my phone. I was about to head back to get my wallet.'

We laughed and paid, collecting our beverages and settling down in our usual spot in the near-empty café.

'I don't mind a croissant,' she said in true Chhaya style as soon as we were seated. 'I haven't had breakfast.'

I picked up her purse and got her the croissant. If she went to the counter, she'd debate on a plain or almond croissant for 10 minutes, and before I knew it, it would be time to get back to work.

'I've something to tell you,' she said, beating me to the bell.

'You go,' I said, laughing.

'Actually, two things to say,' she said, wagging her digits. 'Maybe three.'

'Spill the tea.'

'I saw Meena and Ravi together,' she said, holding my gaze. Then added, 'They were holding hands and looked quite into each other.'

Chhaya had met a distant cousin the previous night for a business dinner at the downtown five-star, where she spotted the new lovers.

'Ouch! That was quick,' I said, laughing.

'You were faster,' she came back.

'This was easy for Ravi,' I said. 'He always worried about women hitching their wagon to him for his money. Meena has enough of her own, so they start on level ground at least.'

'Meena's father is an IT professional. While I'm sure Mr Iyer is wealthy, I'm not sure they're quite in the same league.'

A few zeroes more or less. I shrugged.

'Andrew was also there,' she said. 'He was having dinner with two oldish-looking men.'

I didn't want to think about Andrew's reaction. It was not my business. I was getting out of this space for that very reason.

'I'm not sure if the lovebirds saw Andrew or me, but as I exited the place, my eyes met Andrew's. I'm pretty sure he had seen them, too. Their table was in the centre of the room. It was like they were making an announcement.'

'Bloody! Reporting from ground zero, where hope was so thoroughly squashed.'

Chhaya laughed, and I joined in her raptures, not quite sure why.

'And?' I asked Chhaya, taking a sip of my coffee. 'I hope you have something more interesting to say than this roulette of friends and lovers.'

'Well, there's this guy,' she said, her face colouring.

'Now you're talking…'

Hussain Malik, a Bollywood actor–director was hitting on my friend dearest. He was about 33, a divorcé. He wasn't the best-looking man on the planet, not even a sharp dresser, but he was a crackling artiste. It didn't hurt that he was an extended branch of the industry's first family. They had bumped into each other at the Mumbai airport lounge a couple of months ago. Chhaya had missed her flight, not an uncommon occurrence with her, and he was early for his. (I prayed that if he was the punctual kind, that he also be blessed with a lorry load of patience should this dance go into the second song.)

Hussain had approached her, telling Chhaya he knew who she was before introducing himself. They sat together at a long table, shared pizzas and exchanged numbers.

'This time when I was in Delhi, he came over.' She took a bite of her almond croissant and looked around her.

'Because he had work there?' A question befitting a second-grade first-bencher.

'No, Bae, to see me!' my friend said, gulping down her tea to keep from spattering it over me.

Hussain was the relief in the chaos Chhaya's life had become in recent months. If she was not working, then she was caring for her brother, and the only time she got away from it all was when we met, and we hadn't met much. Men were always chasing her, but either the timing wasn't right or the person was 'a little off centre', as she put it. Whose centre, I didn't ask.

She longed to be young and get knotted in a romance. A careless affair. At the very least, I thought, Hussain would be a worthy spoiler.

'If this were a movie plot, where would it go?' My voice was weak. I took a deep breath in a bid to replenish it.

'I don't know,' she said, smiling. 'It's just the beginning. For the time being, I just want to enjoy it.'

'Some beginning it has been! Comprehensive.'

'Is there any other way to start?'

'Outside of all bases covered? That would be unprofessional,' I said, winking. A tear escaped my determined guard, a sob followed. I had held on for too long.

'What happened?' Chhaya asked, moving forward in her seat. 'Why are you crying?'

'I've put in my papers.'

'At *Morning Herald*,' she said. It was not a question.

I apologized to Chhaya. She was finally enjoying a romance and I couldn't even hear her out. Wait until she had said her piece. Wow!

'Why?' she pressed after dismissing my admission of guilt.

'I can't work with Andrew any more; I shouldn't be around him. I need to get away.'

'Shouldn't?'

I shook my head.

'What happened, Myra?'

'It's not the same any more.' I wasn't going to bring up the messages; they were only a trigger for the decision. Pooja wasn't the reason.

'What?'

'Us?'

She was chewing at her croissant furiously. I heard it.

'He doesn't see what his affair has done to me, to us.'

'But why did you quit *Morning Herald?*'

'I wish he'd returned to India with a wife and three sons. It would've been a kick in the gut, but I would've managed. I'd have recovered.'

'When exactly did this happen?'

'A month ago.'

My friend looked at her watch; she was checking the date. She was in Delhi. 'I assume you have told him.'

I recalled the entire process, from the first texts I had sent out looking for a job to telling Andrew.

She watched me reach for her half-eaten croissant and take a slurpy bite. It was salty.

What we had was special, Andrew and I. I see that now more than ever.

We put the other before *I*, unconsciously.

We were completely in tune with each other – the pen in the far corner of his left trouser pocket, the unopened bottle of water in my hand, which he reached to open. Not because I couldn't open the bottle or he didn't know where his pen was.

We knew each other interminably.

'And he regrets what he did because of what that cost him and not the two of you.'

It sounded silly when put like that. 'It's not like him not to get it, Chhaya. It's not like the Andrew I know.'

'Maybe she screwed him so badly in the head.'

I shook my head. 'I don't think she has anything to do with it.'

'What kind of an idiot falls for or has affection for a person like that? Not once but twice. It can be hard to swallow.'

I nodded. *No!* I told myself. *Andrew is no longer my problem.*

'But that is not your problem,' my bestie said. 'Somewhere, this line was crossed, and it's not yours to uncross.'

I exhaled. I couldn't agree with her more.

'I don't want to quit this job, this city, my home, you. But what choice do I have?'

'Where are you going?'

'Mumbai.' I gave a stunned Chhaya the details of my new job.

I slipped into my apartment quietly. I had passed the pages of the weekend edition; it was my last as the boss woman. Like always, I carried the page proofs home with me to read them after sufficient time had elapsed, examine them with refreshed eyes, ensure they were error-free.

Chhaya had chatted with me from the moment I got out of office till I reached home. In fact, we had spoken so much on the phone these last couple of days, it was more than we had done in all these years. She was still adjusting to my decision, oscillating between, 'Think about it,' and, 'I'll stay with you when I come to Mumbai.'

'I'll bring Huss,' she said, just before I pressed the lift button.

'Oh! Huss, is it?' I asked. For some reason, maybe it was for the relief we needed, both of us chose to laugh at this boogie move.

The house was dark, as it usually is at this time of the night. It was late enough for my dad to be asleep. Actually, any hour was good for my father to call it a day once the sun had done its job in this part of the world. I placed my car keys on my dressing table. I usually leave it in the key bowl on the dining table, just in case my father needed to use it in the morning. Not that he's averse to walking into my room and picking it up from my dresser, so I let it be. He knew my schedule, and I was aware of his.

I was standing up, poring over the proofs, which I had laid out on the floor. The position helped with checking the balance. I usually did this bit in office, when there was still time to shift, cut and correct, but this evening, I grabbed the pages and left in a hurry. I didn't want to cry in my cabin.

My usual routine included a wash, changing into my pyjamas and pouring myself a glass of white wine, taking not-so-delicate sips as I scanned the pages.

Just as I turned to go to the washroom, I heard a rap on the door. 'Papa,' I called. Who else could it be?

My father was looking older than his 60 years. He dragged his foot, something he never did. My mother and I own a quick step, but we both dragged our feet when we got out of bed in the morning. He settled himself in the only single-seater sofa in the room, and I made myself comfortable on the floor opposite him. He wanted to talk.

'I'm rethinking this decision of ours, going with you for a week.'

It was not a week. We had settled on a few weeks, which I hoped would stretch into months.

It was weighing on him. I could tell by the lines on his face, which were deeper than when I last noticed them.

'I don't want to lock the house Amma bought for us, even for a week.'

'Why, Papa?'

'This is our temple, Myra. We can't just leave this and walk away. I know Amma would've wanted me to go with you, but somehow, I can't get myself to do this. I just can't.'

His eyes were waterlogged. He was torn between this house, our home, and his beloved daughter, whom he would now have to send off on her own. I cursed myself for putting him through this.

'Can you manage here, Papa?' What else could I say?

'Andrew will be here,' he said, rising to his feet. Had Andrew Brown been standing before me, I'd have pushed my fists through his skull.

As I watched my father leave my room, it occurred to me, I could lay down the gauntlet, tell him I was going, force him to come with me. For a few days, a week, take a chance, but that would be two unhappy people forced to live in a place that wasn't home. Better that it was just one of us.

I could stay back, too, find a job or a new profession. The bar beckoned. A barmaid?

We spoke again the following morning. He was sure he was not moving. He gave a fair hearing to everything I had to say – the positives of moving to India's commercial capital, maybe I could get another job in Bengaluru in a year even – but he was firm. He didn't stop me, but he had made up his mind.

My father's business ideas may have all been wishy-washy, but it wasn't the result of his heart not being in the right place.

I was raging inside. I had become a pawn in this game I was forced to play. Andrew, who had screwed me over for my best friend of a distant time of my life – even the act itself was no longer the point of contention – was living his life. If he wasn't already executive editor, he would be that and more soon. He had a great reputation and had made good money. While I, who was just beginning to make stellar moves as a professional, had to flee not just the job that had given me a platform but also the city of my birth, like those criminals I've covered.

I called Chhaya to update her on the situation.

'I'll go with you, Bae, for a week, help you find a place. If you're sure this is what you want to do. We can use our guest house for some.'

I took a deep breath. I didn't want to cry.

'To make up, you can sleep on the pavement when I invite Huss over. You can wash the sheets the next morning.'

I'm loving being passed up for a man named Huss! 'Do your own laundry at least, Chhaya Mehta.'

We giggled.

'Wednesday breakfasts with Myra! Let's break with tradition and do Airlines' dosas tomorrow?'

'Let's binge our achy-breaky hearts away. Not yours, sorry, just mine.'

I heard her laugh. She's manic about laughing.

Chapter 29

It was early on Saturday. The office was empty, save for the cleaning staff. The heavy scent of phenyl, frenzied physical activity and occasional chatter notwithstanding, there was a serenity about the space that is otherwise alien to a newsroom.

I couldn't quite recall if, in all my time in *Morning Herald*, I had ever been in office on a Saturday morning. Maybe once. I had drifted in not fully awake, waited for the pick-up to drive me to the neighbouring district for an assignment.

Saturdays were light, the perfect time to clear my cabin. I didn't want to run into colleagues, one of them in particular.

I hadn't yet broached the subject of the broken keepsake mug with *he* who cannot be named. I wanted to apologize. I would message him perhaps.

I had carried bits and bobs of my belongings each day when I swiped out, making the job of leaving my professional habitat easier on myself. Still, I needed two nine-by-six inch packaging boxes, which would be filled with books, papers and photo frames.

I had a month left of my notice period, but I wasn't required to come into work. It was an in-between time, something like the midi dress of the eighties, not too short, not too long. A demure calf length that covered good legs. I couldn't join my new workplace, but I wasn't needed in my current job either. I could 'chill', some of my colleagues had told me rather enviously.

Watch Netflix and do nothing. Let's just say, I'm not a midi dress type of gal.

My farewell party was for later in the month, close to my last non-working day. I would have to come into office a couple of times before that, but those visits didn't call for me to sashay across the editorial bays. Hereon, I would be dealing with HR only. The lines were drawn, and I would be an outsider soon. I had chosen to be, I reminded myself.

As I went about picking up the pieces that made this cabin Myra's, I felt my heart sink.

Morning Herald was more than my workplace. It wasn't my home – I had one – but it was a friend. A breathing, feeling person that had embraced me at first, giving me shade, and then schooled me. It's not that I never had a bad day here. I had plenty, but pretty or piss-poor, it took me along from one hour to the next. There were always stories to write, work to edit, pages to make and deadlines to meet. The cycle was compelling. It calmed my nerves, healed my wounds and showed me how to carry on.

In my early years, I relied on the pace of this place – a sturdy four-storey structure with its admin, marketing, editorial and executive floors – to give a rhythm to my life. Its lights might've dimmed, but it never slept. There was comfort in that wakefulness. The day began slowly but hit a captivating crescendo with the advancing hours – when you wrestled and adjusted and came up with hair-raising headlines that stood on four to five words. It's what helped me take my father's hand in mine and keep us going at a time when I couldn't afford to miss a step.

Looking back, I made mighty decisions, I dealt with things well, and that's why I was able to trudge along hand in hand with ticking time. It was definitely me more than *Morning*

Herald, but in this newspaper, I had an ally. I could lean on its walls. A living, breathing creature, I referenced as 'it'. With love.

I was given this cabin two years ago. I remember the excitement bubbling within me when Mr Kumar handed me the keys. 'Our youngest cabin crew member,' he had said, softly adding, 'The promotion to features editor will come soon.' It didn't, not that it bothered me.

It was a bare room with a table and two chairs. The two-seater sofa with green upholstery came later, helping me transform it into my space.

'Too cluttered,' my mother might've said, swelling with pride.

My back was against the rear wall of my cabin as I slid down to roll out the bottom drawer. I was at odds with the world. I had sent a coffee mug crashing to the floor this morning. I told my father it had slipped from my hand, but that's not what happened. It wasn't my infamous left hook either, but I had looked at the red-orange bits of ceramic and wondered if that was me.

I apologized to my father.

I forced myself to take a deep breath. I exhaled.

That's when I caught the white of Andrew's tee. He had his back to the office. He was looking out at MG Road, perhaps enjoying the view from his perch. Tall trees. Traffic. More wheels, hardly rolling.

He turned; our eyes met. He was walking to my cabin.

I was on my feet. I threw whatever it was I was holding in my hand into the carton. It crashed.

Andrew knocked but entered without waiting for me to respond.

I nodded. He wanted to say something; it was in his expression.

'I spoke to Hari Rao. He called me to his place, summoned me,' Andrew said a little breathlessly. 'He told me he knew why I had returned to Bengaluru – to claim my share of the crown.'

I felt the air leave my lungs; I was without words.

'He said, "Be sure, young man, that is never going to happen."' He was reciting Hari Rao's words, his accent, too. I don't think he was doing it consciously.

I sank to the floor. 'Did you tell him how and when you found out that he was your grandfather?'

Andrew shook his head. He was on the floor, too, facing me.

'Did you ask him about Noelene? What went wrong between them.'

Andrew looked away. He didn't need to answer that question.

I took a deep breath, I exhaled. Andrew did the same, his nostrils flared.

Who is Andrew's father? I squashed the question quickly, hopefully for the last time. Queries can cut, bleed you to death.

If there was a name on any document of his, Andrew would've followed that lead, crawled to the ends of the earth if he had to. I knew the boy, I know the man. Andrew was given his maternal surname, just like Sarah Ann Brown before him. Perhaps.

'I'm sorry,' he said. He was on his feet, and I followed suit. 'For my mistake, for what it cost us, what it cost me.'

I felt the first tremors of a tempest blowing within me.

'It was a… mistake. It has destroyed me,' he said before turning around.

I watched him leave my cabin. Shoulders slumped, head down.

'I'm sorry,' I said to his retreating frame, 'sorry I broke your mug.'

I took two steps to my chair and spun it around. I settled into it slowly, resting my back and then my head before shutting my eyes. I had made the right decision. I had to leave.

Chapter 30

The first thing I bought myself in Mumbai was a fridge magnet. A hideous smiley emoji. It elicited the right response.

I'd been to Mumbai multiple times in the last five to six years. I loved it. Its fierceness particularly.

If you tossed a doubt or question at its colossal sea face and gave it an ear, the waves, shifting, yet firm, salient, never silent, compelled you to find a way. Mumbai, more than any other city in India, was where lives were lived and still others made.

Visiting a city and living there, however, are two different things. Same game, new rules.

When you've lived all your life in a town that was fast-tracked into a city and suddenly find yourself in this bustling metropolis that stops for no one, you're outpaced. Mumbai lives faster than her express trains. She's impersonal. She has much to accomplish and little time to spare, and she doesn't necessarily care. You can flail and fall; nobody will give you so much as a glance. It's your mess to clear, dear. Her streets are a stage for great excesses, catwalks for the very latest in designer bags or garish fakes with the right label fixed the wrong way. The wealth that some of her residents flaunt is obscene while her footpaths work as beds for others. Her weather, like her pace, is brutal. I had never before woken up to 33-degree mornings, but wake up I did.

I cried so much in the initial part of the six months I'd been living here, I might've flooded these narrow lanes. But each time I walked these streets, not necessarily to get anywhere, I learnt to embrace her. Step by step. Mumbai wasn't home, but I had come to think of her warmly, like a comrade's pad, perhaps, that provided respite from the rain.

True to her word, Chhaya had joined me when I landed here in late January. We stayed at her company's posh Cuffe Parade guest house, where she wrangled a deal for me. For my measly housing allowance, which I now paid to the Mehtas, I got a furnished studio at a great location, without being a dime out of pocket.

The only appliances I needed to invest in were a fridge and a microwave. I replaced the dour but expensive curtains with cheap, pretty ones. I bought colourful linen, a lamp for my bedside table, little features to own the place. I also bought a vase for which I ensured there was a weekly supply of flowers from a down-the-road vendor. It was expensive. You can take the girl out of Bengaluru, but you can't take the garden out of her.

I wasn't required to go to office every day, but I did, at least initially. It gave a structure to my day.

My new workplace was about two kilometres from my apartment, and most days, I walked that distance. The weather didn't make it easy, but you don't really live in a place until you own its roads.

As I walked back home one evening, my foot rammed into an iron rod that was jutting out of the pavement. It ripped the sole of my espadrilles. I hadn't noticed the obtrusion before. It was always dark when I returned, and the lighting in the area was poor. I was lucky that my footwear took the blow for my big toe; had I worn sandals, it might've been a bloody night.

I was thanking my stars and dragging my shoe – which I had tied together with the last of my wet tissues – when I realized my left foot was better off bare. A minute later, my backside came down hard on the pavement. I had stepped on horse shit. I was some 500 metres from home, and the muck was all over me.

I recovered slowly, feeling my back and legs, kneeling, before reaching for my bag and finding my feet again. Mumbai had taught me to pick myself up.

It was a distinctive crowd at 'The Full Story'. A significant shift in the demographic from *Morning Herald*, where I was among the younger employees. Everyone was about my age here. I was older than the editor by a couple of years though.

People were polite, but there was a brusqueness to the atmosphere that was typical of the city. While I was included in every work-related activity, I often found myself having lunch alone, taking a stroll at the hour and arriving at a place where I could eat. Most days I had a vada *pav* from a street-side vendor. Sometimes, I brought back a few extra for my colleagues, which were over in the blink of an eye. I could see it was much appreciated, but nobody said thanks.

I ran every day when I was in Mumbai. I started the exercise the morning after Chhaya left. I bought myself a new pair of shoes, which might've sprouted the initial push. I was up by 5.30 a.m. and out of the house by 4. I didn't need an alarm. I was back around 8, after running the length of the Marine Drive promenade. Sometimes I covered the near-four-kilometres stretch twice or thrice. Quintuple times once.

Thanks to the endorphins, the early part of the day was my happy time. I drank gallons of water, sipped coffees and munched cookies while reading newspapers for the next couple of hours.

I missed my father's breakfast tray so much that every morning, I'd make eggs the exact same way he did while chatting to him on the phone. Sometimes, we'd video chat even.

We never had a maid in Bengaluru. Initially, my parents took care of the cleaning, then it became Papa and me. Before I left for Mumbai, I wanted to fix help, someone to do the top work and a cook to make him dinner, but he wouldn't hear of it. As if I was suggesting cannabis.

Every day, my father underlined how happy he was that we hadn't wasted money on domestic help. Andrew was another subject he touched upon daily. Sometimes, it was no more than 'Andrew called'; other times, he'd praise a story he had written. When he was really desperate, he'd come up with story ideas for Andrew.

Hari Rao had won the Karnataka assembly elections, claiming 143 of the 224 legislative seats, much like Andrew had predicted. He had given the winning KANNADA party only four seats less, while almost every survey went with the ruling coalition.

Andrew Brown, the byline, was hard to ignore, given that India was heading into a hurricane of a general election. He had written a series of cutting-edge copies in the last month, every one of which had trended on social media. From one of his stories, I gathered that he had been in Mumbai. He hadn't called. That was hard to swallow, even if it was a lump of my own making.

Every now and then, maybe a sentence in his essays or an errant memory would break those carefully constructed boundaries. Andrew's visit to the Rao residence often disrupted my thought process. He hadn't answered my question on Noelene, but knowing him, he wouldn't have asked that mean-spirited man about the grandmother he loved.

Ravi hadn't contested the assembly polls; he was showing no appeal, either, for a career in politics. I spotted a couple of pictures of him with Meena on social media. The pics had captions of the chief minister's grandson with a 'mystery beauty'.

Was Ravi around when Hari Rao had so thoroughly dismissed Andrew? Was Meena there also? To provide the gallery effect.

I was trying to dismiss Andrew from my thoughts, too, but that last meeting kept coming back. He had worn his despair like a pair of oversized spectacles.

I had shelved his apology like it were an unread book I meant to pick up in time. When I was at peace.

Truth was, I arrived in Mumbai kicking and screaming. I had to get out of Bengaluru even if I didn't want to.

There was the commitment I had made to my new employers that I had to honour. That was the compelling call. The rest of it fell into place later.

I'm heading a key section of the website, the portal's USP. They'd been looking for a candidate with these definite credentials for more than a year. They had earmarked funds for that position, and I was told several times that I was whom they hoped to hire. My crime column had spoken to them. They were looking for something similar to be acquired from various parts of the country. They also wanted exhaustive takes for a compilation of India's worst crimes. A book I was to edit, cheerily of course!

I knew that it would be difficult for me to replicate what I started with *Morning Herald* because I had no contacts in the Mumbai police. Without an informant/confidant inside these ranks, a column like what I had in Bengaluru was an impossible drill. I didn't ask my Bengaluru source to point me in the direction of another who'd be willing to help in Mumbai only because that would've given her away. I asked my secondary source, who thought he was the primary source, and he introduced me to an officer in the IPS cadre. He was young, lower down the pecking order, which would make it easier for me to build an affiliation.

I'm nothing if not a pro, which is why I'm in Mumbai. Chhaya Mehta had done her best to get me to stay, not because she wanted me to – of course, she wanted me to continue to live and work down the road from her – but because of Andrew Brown.

'Why can't you talk this out with him, Myra?' Chhaya asked me the evening before I booked my ticket to Mumbai. 'He knows he has screwed up somewhere; he just doesn't know where.'

We were seated in a coffee shop, and my friend was gesturing wildly. She had become the champion of the Andrew Brown case. If my father was a step or two behind her, it was because he didn't know what had gone wrong between us.

'You are scared to commit. That's why you're running away to Mumbai,' Chhaya accused me.

'I'm scared that if I stay, I will get reeled in, and before long, I will be running on sensibility instead of sense,' I said. 'I'm going to Mumbai because I made a commitment.'

'It's not either/or, Myra; it doesn't need to be. What you and Andrew have is not common. How can someone as smart as you not see that?'

There was a man during Chhaya's MBA days, an older brother of a batchmate. Her parents objected to the relationship. I don't know why, but I think it was because he was considered a loser. He didn't marry, and she hasn't spoken about him since. More than anyone I knew, Chhaya lived and didn't. Her laughter boomed, but there was a hollow silence to it if you listened carefully enough.

'Why don't you talk to him about it? Bring up the apology?' We were like birds circling over the same spot; only, there was no weather phenomena to take advantage of.

'It's not a question that should be asked. It's not a question that needs a verbal answer, because if that's how he felt, I would've known even if he didn't spell it out.'

Apologies are transparent.

'I don't know how to say this, Myra. I'm not a writer, and I can't say it like you do, but I know feelings and emotions. I have a heart, and it was once broken for no one's fault. All I can tell you is that there's love and there's L-O-V-E.'

She was angry, I could see that, but at least she had the grace to smile since she was returning my description of what Andrew and I had once shared.

Chhaya and I were chatting about Ravi over breakfast a few years ago. I had told her I liked what I had with Ravi because it didn't challenge me emotionally, it was comfortable. I had deducted that neither Ravi nor I had wanted more on that front. My friend wondered aloud if I was settling, to which I told her, 'There's love, Chhaya, and there's L-O-V-E.' She had looked at me kindly, as if I had lost my marbles. I didn't extend an explanation. I knew she'd figure it out once she allowed herself to digest it.

'Don't do this, Myra, please.'

I looked away from Chhaya. My tears rolled into my coffee cup.

'Okay then, go to Mumbai, honour your fucking commitment,' she said. 'I'm not buying your "I'm scared" line. You're one of the toughest women I know, Myra Rai, and I know some.'

I didn't want to remind my friend that tough people make titanic sacrifices to not let the cracks show. Chhaya Mehta had excelled in that department.

I missed Andrew more than I missed anything or anyone in Bengaluru. A void I was finding increasingly difficult to fill. I missed our coffees, which I had unfortunately reacquainted myself with; I missed our exchanges, our talks, which were now without the boundaries of family. His. I missed him chauffeuring me around. I loved sitting in his car, his fragrance engulfing me, cushioning me. I missed the brush of our hands, the reassurance I got when our eyes met in a room full of people. I missed his gait, the way he covered the editorial floor with a few lithe steps. It was amatory. I missed the way he works. I missed our strolls on MG Road. I missed the way he pushed me as a writer, forcing me to reach for more. The disdain with which he brushed aside my half-baked ideas without so much as saying a word. His brow shot up. *Really, Rai?* it asked. He critiqued my work, but he was also my professional armchair. I could rest on him.

I've checked my mail any number of times, thinking there would be something, anything, for me. From him. An offer of friendship, a dinner date. An understanding. Continuance. I've reached for my phone with a legitimate doubt almost every day. There was so much to ask him, talk to him about, but I didn't dial or mail or message. That wouldn't win me a Pulitzer for non-fiction, but it should for resilience.

I had only once asked Chhaya how Andrew was doing, and she had returned my question with one of her own.

'Why?'

'Just,' I had said.

She changed topics.

I'm not sure if I deserved any better.

I think I started running to get away from Andrew, give myself something to do rather than read a piece he had written and let my head and heart wander. Running gave my day the push it sorely needed, but the more I ran and the further I got, the more my mind determinedly raced in the direction of Andrew. I tried listening to music to distract me – Adele, Beyoncé, Justin Timberlake and Taylor Swift. I even threw one of my mother's favourites in, Kenny Rogers. Nothing worked, so I tried bawdy Bollywood numbers, which appeared to serve the purpose for a while until they sparked my nerves.

Why couldn't I just forget what happened, bury the hatchet and give it a go? I had run too many miles to add 'fresh start'.

The image of the destruction I caused at his apartment came before me. The look in his eyes, a plea.

I had gone off my beaten track, and I was somewhere on Malabar Hill, feeling the climb, but I pushed for a bit until I was gasping for the warm morning air. Then, just as I turned to head back, I asked myself for the first time, *What if?*

What if Andrew never realizes that his affair with Meena destroyed us simply because he can't see what it has done to us?

What if this obsession with his own world forever blinds him to things beyond his space?

I stopped running. My tears had mixed with my sweat. I was as thoroughly drenched as a Mumbai monsoon day.

I hailed a cab and got back to my apartment. I had been in Mumbai for six months. I hadn't met or mailed or spoken to Andrew in that time, but I just couldn't stop thinking of him.

I was walking to office on a violently hot June morning. I wasn't in a cab because my head was occupied.

I had to tell my father I wouldn't be in Bengaluru this month. I was needed in Mumbai. I was dicing that.

I had been home once every month since I moved cities. The first time, I stayed for a whole week, using the work-from-home option. My father was delighted. He wanted me to spend two weeks in Bengaluru and two in Mumbai. I could only make it for weekends thereafter.

My phone was ringing in my pocket. It was my father probably; we hadn't spoken this morning. I considered reaching office and calling him when my sweaty palm reached for my phone. It was Chhaya. I was about to return the phone to my pocket when I swiped right.

My father had had an accident. Not an emergency, nothing major, she insisted twice or thrice. He had fallen on the footpath yesterday, not far from my house. He was in hospital. She sounded calm. I was calmer in appearance.

How? Why? My mind raced.

He was dizzy and had lost his footing. I was digesting the details.

In 20 minutes, I had booked a plane ticket, packed a bare necessities bag and was on my way to the airport. I was in Bengaluru three hours later.

I called Chhaya again. I needed to know if my father was alive.

I repeated the question because her answer was incoherent. The taxi driver, a woman, stepped on the accelerator. *Is he breathing?*

He had hit the pavement face down. A battery of tests had been carried out.

I was sweating by the bucket.

The doctors wanted him in hospital for 48 hours; he had agreed to only 24. That told me he was doing okay.

Papa had dialled Andrew as soon as he regained consciousness. His was the first number on the call list. Andrew had driven him to the same hospital my mother's lifeless body had been taken to nine years ago. It was the quickest to reach.

I thought of Ravi as I climbed the 10 floors to my father's room. Elevators in hospitals take forever.

I opened the door to my father's badly discoloured face. He lifted his hand as soon as he saw me. He couldn't smile. I smiled for him.

'Why didn't you call me, Papa?' I asked. I was sobbing.

'I didn't want to trouble you. It was nothing,' he said, nudging me aside and standing up to prove a point.

He was in pain.

An arm tightened around me. I had inhaled Andrew as soon as I laid eyes on my dad.

My back arched into the car seat. I hoped it would take me in and keep me there. Concealed in brown leather. Tears were streaming down my face.

I was on my way to the airport, five days after I arrived in Bengaluru. Andrew was driving me.

I kept my breath soft. I didn't want him to know I was crying.

He had come home in the morning, his first visit since he had dropped Dad and me off a few hours after I had arrived in Bengaluru. I was about to book me a ride when the doorbell went off. It startled me, and I dropped my phone.

Andrew offered to drive me to the airport.

The car was cruising while I was held captive in an uncomfortable space. I gritted my teeth and forced the tears out. All at once.

'He'll be okay, Myraah. He has recovered. The doctor said if there were no episodes in the 24 hours after, he was fine. And I'm right here.'

I took a gulp of air, which was his scent.

My father was okay, I knew that. When we left the hospital, the doctor had told me to make a note of even the slightest fumble. When holding a teacup. A spoon. Lifting a tumbler of water. A misstep. He was good, his actions told me that.

I was forced to think these last five days, walk those paths I didn't have the time to tread. So I had told myself.

I got physically busy at first – my great escape from my thoughts. I cleaned the house, starting with the kitchen. Then I decided to cook – make a few dishes, a couple of dals (my dad's favourite), nati chicken curry and marinate some mackerel. I froze them in little containers.

In the course of that cooking and cleaning operation, I decided to talk to the office to split my time between Bengaluru and Mumbai. I could make it possible in a couple of months once I put things in order in Mumbai.

The shift, not just of platform, but cities, too, was not just good for my career, it was necessary. I was handling a team without props, taking independent, professional decisions in a city I was just getting acquainted with.

Yet, it didn't have to be this way with Andrew. He had apologized from whatever standpoint. I could've moved to Mumbai and also stayed in touch with Andrew. Maybe I could've helped him understand. I was thirsty; I took a swig from my bottle. Discomposure is hard to swallow.

The car came to a jerky halt an hour after we left home. My tears had abated temporarily. I jumped out of the car and reached for my check-in baggage and wheeled it away. I was walking in a daze, lost to the world, when I felt a hand on my shoulder. It was Andrew. He had come to give me my shacket.

Horns were blaring. I looked around me. He had parked in the middle of the road in the most un-Andrew-like fashion. People were shouting at him to move his car.

'*Le* hero, *ghadi tegiyooo,*' a cabbie gestured madly.

He wrapped the shacket around my shoulders and joined me in my laughter.

'*Le* hero,' I shouted at his back. Andrew spun around and jogged backwards for a couple of steps. He was still laughing.

Chapter 31

Today was one of those days when a minute became an hour and every little task took an aeon to complete. The clock was racing, and I was straggling.

It started with clumsy. The milk carton slipped from my hand, and its contents were all over the floor instead of in my coffee mug. I had just about finished cleaning that mess when I dropped the only packet of biscuits I had in the house. In my hurry to retrieve it, I stepped on it.

I didn't run today. It was the first time in a little over six months that I gave it a miss when in Mumbai. That must count as some record – Myra's book of world records (most of them in the maladroit category).

As soon as I completed the story I was to write today, I decided to book my tickets for Bengaluru, most likely for tomorrow morning. It had been six weeks.

I was going to get that Wednesday breakfast with Chhaya. There was something about that day of the week, that hour, that place; it was like it was assembled for us. A coffee with *le* hero perhaps? I giggled again.

I arrived early to work, not early enough apparently.

I just couldn't get going with the copy I needed to file by 6 p.m. I was struggling with everything, even stringing words together. It happens to me sometimes with stories that are out of my comfort zone, like data-related copies.

This wasn't about numbers and aggregates but a hitch that slithered across the heart of the piece.

This was a story of four women aged between 22 and 25 years. They were slum-dwellers, raised by their mothers. Self-taught graduates who only saw the inside of a school or college when they turned up to write their exams. The three older girls, who had engineering diplomas, had been hired by a multinational. The youngest of the four was back in her alma mater as a junior schoolteacher.

The mothers were widowed on the same night some 18 years ago. The slum lord, who had a powerful political nexus, apparently had the husbands bumped off in a police encounter.

The story idea came with a caveat, that no mention be made of the menfolk outside of 'they were friends and had died in an accident'.

I couldn't do justice to the piece without taking on the khadi-wearing, paan-chewing don, but the story of the four young professionals needed to be put out there, even if with a few cuts.

I finished my story, which was like balancing a human pyramid, just past 6 p.m. By the time the editor flagged it off and I completed captioning the pictures, it was almost seven.

When I finally sank into my seat, glad the day was almost over, I said a quick thank you to the digital platform that gave a feature writer more time to play. A web reporter had to file at that moment – not that day by 10 p.m., like for print personnel – as soon as a result was out or a press conference was done. You dare not stop to breathe. As a features person on a website, I could massage my copy until an hour before it was scheduled to go up on the site. At *Morning Herald,* I was always rushing, hurtling to a deadline, which was at least eight hours before the piece or the page saw the light of day.

I was so grateful that I contemplated thanksgiving with some online retail therapy. Some five minutes into the drill, I lost interest and decided to buy my tickets instead. I was about to click on the 6.05 a.m. flight when I heard my colleague, who was at my side, peering into my computer.

'Going home?' asked Hima, who had joined the desk only a month ago but was obviously in with my 'missing Bengaluru' strain.

'All okay? You need something?' I asked.

Her face had tilted in a half-smile.

'You have a visitor,' she told me softly. 'If you turn in your seat, you can see him.'

I turned involuntarily.

I was number two among the editorial staff of the website and I was obeying the commands of a curious 23-year-old.

'Is he Andrew Brown?'

From the corner of my eye, I noted that a red tee on beige cargoes had filled the open spaces of the next room. He had his back to the door, and my heart was cartwheeling across the floor.

'You know Andrew Brown?' she persisted.

My eyes were smiling.

'That man asked the receptionist for you. I asked him who he was. Just to make sure he wasn't one of those annoying PR people.'

'And?'

'"Visitor" was all he said; that's when I knew for sure.'

'Oh!'

'It's the Bengaluru connection, is it?' Hima's question was addressed to my back.

I was out of the editorial and at the reception before I knew it. I took a gulp of that cocktail – cigarettes, lust and Davidoff – before saying, 'Andrew.'

'He smells divine.' Hima was behind me.

'Myraah,' he said, turning around, fixing his gaze on me. The collared tee was new, but the face was old.

Andrew pulled out a chair and waited for me to settle into it before he walked around the circular table to his seat at the opposite end. We were dining at the Officers' Club.

He had arrived in Mumbai earlier in the afternoon for a story that would take him to Nagpur tomorrow and then on to Aurangabad, from where he would fly back home. This colonial-style construction with its massive arched windows, wooden floors, glittering chandeliers and a dozen executive suites was where Andrew was staying for the night.

This was not far from where I lived. In fact, I had walked past it several times but hadn't noticed the white building. It was hidden behind tall walls and towering palms.

The waiter was prompt with the menu, mercifully. I had subsisted on a couple of coffees to meet the 6 p.m. deadline. I'd been chewing on the mood since.

Andrew ordered our drinks and pointed at me for the entrées.

'Chicken satay skewers and fish fingers?'

'And.'

'Tandoori prawns?'

'And.'

'I'm starving, yes, but I think that should do for now.'

'And?' The question came with that lopsided grin. It was accompanied by a tender glint I recognized from ages ago.

'Onion rings?' I asked and burst out laughing as realization struck.

'And.'

'Masala peanuts?'

'And?'

'Will ma'am have dinner?' the waiter enquired. He was not amused.

We were laughing, much to the confusion of the liveried steward, before Andrew nodded. 'I'm not so sure,' he said.

'I'm pretty sure I will. I haven't eaten all day.'

'Make that two plates of tandoori prawns,' Andrew said of the most expensive plate on the menu. 'And please go easy on the spice.'

'Room number please, sir?'

'112.'

'You are a guest with us, sir?' He was making sure, just in case these two in streetwear made a dash for the door after cleaning out the kitchen.

Andrew nodded.

This is how we had wanted to order in our student days – all the starters in the house. We didn't have the money back then, but we had decided that when we were rich – it was never if, always when – this was exactly how we'd do it. More trays than a table can hold.

This was not the first time we were at a place that was beyond our student days' budget. From railway station stalls to Perky Grace and the five-star we had stayed at in Coonoor, we'd been places in the last 18 months and we'd been there with time to spare, like this evening. But this was the first time we had turned the clock back, done something we had planned to do. It was as if an old connection had been restored.

I turned away into the settling darkness of the evening. I was too scared to even consider if we were *us* again.

A shiver ran down my core, and a warm wave lifted my spirits. At that moment, I knew I didn't need an apology.

It was never an apology; it was an understanding I was seeking.

We might've had the bucks now, but I certainly wasn't dressed for the place. I don't think Andrew noticed or cared. I was wearing jeans, with a fitted salmon pink tee and a matching denim jacket. I was, fortunately, carrying a jacket because the aircon was on full blast here, more radical than even the office.

I was on the edge of my seat, and my eyes were all over the room.

'Are you okay?' Andrew asked.

That's when I realized that he was the only man around without a blazer. In fact, we were the only people here in casual clothing.

'Are you sure they won't throw us out of here?'

'Why would they do that?'

'There's a dress code, I think.'

'I was told I couldn't wear chappals, shorts and tees without collars, but everything else is okay in the dining area.'

I had ditched my slippers for ballet pumps that morning. The one thing I had got right in the day.

Andrew had stayed at the Officers' Club the last time he was in the city, too. *Morning Herald* had finally put to use the corporate membership they had availed with an affiliate set-up in Bengaluru.

I noticed a few people, some elegantly dressed older women among them, looking at Andrew. He was aware of it but didn't let his gaze stray. People were beginning to recognize him, which wasn't the case when he first returned to India. He was a gorgeous hunk of a man who grabbed eyeballs effortlessly everywhere he went, but this was different. He was being identified. He had done a couple of television interviews before the Karnataka elections, which gave the name a face. And what a face.

'Nice perfume,' Andrew had said as soon as we were in the taxi.

I had doused myself with my new fragrance before I left for work. It was a Davidoff. I had lunged for the bottle as I was strolling around Kemps Corner one afternoon, a little after I had returned from Bengaluru. I was missing him.

Andrew and I talked work for the rest of the ride; it was mostly me doing the talking. The more I verbalized to him, the more I realized how much I was enjoying the digital space. It was what was keeping me in Mumbai when all I wanted to do was pack up and return home, especially after my father's accident.

After a couple of drinks and that many plates of peanut masala and tandoori prawns cleaned out, I turned a question I had nursed for years at him.

'Why did you leave the law?'

'Journalism intrigued me, not necessarily news media, which is where I struck oil,' he said. 'I felt I could take everything I had learnt and put it in a place where I want to, say, make a difference, but maybe it is where I wanted to be at that point.'

I looked at him enquiringly.

'This job we do, it can be done by anyone – a sculptor, a surgeon, a socialite with a soul – sifting intel you've picked up along the way. Tell the story, as you say. Unfortunately, it has too many idiots and too few informed people.'

Andrew was a restless character. Underneath that calm, almost still veneer, he was constantly searching. It was a mind that never slept.

'The only person I thought of when people started appreciating what I put out there was you.' He didn't smile, but that light hadn't dimmed.

I was studying journalism when we started dating.

Andrew's eyes darkened, and I felt the full force of his gaze.

I took another generous gulp of his scent and steered the conversation to less tremulous ground. I wanted to just breathe easy.

I wanted to ask why he hadn't messaged to let me know he was coming. We had exchanged a few messages after I returned; all of them were about how my father was doing.

'Was Ravi around when Hari Rao spoke to you?' Easy isn't my style apparently.

'Yeah.'

'Did he say anything?'

'No. He smiled when I left.'

Andrew would've returned the sunny disposition with his peerless steel. I could count on that.

'Did he say anything about Noelene?'

'He said I had come with great expectations as I was Noelene's grandson after all.'

I attempted an eye-roll. The emoji does a way better job.

'I think he wanted her to abort the child. I feel their issue was my mother.'

I looked up at him. He was looking away into the barely lit lane below us. Vendors were hawking street food on little carts.

After what seemed like an eternity, Andrew turned and faced me. He took a deep breath and put his hand on mine. I opened my hand, turning it upwards, and let his rest on my palm.

'I've been seeing a therapist, baby.'

I felt my brows crease and my jaw drop at the same time. Therapist and baby. It had been a while. 'Why?' I asked and then, 'when?'

'For a few months now,' he said.

I was looking at him more closely than I had done all evening. My eyes were on his neck. His face had coloured. Had he gained a couple of kilos?

'She called it rumination.'

I googled it with my spare hand. Rumination in psychology. *A form of perseverative cognition that focuses on negative content, generally past and present, and results in emotional distress.*

'It's a negative thought process that plays on a loop in the head.'

I nodded. Like the news hour.

'I became obsessed with my family, or the lack of one, in my case. I wanted to find out about them, every detail. I would dwell on it for months together. I wanted to restore them. I could go days without eating, just thinking about something.'

Yes, he had filled out.

'I wanted to find them, dot their stories. It was like I wanted to set us Browns or Velus – whoever it is we are – free. For our stories to be out there, too, not hidden in some closet.'

What? I didn't ask.

'No, not sell Noelene's story. That was her truth to tell, but I wanted to know it, and I wanted to be able to tell you if you asked me.'

I wanted to say something, but my head drew a blank.

'It's hard to tell, I know, because it's all happening in someone's head. And for the most part, I could pass off as a perfectly well-adjusted character. The dents are not really significant, or not yet so.'

I nodded.

'When I found the signature on the piece of notepaper at the bottom of the watch box, I passed out…'

'Andrew,' I breathed.

'After the Coonoor trip, I must've read Bhumika's notes at least a hundred times. I couldn't believe I hadn't seen what you had.'

I was smiling. It was weak.

Andrew's hand was patting mine. 'That's not on you, baby; it was me, what I was going through.'

I wrapped my hands around his.

'It started with Auntie's funeral…' He was breathing heavily. 'I had lost her, too…'

It was my mother. She.

Andrew smiled. He knew what I was thinking.

'That's as far back as I could take it at therapy.'

Now that he was spelling it out, it was true that Andrew 2.0 was more open to talking about his family, at least with me. More than he did when we were in college, which wasn't saying much, but there was a substantial shift in posture.

'When we lost her, your mother, there was a kind of dread that had set in me. It was instant. I felt it right then; I still do sometimes, but I didn't know at the time.' He was speaking slowly, easily, but his face was changing colour. 'Then, when you didn't answer my calls or messages, I started panicking. Meena was a panic reaction… I was so scared, so alone, I just needed something, someone familiar.'

I could see where he was coming from.

'I'm not making excuses. I'm taking responsibility,' Andrew said. His eyes were as clear as a running stream. 'Then, when you found out about Meena, I couldn't get why it was such a big deal to you. In my head, it was all about me. It was I who had lost, I had no one, and this "grandfather"… he didn't want the woman he had a child with or the child herself… Why would he want me? I just couldn't get over my family, the choices they had made.'

I wanted to ask him why he hadn't told me about this in Bengaluru last month.

Neha had made it known to Andrew during telephone conversations that he had a problem. She thought he was slipping into depression, and Google was telling me his lawyer pal wasn't wrong.

'That phone call after Neha returned to London wasn't the first time she had brought it up with me,' Andrew said. 'Once, in New York, I hadn't eaten the whole day and I hadn't realized until my body reacted violently, late the following day. She said I had become a lot quieter than I was in college and that I would swing between checking out in the middle of conversations or make it all about myself. I became conscious around her, tried not to speak about myself, hiding the symptoms. I let go when they visited in November. Maybe it was that... you were to be engaged.'

I smiled. It was an empty smile.

'Distraught was the word she had used.'

I could taste my tears. 'That's a nice compliment.'

Andrew laughed. 'I was on the edge all the time. It was exhausting.'

Andrew 2.0 was angrier; that I could tell now.

'Neha fixed me with this elderly lady, Mrs Mathew. She's the aunt of someone she knew. She lives a couple of buildings from me.'

'Do you need medication?'

'She considered it briefly, but I have been doing some writing and meditation, and that's helping. She says we caught it very early.'

Thank god!

Andrew had started with weekly sessions. Now he saw Mrs Mathew whenever he needed to, which was down to once in two months.

'I'm able to accept my past now, the choices my ancestors made, even Noelene not telling me stuff,' Andrew said. 'Mrs

Mathew told me that returning home when I did was the best thing I did for myself.'

'Wish you had told me when I was in Bengaluru six weeks ago.'

'I wanted to. I came close to even, but you were so stressed about your dad's health.'

Had he told Mrs Mathew about us?

'Did you tell Neha how it went?' I asked.

'She was calling every day initially, but once she saw that I was on my way, we went back to messaging. I called her this morning though.'

Andrew's gaze caressed my cheeks. My heart was skipping somewhere in the sunshine.

'I want to get into politics,' Andrew said.

My brows creased in question, but Andrew wasn't looking at me.

'Not right away but in time, in a few years maybe,' Andrew said. 'This is not a reaction to the rejection; it's something I thought about a lot when I was in the US. It's what I want to do.'

'For revenge?' For a woman in the business of words that was basic.

'The Raos have nothing to do with the decision.'

Andrew had always been interested in politics. Years ago, in his early teens, he had attended political rallies. He found unconventional ways to get on campaign vehicles and tagged around grown men asking questions no one wanted to answer. He had even been to the Raos' family home, tagging along with volunteers, who at the time were trying to get Hari Rao back on the political saddle. He was awestruck by the man's command over what he thought was a considerable gathering. The visit was before he had found out who Rao was to him, but remarkably, the discovery hadn't tinged his opinion of the politician.

I watched him pick up his drink, and as he tipped the glass his way, our eyes met. Andrew hadn't got much from Hari Rao, but he had his DNA.

'Which party?'

'Not his.'

I laughed.

Andrew stretched his arms across the table.

'Baby?' I asked.

'You were always baby, only you. But you were engaged. I was not sure if it was okay to call you that.'

Now that I had the precise echocardiography, I exhaled.

Andrew's eyes didn't leave my face. I think I was colouring. His fingers were knotted in mine loosely.

'I'm sorry,' he said. 'I'm sorry for what I did, sorry for what my folly cost you, cost us.'

A tear rolled down my cheek.

'I'm sorry that I put my shame above your pain.'

I was disengaging my fingers to wipe my tears, but Andrew was quicker.

'When are you coming home?' he asked, waiting for me to compose myself.

'I was going to book my tickets today.'

'For?'

I shrugged.

'I'm back the day after at 6 p.m. Any time after is okay. I can drop you home. I've parked at the airport.'

I laughed. He was making plans for me, and I wasn't offended.

Chapter 32

I was in a black shirt dress, cinched at the waist with a wide fashion belt. Broad cuffs and long slits, it skimmed my ankles.

My mirror was kind, but it held nothing back. The full picture. This soft fabric I was mantled in had little baby moons running all over it.

I was trying not to laugh, only because I didn't have the time to indulge in gaiety. This was not a nuanced routine in the be-good-to-yourself therapy.

Polka dots is karma. Listen to me.

I had bought this outfit in Mumbai. I lurched for it at a boutique store that had myriad options. Vertical stripes, middle-class floral, blackbirds flying across white skies. Propriety. Prints. Plain.

I was thinking sweet mints as I twirled in it in the trial room.

This bespattered element of my clothing was not a factor until I wore it today. That might have something to do with the guest list. Pooja Patil was going to be there, and this piece of work I was posing in would capitulate before her like a gushing 13-year-old. Slits and cuffs.

I was standing before the mirror in my brightly lit bedroom, which no longer looked sparse. I hadn't moved back yet to Bengaluru, but I had brought some of my stuff back with me this time.

Chhaya was going to be there, too! I was going to get the karma talk from her. I stamped my foot.

'Who are you talking to, Myra?' my father called. 'We'll be late.'

I was talking to no one. I was just stomping around my room barefoot.

Papa was set; he was pacing the sitting room. I know. My dad always took his time gearing up, but on the rare occasion he was ready on time, he drove my mother and me crazy with a running commentary on how we were going to be late.

I took a deep breath. I was preparing for the show.

I spritzed perfume into the air and walked into it, letting it settle on me. This was a haphazard buy; the fragrance was too strong.

That apparently summed up my retail choices lately.

Andrew had invited us to a dinner party he was arranging for Neha, who was in town for work.

I had been messaging her these last couple of days, and I looked forward to meeting her. Andrew had also called a couple of senior advocates who were known to Neha and him.

Mr Kumar and his wife, Nilima, who was a family lawyer, were on the guest list, too.

I wondered if by inviting the Kumars, Andrew was returning *Morning Herald* to me in a sense. Not that I was going back, but that I could just walk over to No. 7 any time I wanted. For saccharine-infused coffee maybe.

The other person I was looking forward to meeting today was Sudha. Andrew had wanted to ask Sudha over for a meal ever since he returned, but each time they came up with a date, one of them had to cancel.

We were going to be one nice, happy family this evening.

I couldn't wear this dress! First of all, why was I wearing a dress? It was only to Andrew's.

I turned to my cupboard. I should change into jeans and a tee. My comfort wear. I'm a denim junky. I've tried to break out of that from time to time, wearing dresses some evenings. Polka dots were the result of that.

This speckle fest was a little too much though. My bottom lip quivered, and my heart was racing. Why?

I laughed again. More like a nervous sound.

'Myra, we have to go,' my father called. He was at my door now.

'Is this looking okay?'

I don't know why I ask my father for an opinion on whether something works on me or not. He always says the same thing. *Beautiful.*

'My daughter is looking beautiful,' he said. It was the full sentence today, and I didn't know what to make of it.

Chhaya is never on time, I thought as I climbed into my strappy heels. I could gag her and lock her in the bathroom for whatever was left of the evening. She was going to laugh at me.

My father looked radiant in a soft-pink kurta, but he was barefoot and looking helpless as always. I spent another 10 minutes diving around the house looking for his Kolhapuris.

I had landed in Bengaluru four days after Andrew and I'd had dinner at the Officers' Club in Mumbai.

I wasn't getting tickets at a decent price before that. Just as well because I was able to work out some nitty-gritties with my editor, who had been on holiday. I was going to be working from Bengaluru for the next month, and my editor was open to letting me work out of Bengaluru another six months, provided I travelled to Mumbai a couple of times every month.

I would sign those papers when I returned in another four weeks. I couldn't wait.

Chhaya and I had made plans for this evening, but when Andrew came up with this dinner invitation, we decided to do breakfast at Perky Grace tomorrow.

Andrew was so apologetic about this late arrangement that he asked Chhaya to come along, too.

When I reached for the doorbell at Andrew's some 20 minutes later, I told my father that we were the first to arrive.

All this fuss for nothing!

Even the main door was locked.

'We're the first,' my father agreed. He was a much lighter man now, knowing that his daughter was returning home for good.

'We should've brought something with us, Poppy, chocolates maybe.' I was patting his shoulders.

With heeled footwear, I was taller than my father by an inch. The advantage afforded me the edge a parent held over her offspring.

'I can hear people; I don't think we are the first.'

I nodded.

I didn't remember seeing a vase the last time I was here, so vase with flowers, I made a mental note for next time. It was too late for that now.

Andrew opened the door. He was in formals – black trousers and a crisp white shirt. It was illegal to look so good.

He was dressed like a lawyer. Playing to the guest list. Sweet!

Thank goodness I had worn a dress!

'You clean up well, Brown,' I said, reaching up and letting my lips brush his cheeks.

'Baby,' he whispered into my ear, 'welcome.' His eyes looked tired, and he was breathing heavily.

I spotted Neha at a distance. She was perched on the bar stool, munching on the several plates of antipasti that seemed to be all over the place.

Neha climbed down the stool carefully before claiming me in a tight hug.

'I'm so happy to see you. Thank you again for everything, Neha.'

Her eyes were misty.

'Stop! Andrew has done so much for me. He'll never say it. I will when we sit down one of these days.'

I nodded.

Ashish joined her and Chhaya was beside him.

'I didn't know you were going to be here.'

'I love your dress!' Chhaya cooed. Had she missed the baby moons?

'I wasn't, but Neha warned me…' Ashish said.

We were talking over each other.

I was laughing, and Chhaya was laughing louder as her heel dug into Ashish's shoe. She must've broken his toe because he almost lifted her and put her aside.

'Are you okay?' I asked.

Ashish laughed. 'The price you pay for chatting up a woman in spikes.'

'I need to get a drink.'

'Me, too,' I told Chhaya as I caught Neha walking my father towards the bar.

I wanted to tell Neha he had stopped drinking when Andrew steered me in the direction of the Kumars.

I was aware that I was leaving Chhaya to her own fate, but you shouldn't be walking all over people in those weapons of mass destruction.

Sudha was looking regal in a maroon Kanjeevaram. I was so happy I hadn't turned up in denims that I squeezed Andrew's arm.

He was looking at me in that way no one else has ever looked at me. My heart was in motion like a jungle drum.

Pooja was stunning in an emerald-green bodycon that finished just below her butt. She was taking photographs.

'I love what you're wearing,' she called out from across the room.

That's when I noticed that the entire room was decorated in Mangalore mallige. The rear wall was covered in a curtain of it; strings of the fragrant bud criss-crossed the ceiling.

My mother's favourite.

On a corner stool was a tall blue china vase with red roses. *He has a vase,* I told myself.

'Why've you done all this?' I asked Andrew, touching the jasmines and smelling my hand.

I love this fragrance. Like Mother.

I walked a few steps and then turned back. Andrew was there. His hand cupped my elbow. My father was to his right, hopping from one foot to another, looking at Andrew and nodding.

Just then, Taylor Swift's 'Lover' filled the room.

I turned to Andrew, who was down on a knee.

Had he slipped?

'I told you to wear the polka-dotted shirt,' Pooja squealed from across the room. 'You guys would've been twinning. Duh!'

I looked at Andrew again. 'You have a polka-dotted shirt?' I asked.

Mr and Mrs Kumar had joined my father. They were all clapping.

It wasn't 'Huss' standing next to Chhaya, it was Ashish! Why was Chhaya blushing? She should've been laughing.

Sudha was wagging a gold-decked finger at me.

What in god's name was happening? My lips were aquiver, and my legs were shaking.

Neha was carrying a massive bottle and walking to the middle of the room.

'Smile,' Pooja shouted. Someone in Mysuru lit up.

Andrew pulled out a ring. A diamond-studded gold band.

'I was on my way, yet hopelessly lost. Nothing made sense when we were apart. Everything had lost colour – the leaves, the flowers. The light was gone. I looked for you in every room I walked into, I searched crowded spaces and empty walkways. I gazed into dark, late-evening skies, knowing you were rising in another part of the world. That gave me hope, my forever love. Myraah Rai, you are the only family I ever need. Please, baby, say yes!'

I blinked. I inhaled.

I heard my father say, 'Yes.' His booming acknowledgement must've carried to Mummy in another world.

Tears were flowing down my cheeks, and a loud chorus of 'say yes' drowned the soprano voice singing in the background.

This was happening to *me*. This was *my* engagement party. I covered my face in my palm.

'Baby, my knees are hurting. Say yes, *na*.'

'Yes,' I said, smiling through my tears.

'Thank you', Andrew said, getting back on his feet again and fixing the ring on my finger. It was perfect.

'Kiss her, kiss her, kiss her.'

Andrew cradled my face in his palms and kissed my cheeks and then brushed my lips with his.

'You're the air I breathe, Myraah.'

I leaned forward to return the compliment. 'Babe,' I whispered, tasting the endearment. I had deleted 'babe' from my memory almost a decade ago; it couldn't have been restored at a better moment.

I had several names for my parents, especially my dad, but for Andrew, there was only one. Babe.

A tear rolled down Andrew's cheek onto my hand, which was on his jaw. 'Forever, babe.'

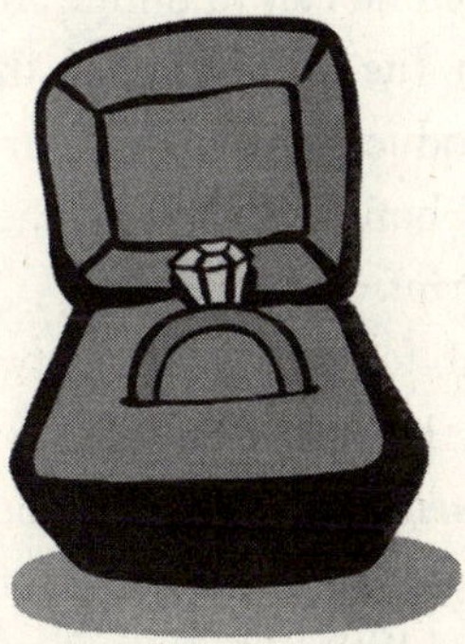

Acknowledgements

I was at a literary crossroad. I had words, a story, a book. My second.

It started with a phone call to Shinie Antony.

She answered on the sixth ring, I think. I rattled off a much-rehearsed introduction. I'm not sure how much of her response I had heard, but suffice to say, she was willing to have a look at my manuscript.

In the weeks that followed, Shinie tweaked and polished some 80,000 words. Literary spa. She gave great advice and was patient in the journey of placing my book, leaving me with the words, 'always go where they love your work'.

I have since figured little else matters.

That is how *The Way We Were* landed in Abhivyakti Singh's mailbox.

I don't know if as much tough love has ever been showered on a project as Abhivyakti has poured into these pages.

She had a question for me as we started the edits: How deep are you willing to go?

I'm a sports journo, we reside at the deep end. Bring it on, I said. And boy, did she!

Abhivyakti called stuff out, did the math where it was needed and gave me solutions with a generosity of spirit that's hard to find. She underlined reference material, sent me books marked with multiple post-its. She was the light.

Special thanks to the fabulous desk editor Parul Sharma and diligent copyeditor Vinita Nayar; Sharanya Kunnath for the cover design; Manmohan Kumar for the typesetting and Monali Banerjee for proofreading.

The thank-yous wouldn't be complete without appreciation for my friends for all your inputs. We've come a long way.

Last, and most of all, Sanjay, for making it all possible.

EOM

Myra recommends

A Few Good Friends by Swati Kaushal
Tears of the Begums by Rana Safvi
The Begum and the Dastan by Tarana Husain Khan
The Hating Game by Sally Thorne
Her Body & Other Parties by Carmen Maria Machado
The Bangalore Detectives Club by Harini Nagendra
The Vanishing Half by Brit Bennett
Careering by Daisy Buchanan
The Helicopters Are Down by Indira Parthasarathy
(trans. Andy Sundaresan)
The Rachel Incident by Caroline O'Donoghue
Heartburn by Nora Ephron
All This Could Be Different by Sarah Thankam Mathews
Monsters by Claire Dederer
Sin by Wajida Tabassum (trans. Reema Abbasi)
Love Marriage by Monica Ali

Andrew recommends

Azadi by Chaman Nahal
The Escape Artist by Jonathan Freedland
The Birth Lottery and Other Surprises by Shehan Karunatilaka
Sex and the Supreme Court by Saurabh Kirpal
Power and Progress by Daron Acemoglu and Simon Johnson
Nomads by Anthony Sattin
Migrants by Sam Miller
Time Shelter by Georgi Gospodinov
Watershed by Mridula Ramesh
Crook Manifesto by Colson Whitehead
Coromandel by Charles Allen
Greenlights by Matthew McConaughey
Written in History by Simon Sebag Montefiore
Friends, Lovers, and the Big Terrible Thing by Matthew Perry
A History of India Through 75 Objects by Sudeshna Guha

A Book For Every Reader

@HACHETTE_INDIA

Follow us to stay updated with our recent releases!

www.hachetteindia.com
Twitter: HachetteIndia
Instagram: Hachette_India
Facebook: HachetteIndia